FOR MY COUNTRY

FOR MY COUNTRY

SECRETS
BOOK 2

P. A. DUNCAN

Printed in the United States of America.
ISBN: 979-8-3302-8099-5 (Print Edition Only)
FIRST EDITION: June 2024
Published by Unexpected Paths. www.unexpectedpaths.com
Edited by Sylvan Echo Editing.
Cover art by: www.SelfPubBookCovers.com/geekartbyzentner
Created with Vellum.

DEDICATION

To every writer who has inspired me. It's a long list.

EPIGRAPH

I've met enough KGB colonels in my life.

— GARY KASPAROV

CONTENTS

AUTHOR'S NOTE

Secondary characters have jobs to do in a novel: give us a break from the antagonist and maybe the protagonist; give a different perspective or point of view to the story; and aid in advancing the plot to its logical conclusion.

I've always been careful to flesh out my secondary characters but not let them take over the story. My readers had other ideas.

Among the feedback I've received on these secondary characters were suggestions that three specific characters needed their own stories. One of those characters was Olga Lubova, who was an au pair/bodyguard for Alexei Bukharin's granddaughter. But before that for 40 years, she served in the KGB's Training Directorate, eventually rising to become Colonel Olga Lubova.

I've called this a memoir, but can a fictional character have a memoir? Of course. Think of this as a memoir's rough draft.

For My Country is not a spy novel, per se. It is, however, another novel from the ***Secrets*** Box Set about the people behind the scenes of a spy's life—notably those who train others to be spies from love of country.

1

REVOLUTIONS ARE ALWAYS
VERBOSE

1957

The Lubyanka
KGB Headquarters
First Directorate Training Unit
Moscow, USSR

Before I, Lieutenant Olga Yevgenyevna Lubova, knocked on the door, I gave my uniform jacket a tug, set the belt precisely at my narrow waist, and smoothed my skirt. My sensible but chunky shoes had a high polish, as did the brass buckle on my belt. This morning, I made sure to place my collar tabs and epaulets per regulations. The buttons on my jacket gleamed. I had worked on ironing, polishing, and cleaning everything most of the night before. The olive-gray color of the uniform was not flattering for me, but it was what it was.

With my regulation hat tucked under my left upper arm, I checked my hair for loose strands. From the judicious use of hairpins, every hair stayed in place. My makeup was minimal, barely a touch of lipstick, and I hoped I radiated professionalism.

I took a deep breath, cut off by the damned regulation girdle, raised my clenched fist, and knocked.

"*Voidite!*" came a woman's brusque, raised voice. Of course, a woman. This was the typing pool—not the most exciting job in the Training Unit, but it was a place to start now that I was fresh out of my own training.

My back stiff and straight, I opened the door, took two steps inside, and closed the door behind me. I came to attention and saluted the woman standing at a desk. The woman returned the salute then held up a hand to others in the room and shouted, "*Stoi!*" Stop.

The sound of typewriters faded, and a series of clicks told me the tape decks had been paused.

Before I could announce I had reported for duty, the woman said, "You must be Lieutenant Lubova. I am Captain Mikhailov-na." The captain's eyes narrowed at me. "Is that your natural hair? We will have no dyed hair here. That is a decadent perversion of the West."

"Yes, Captain, it is my natural color," I replied, tone neutral. Not the first time I'd been asked. Auburn-haired Russians were beyond rare.

"I see. Of course, your mother had the same color. I always believed it was dyed, given your mother's . . ." A turned-down mouth. "*Profession.*"

No one laughed, but I saw the smirks, the side glances.

My mother had been an actress, a star of Soviet propaganda films made during the Great Patriotic War, and a director of films about the glories of Soviet life post-war. If you watched her war films, and I had in my teenage years, you would think my mother had killed more Fritzes than the entire Red Army.

From the fire my father had ignited to rid himself of my mother's belongings, I saved one scorched picture: my mother receiving a medal from Stalin himself. All the men in the picture gazed at her with adoration except my father. He scowled. Fortunately, Stalin was in the part of the picture eaten by the fire. I trimmed my father away from what was left.

When my father had denounced my mother, he called her a *prostitutka*, and the number of her "lovers" arrested at the same time gave that insult credence in an attempt to save themselves. That was the current official conclusion about my mother. Her fame had corrupted her, and she had given her Soviet-owned body to men other than her husband for the money and gifts they could give her. Capitalistic vanity.

"Follow me," Captain Mikhailovna said and marched down the long room of busy typists to an empty desk in a corner far away from anything of importance.

I marched smartly behind her, noting how the others snuck glances at me.

"This is your station," Mikhailovna announced.

A squat, black Cyrillic typewriter sat in the middle of the wooden desk. Beneath it was a thin, green felt blotter for noise mitigation, I assumed. Beside the typewriter sat a reel-to-reel tape deck and a pair of heavy headphones.

"You were instructed on the procedures here?" Mikhailovna asked me.

"Yes, Comrade Captain."

"Recite them to me."

"I transcribe what is recorded on the reel, word for word. When I finish the transcription of the reel, I remove it from the player, return it and the typed sheets to you, sign a form that I returned it, receive another reel from you, sign that I received it, and repeat the process."

Mikhailovna waited, an eyebrow raised.

"And forget everything I have heard while transcribing."

"Very good, Lieutenant. You will find one ream of paper in the upper right drawer. When you need more paper, pause the tape, stand at attention at your desk, and I will bring you another. At the end of the day, return all unused paper to me along with your final reel, whether it is finished or not. You will note we have no trash bins. Your purpose here is errorless, accurate transcription. I will count your errors. If you do make an error, pause your tape, type over the error with Xs, rewind the tape past your error, and resume. You will receive a ten-minute break morning and afternoon. Long enough to use the toilet but nothing more. Half the group goes to lunch at noon and returns at 1245. The other half at 1300, returning at 1345. You are new. You are in the second group. For lunch, you must use the commissary here. You may not bring in your own food. You may not leave here for food. No phone calls to or from here. No visitors. No fraternizing with our male comrades during work hours. We conclude at 1700, and if you do not finish your last reel, you will resume with that reel the following morning. Any questions?"

"No, Comrade Captain."

"Get started, Comrade Lieutenant."

I set my hat on the upper right corner of the desk, as had every other woman here. I sat in the armless, stiff-backed, and cushionless chair and donned the headphones. I pressed "Play" and began to type. Mikhailovna hovered for a moment before she marched back to her desk.

Despite the droning monotony of the recording—an instructor reporting on the progress of his trainees, who were only identified by a three-digit number—I did not get bored. The details fascinated me, and, contrary to what I'd told the captain, I absorbed them. The morning passed quickly, and break time arrived. Each typist stood at attention at her desk and filed out at Mikhailovna's command to form a long queue. With military precision, the line made its way to the women's toilets and stalled almost at once.

After several minutes, I checked my watch.

"Do not worry," came a voice from behind me. "Comrade Captain knows we have but two toilets for all of us. She will excuse a few minutes of tardiness, but we must make sure we tell her there was a line. Each of us. Otherwise, she deducts how long you were late from your lunch time. Do you smoke?"

I glanced over my shoulder. A diminutive girl with a narrow face and mousy hair. No makeup at all, but she did not need it. She was the typist who sat to my immediate left.

"No. Why?"

"Why, I was going to . . . how do the Americans say? Ah, yes, *bum* one off you at lunch. I am Masha. Pardon me. Lieutenant Vashnikova, and as we all heard, you are Lieutenant Lubova. You are on the back row because you are new. I am there because of my typographical errors. Keep typing like you are, and you will be right up front, next to the Comrade Captain's desk." Masha winked at me.

The line inched closer to the toilets.

"How do you know how well I type?" I asked.

"You are close enough I could see you have not backed up to cross out any errors. So, your mother was that famous actress, *da?*"

My jaw clenched. "She was an actress, *da.*"

"I have seen all her films. They were too good to destroy, you know. They simply removed her name from the credits. You look like her."

"Sometimes not a positive aspect," I murmured. "She died in a gulag, where she belonged."

A brief silence, then Masha's voice came from close to my

right ear. "No need to be socialistically precise around me, Comrade Lubova. 'Revolutions are always verbose.'"

Stunned, I almost didn't step forward to close the gap in the line. Comrade Lieutenant Maria "Masha" Vashnikova had spoken the latest code phrase of the Red Circle, which meant she knew my status before I arrived.

Now, I asked myself was, is she here to assist me in my part of the Red Circle's plan, or is she here to spy on me?

2

CALCULATIONS

63 years later . . .

November 2020
Cologny, Geneva, Switzerland

I stood on a dock jutting into Lake Geneva and willed myself not to shiver. The average Geneva winter temperatures were balmy compared to the Siberian winters of my youth; however, my bones, now in their ninth decade, were fussy. They preferred warmth.

I had tired of being indoors, and the mild day invited me outside. Geneva had gone into lockdown at the end of February, and for nine months, I had rarely stirred from my apartment attached to Natalia Bukharin's house. Natalia, for whom I was personal security when she was a child, arranged for the delivery of my groceries and medications. The apartment had a strong WiFi signal and a smart television. I had no reason to leave the safety of my quarantine.

Today, I craved movement, and pacing my apartment for hours on end had grown tiresome. Because of that scant exercise, my legs were firm beneath me as I'd descended the stairs from the house to the end of the dock.

The constant breeze off the lake lowered the mild temperature a few degrees, and my wool coat with its lining should have been sufficient. Yet, I felt the breeze like needles of ice in my knees and shoulders. To alleviate that, I focused on the sun glinting off the water and brought to mind what I'd learned on the Internet.

The average water temperature of Lake Geneva in winter was fifty degrees Fahrenheit.

How long before submersion in fifty-degree water would render me unconscious?

I brought to mind the hypothermia chart I'd studied. Thirty to sixty minutes.

The thirty was not so bad. The sixty was long enough that I might change my mind.

No, I am a patient woman; I am Russian, after all. I was KGB. I could wait as long as it took for the Matterhorn to erode.

I should go into the water face down. Face up, I would float for a while, and, per my calculations, that would mean an hour to die, long enough for someone to miss me and come looking. I don't want that humiliation. I want to lose consciousness quickly, fall to the bottom of the lake, and be food for the fishes.

But, I had not written a note. I should do that. So no one would wonder. So no one would question my fate. I should make clear this was my decision, that this was not a plot by the Russian security services to eliminate me, that this was my choice after weeks of internal debate and no one's fault.

Why was I doing this, this suicide ideation?

I am eighty-one years old. I am a widow, not from natural

causes but from murder. I took revenge for that, and to my surprise, the satisfaction had been brief, too brief.

I had assumed that elusive thing called closure would have shut the door on my old life, the one where I was happy, the one I had come to love, to need. Not long after my wife Olive's death, I sold our house in Oregon, brought our belongings here to Geneva, and put them in storage. Olive's son would want some items—family pictures, a few pieces of his mother's furniture, and Olive's jewelry for any bride he might have. I have carefully labeled all of that. The rest, the things that I used to furnish my apartment, Natalia could do with as she pleased. After.

My loose ends neatly tucked away. My will was up to date, as were my medical directives. A recent physical had revealed me to be healthy and hearty, despite aches, pains, and the annoyance of persistent insomnia.

"You could live another twenty years!" the doctor had declared with a bright smile.

The truth is I honestly have nothing more to tie me to life. In some ways, my authentic life began when I met Olive and understood, through her love, who I am. Was. If I count only the length of time we were together, living that life I loved, I would only be sixteen years old instead of an aged and useless woman.

Why has it taken me so long to get to this point?

I realized people would miss me. At one time in my life, that would not have mattered to me. Now, it did. How could that have happened? All my training, my life's philosophy had insisted on no encumbrances. I had imbued that in all my trainees. Most of them had listened to me. The ones who had not? Some died because encumbrances could also mean betrayal. Others had hidden their encumbrances well, and the one notable exception for enjoying life's encumbrances was my *staryy droog*, Bukharin.

I narrowed my eyes at the water. This was what I wanted, what *I* had decided to do.

"What do you wait for, *starushka*?" I murmured.

The depth of the water at the end of the dock was fifteen feet, and if I swam far out into the lake, unconsciousness might come sooner; exhaustion might drag me down. Despite the doctor's optimism, such exertion might give me a heart attack.

All I had to do was take a step or two, and the water would embrace me.

I took the first step, but other footsteps behind me stopped me from taking another.

3

OLD HORSE

I turned to see the two moderately steep, wooden staircases that ran from the main house and the guest house to the dock. Whereas I had easily negotiated the one from the guest house, albeit one step at a time as a concession to my arthritic knees, a tall, red-haired woman seemed to glide down those stairs. The woman's riding boots had heralded her approach, and she wore a knee-length tweed coat with a hood over her hair, though plenty of it escaped. A pair of oversized sunglasses covered the top half of her face, a KN95 mask the bottom.

I looked back at the lake with a sigh and pulled my mask over my nose and mouth.

Hands in her pockets, Natalia Petrovna Bukharin-Terrell stood next to me, Olga Lubova, her former au pair/bodyguard.

"Contemplating a long walk off a short pier?" Natalia asked.

I had noticed this girl's fierce intelligence upon our first meeting nearly thirty years ago. I gave Natalia what the girl would expect—a shrug.

"Well, after watching you from my home office window for

the last fifteen minutes," Natalia said, "I decided it was time for a break so I could come down here and stop you."

"Why would you think I contemplated such a walk?"

"Let's see. You sold your house in America, arranged the distribution of your belongings, and updated your will and medical directives. You showed me where to find all that paperwork, and you hardly ever leave your apartment. You haven't been to my house, only steps away, for more than two weeks. Shall I continue my presentation of evidence?"

"Perhaps I have had bad news from my doctor?"

"Since I'm your designated next of kin, and there's no HIPPA law here, I checked with your doctor when you didn't say anything. You're healthy as a horse."

"*Staraya loshad'* perhaps." An old horse.

"Whatever. What's wrong?"

"Nothing is wrong. Merely seeking a simple conclusion for a long, complicated life."

"We all hope for that, Olga. No need to hurry it along," Natalia said.

I shrugged again. "What is there for me now?"

"For one, my kids, who fucking adore you. Mums and Popi's son, Ivan Alexeivitch. And speaking of my grandfather, he's the reason you can't die for a long time. He's only four years younger than you. Don't give him any ideas about mortality, okay? Not only do I need him, and my kids need him, but Mums and his kid need him, too."

"I have nothing more to accomplish."

"Relaxing and enjoying life is something to accomplish. You've earned it." Natalia smiled. "I mean, dealing with my shit all those years means you deserve a long, fruitful retirement."

When I didn't reply, Natalia turned to face me.

"What? You think there's an afterlife where you'll see Olive again?" Natalia asked, with sarcasm worthy of the woman—Mums, Mai Fisher—who'd raised her.

"Of course not. I am a good, atheistic Communist still. It is merely that . . ."

Another pause seemed to trigger Natalia's impatience. Her "What?" was abrasive, insistent.

"I have nothing to do. I am too old to be bodyguard to your children or Ivan. I have read every book in my apartment and in your house. I have streamed every television program of interest to me. I have one friend my age left in this world, your grandfather, Alexei Nicholaivitch. What is there for me to do? Nothing!"

"Mums would be hurt you don't consider her a friend."

That made me snort at the absurdity. "Maiya has no feelings to hurt, and she was my employer, not my friend."

"Wow, you are so totally a cynical Russian today. So, what can we do to help you realize life is worth living?"

"You have your own family to worry about. Never mind me. It is what it is. I could die tomorrow. Next year. A decade from now. But I know which I want it to be."

"You're giving up," Natalia snapped. "On life. On yourself. On me."

"How is this giving up on you?"

"Apparently, I'm not important enough to you to keep you here. Olga, you were always more than my bodyguard, and you know it. When I needed it, you were teacher, mentor, mother, and father to me. Yes, I'm forty, but I still need that from you."

"You only think you do. Time to let go of childish things."

"Fuck that."

"Ah, it is obvious who influenced you more than I did. Maiya, who never met a profanity she did not like. What would you have me do, Natalia? Knit socks for your children? Read them bedtime stories? Put plasters on skinned knees? Bake them cookies? They have a nanny for that. You are a grown, strong, powerful woman. A magnificent lawyer who has won rights for people who did not have them. You have a husband you love and who loves you. You have a country to return to when it rids itself of its petty dictator. I. Have. Nothing."

The silence between us was almost a barrier. Natalia turned away from me, her posture echoing mine as we stared out over the lake. Natalia's mouth had twisted into a moue of frustration, and I thought she took a long time to collect her thoughts. So long, I hoped she would tire of the stubborn silence and leave me alone. But this child, this girl, this woman whom I helped to raise, was too much like her mother figure, Mai Fisher. She and I could end up standing here, mute, for hours, if not days.

"You do have something," Natalia murmured, bitterness obvious in the emphasis she put on "something."

"Enlighten me."

"You have that long life you mentioned. You were a woman with an unusual career, and you rose high. Then, you gave that up and took on a second career so different from the first that it was neck-wrenching. Look at the sexism and misogyny you overcame. Look at how you adjusted to a completely new life and country, not once but twice, and helped make me what I am today. Think of how many other women and girls could learn from, be inspired by, your example."

"What? You want me to go onto the YouTube and blather about meaningless trivia, like the strange gamer people whom your sons listen to."

"No. Write it down."

"Write it?"

"Yes. Write a novel. A spy novel. Even if you touch on old state secrets, it's fiction, but make it autobiographical. You know, a *roman a clef*. Or..."

Natalia took me by the shoulders and turned me to face her.

"Or what?" I asked, hoping Natalia could perceive the utter contempt this ridiculous idea deserved.

"A memoir. Think of all the history you witnessed. World War II—"

"Great Patriotic War."

Natalia rolled her eyes. "Whatever. The Cold War. Sputnik. The Berlin Wall. The fall of the Berlin Wall. The dissolution of the Soviet Union. You could give others an inside look at those events, how they affected the people in your country, how they affected you. People need to know how you survived in a country that sent people to gulags for walking on the wrong side of the street."

"You forget, I sent some of those people to gulags."

"So, explain why you did that."

"Because they deserved it. Yes, many did not deserve it but were sent because they were out of favor, but every single person *I* sent to prison deserved it."

Natalia's hands tightened on my arms. "*Why* did you do it?"

"I did it for my country."

"That's it! That's exactly it."

Natalia pulled me into a tight hug, one she held for a long time before releasing me.

Her hands back in her pockets, Natalia said, "You don't have a choice about dying. Not yet, at least. Not for a long, fucking time. Last week, I bought Rachael M a new laptop. I scrubbed the hard drive on her old one, and before I came down here, I put it on the desk in your living room, waiting for you to tell your story. You can start right away, but don't forget dinner is at seven. You're joining us this evening and every evening indefinitely. Now, I'm going back to work before The Hooligans get done with virtual school and the noise level in the house exceeds safe limits. See you at dinner."

I watched Natalia head for the stairs. She stopped a few feet away and turned around, fixing me with a stare that could have come from Mai Fisher herself, one full of steel and danger.

"Don't think I'll forget you were contemplating killing yourself in a place that would remind my kids of it every fucking day of their lives."

Natalia climbed the stairs.

In Russian, I murmured, "That apple did not fall far from the Mai Fisher tree."

I MOVED my desk with the laptop closer to the window where I could see the lake. That could be my solace, knowing it was still there while I pretended to indulge Natalia's fantasy. However, I did have a title for whatever this will become, inspired by something I said to Natalia: *For My Country*. Not snappy but accurate.

I sat for several minutes, my fingers poised over the keyboard, and though this compact laptop was so different from the first typewriting device I used, it took me back to my first day as a transcriber in the Operational Training Unit of the First Directorate of the *Komitet Gosudarstvennoy Bezopasnosti*.

The KGB.

I remembered my first day in that typing pool. That officious Captain Mikhailovna. Masha. Others.

No, I was not ready to write about some of them.

I flexed my fingers and typed, "The guest house at my friend Bukharin's house . . . That is to say, my friend Bukharin's wife's house . . ." I backspaced over those seventeen words. This was pointless, futile.

"*Boizhe moi*, let me try this again."

4

FOR MY COUNTRY
ENTRY 1

The guest house where I live now is almost as large as a "McMansion" as they say in the U.S., and it holds the family of Natalia Bukharin and Alex Terrell. Natalia is my friend Bukharin's granddaughter. Her and Alex's children are Alex Jr. and Barrett Edwin—twins, twelve years old—and Rachael Maitland, who is almost ten but with the attitude of a teenager since she was three.

Also living there is the children's bodyguard, what was my old job for Natalia. The bodyguard is Dana Armbruster, a former FBI agent. Tough. Competent. She and I have had many long talks about security, and I like the way she thinks. For an old, Cold War adversary, she is not bad.

This guest house has a three-car garage attached, and above that is my apartment. That apartment has its own entrance up a flight of stairs from the garage level, but I can also go directly into the guest house's main level by a connecting door, like that of a hotel room.

That apartment is a perfect size for one person. A large, open floor plan, a nice view of Lake Geneva and the city beyond. My kitchen is small but well-equipped, and I have always loved to cook. Natalia indicated she wants me to eat more with "the family." But, my family is gone. Every family I ever had. My mother. My father. My brothers. The KGB.

Olive.

I must be a good writer. See? In a few paragraphs, I have condensed eighty-one years. I am done, yes? No. This would require too much reading between the lines for the details of my life, such as they are.

Of course, I thought this idea of Natalia's to be ridiculous. I still do. I sometimes do not remember what transpired yesterday or what I had for breakfast. How could I remember what happened long ago? But this is not a comprehensive autobiography. Indeed, if it were, the footnotes and bibliography would be classified still.

After my conversation with Natalia, the one where she thwarted my "long walk off a short pier," I returned to my apartment, made tea, and went to the computer she had provided. She had opened it, turned it on, and opened a word processing program. I will, of course, fix it so no one can read what I have written here except me; old habits die hard.

So, here I go.

"Before I, Lieutenant Olga Yevgenyevna Lubova, knocked on the door, I gave my uniform jacket a tug, set the belt precisely at my narrow waist, and smoothed my skirt. My sensible but chunky shoes had a high polish, as did the brass buckle on my belt. This morning, I made sure to place my collar tabs and epaulets per regulations. The buttons on my jacket gleamed. I had worked on ironing, polishing, cleaning everything most of the night before. The olive-gray color of the uniform was not flattering for me, but it was what it was.

"With my regulation hat tucked under my left upper arm, I

checked my hair for loose strands. From the judicious use of hairpins, every hair stayed in place. My makeup was minimal, barely a touch of lipstick, and I hoped I radiated professionalism.

"I took a deep breath, cut off by the damned regulation girdle, raised my clenched fist, and knocked . . ."

AND THAT WAS my first day as a typist in the KGB. Not terribly exciting, was it?

I suppose before I get too far along in this ridiculous exercise, I should explain something called the Red Circle, but, in truth, that could encompass its own book. Also, its primary members, a great many of them dead now, decided after the dissolution of the Soviet Union that their objective had been achieved and that no one would much care whether the Red Circle had existed or not. They destroyed all records of their existence, and the Red Circle became a mere rumor, a legend.

I will write about it what I know, what was explained to me when I was recruited.

First, a history lesson.

As Stalin rose to power after Comrade Lenin's death, a group of dedicated Leninists and Trotskyites formed the Red Circle, veterans all of the October Revolution and dismayed by Stalin's perversion of Marxism for his own aggrandizement. Slowly, they expanded the Red Circle into the military, government, even the various versions of Soviet state security: the Cheka, the OGPU, the NKVD, and their successor, the KGB. The key members of the Red Circle, the leaders, met sparingly and in secret to devise their plan to overthrow Stalin, only Stalin. They did not want another revolution. They wanted to restore the ideals of the original and return to solid Marxist principles.

Stalin's purges almost blockaded their plans.

Whether by accident or design—or a bit of both—a good number of the original Red Circle met their deaths in forced labor camps, in the basement of the Lubyanka, and even in places of exile around the world. Then, the Great Patriotic War meant putting aside the Red Circle's plans and Stalin's purges to work with the devil to save *Rodina* from the Nazis. With casualties of war and Stalin's shipping of any opponent off to gulags, the Red Circle had to be rebuilt and their plan refined.

After the end of the war when the possibility of mutually assured destruction by nuclear war arose, the Red Circle could at last put the pieces of its plan to work. Countless small operations began: specific people in specific jobs defected or became western agents; specific people were placed in key government and military positions to enact reform in a slow and careful manner; certain policies were designed to be belligerent and others benevolent. Sabers rattled for small affronts and were sheathed for major confrontations. When a general lobbied against an incursion into Afghanistan in 1979, knowing the Soviet Union was headed for an economic collapse (another of the Red Circle's operations), Red Circle members in key advisory positions won the argument for invasion, knowing it would hasten the end.

And the rest, as they say, is history.

Yes, I have used a cliche. Writing a memoir to prevent one's suicide is a cliche, too.

5

I AM BORN
ENTRY 2

I am born.

On August 23, 1939, a date of significance in my country. That was the day Soviet Foreign Minister Vyacheslav Molotov and German Foreign Minister Joachim von Ribbentrop signed the German-Soviet Non-Aggression Pact.

People celebrated all over the Soviet Union because of this, but, later, my mother would tell me the whole country had been celebrating my birth.

I can remember happiness, hers, my father's. After three boys in a row, a baby girl was a joy to them. Someone to spoil and prettify, but my mother was gone often, given her duty as a Soviet propaganda tool. I ended up as much a boy as my brothers. They taught me to fight dirty, taught me how to shoot, how to hunt and butcher my kills, all skills I would use in the KGB.

My mother would come home with pretty dresses and dolls for me, and I would wear the dresses and play with the dolls out of respect for her. They never held my interest as much as a hunting rifle or a good knife.

Some might say that behavior portended my late-in-life realization I was a lesbian, but I do not think so. I believe I was what they now call an ACE, an asexual, because my focus was on achieving my career goals. As a teenager, when most girls I knew focused on procuring a boyfriend, I worked almost without ceasing on my martial arts, all for the purpose of joining the KGB.

Many years later, my wife Olive explained that perhaps I was not asexual and maybe that was because I did not have a cultural concept of being a lesbian, that at the time I lacked the option of being a lesbian. Olive and I talked about this often, and she also suggested I might have been asexual or demisexual where I was attracted only to people I had a connection with, like Olive. Once that connection happened, I was . . . I became a lesbian? Yes, I have had to almost learn a new language.

Dmitri Kargin likes to tell the story of how he wrote to the KGB as a boy and said he wanted to be a spy and how he became a judo champion to ensure a position in the intelligence services. He stole that from me. When I was eleven, I already understood what my father did for a living—I was good at hiding and eavesdropping. I told him I wanted to follow in his work. He did try to talk me out of it, but once he encountered my stubbornness, he did what he could to help me prepare.

But again, my birth.

I remember seeing photographs of my mother and me when I was an infant. She was always smiling. She and my father looked happy, but as I grew older I became aware of the tense arguments behind closed doors. Part of that stemmed from my father's desire —now with four children in the family—for my mother to stay home and be his wife and our mother, for my mother to give up her "movie-star" career.

My mother, of course, had no say in whether to quit acting or not. Her performances were so loved, her popularity so enormous, the propaganda ministry could not afford to lose her, especially when the Great Patriotic War came along. Her work also brought her status and more privileges for her family, status and privileges we would have lost had she left it all to perform her "socialist duty as a mother to rear [and, of course, indoctrinate] the next generation of Communists."

For some time, I thought my father was simply jealous of the attention she received. That was true in a sense. My mother attracted the attention of highly placed men in the Party, and my father was jealous of that. Papa was a senior and well-respected officer in the NKVD, so he had status and privileges, too. As he aged and vodka made him more verbose, I understood he loved her and simply wanted her to be with him. Of her feelings in that regard, I am unaware, but for a long time, I suspected her frequent absences were indicative.

I remember with more than a child's clarity the day my father's men came to take her away. She looked to me as she walked away, her arms held fast by these men, her eyes pleading. What could I, a ten-year-old, have said to stop the inevitable? Nothing, but I could have told her I loved her. She could have gone to the gulag with the love of her daughter in her memory, but I stayed stoic and silent like my brothers and my father. I do not remember if I cried after she was gone or when, two years later, my father told me she had died of some epidemic that swept through her prison.

I should have cried.

Nor did I weep when I found my wife's exsanguinated body. I was too busy planning my escape before the attackers could return and correct their mistake.

The only time I remember crying as a child was when I was five or six and because of some slight my oldest brother had perpetrated on me.

So, perhaps the KGB did not take my soul. Perhaps my mother's absence did.

I was born. I was a normal baby in every way. I achieved all the standard milestones for talking, walking, and learning within the expected timeframes. Actually, I exceeded expectations. Until my mother went away, it was a good childhood where I played with my brothers, played with the puppies my father bred as a hobby. As all good Soviet children of that era, I dedicated myself to being a good Communist. I truly believed in the socialist state as it was presented to me, but I came to realize it was a veneer, a Potemkin Village on a national scale.

I realized it had to be reformed. No, restored to its original purpose, but I also learned to keep my thoughts about that to myself. My father taught me that, though in my youth, we had many quiet and deep conversations about the state of socialism in the Soviet Union.

I wondered more than once if Papa was a member of the Red Circle. How else would they have recruited me? At times I was certain he was; other times I decided he was not. I never tried any of the code phrases on him. Not that I was afraid to; rather, his response might have been one I was not ready to hear.

Still, you might ask, how did a happy baby, born to two well-positioned apparatchiks, become someone who taught people how to kill?

6

PRESUMPTUOUS

ENTRY 3

Did you think it presumptuous to title the previous entry the same as the first chapter of Dickens' *David Copperfield*? Do you believe I know nothing about decadent Western literature?

I had quite a collection of books in my Moscow apartment. Not my first one. That was barely big enough for a bed and a kitchen table. I speak of the apartment I received for my service to the state. The previous tenant, who collected them for his study of "pernicious capitalistic influences in non-Soviet literature," had left the books behind. I believe he intended someday to sell them and line his pockets.

Many of the books were rare first editions, likely taken from the libraries of the bourgeoisie and the nobility after the Revolution. He would have had quite the retirement nest egg, but I suspect he ended up in a gulag—how I got the apartment on the top floor of what had been a minor noble's house in Moscow.

Whether the previous occupant had been sent to the gulag to

vacate the apartment for me, I do not know. I could have found out. I chose not to.

You think perhaps that was because it was of no consequence to me? I was not, I am not that heartless, but I had to appear that way. That was my role to play, and I played it well. My mother, after all, was an actress. Perhaps talent is hereditary.

I added to that extensive collection of books over the years, usually banned books confiscated from counterrevolutionaries. To assess them, of course, to confirm their inappropriate content. I had to keep them—for reference purposes. Yes, the authorities believed that. Again, I was convincing.

Of course, those rare books eventually enabled me to live comfortably when I left the Soviet Union. My trainees thought they were learning tradecraft when they couriered a book at a time to rare-book sellers all over Europe. They also thought the money they brought back went into the State treasury.

A risk? Yes. A tremendous risk, but the Red Circle protected its operatives. Most of the time.

I had few regrets about leaving the Soviet Union. Rather, I felt as might a rat leaving a sinking ship, but think on this: The rat leaves the ship to survive. That is what I did. I survived. When the Soviet Union dissolved and the Red Circle's goal was essentially accomplished, my usefulness to the cabal came to an end. Granted, the Red Circle would not have done to me what the KGB would have had the coup against Gorbachev succeeded.

This is not to say the Red Circle would not have sacrificed a member if The Plan required it. However, it would never have eliminated us post-dissolution to hide its existence. In fact, many members of the Red Circle became part of the subsequent governments. Now, if the Red Circle is mentioned, it is likened to a fairy tale or a conspiracy theory about counterrevolutionaries and spies.

Had Boris Yeltsin not thrown a spanner into the works in the form of Dmitri Kargin, the current president of Russia, I believe my country would have been much different—a modern, efficient country, not a country of oligarchs, not a government whose purpose is to line the pockets of its leader and to suppress those who would criticize him.

I remember when the American President Arbust, the second one, announced he had looked into Kargin's eyes and seen his soul. I laughed. Kargin had been KGB. He had no soul. That is the first thing the KGB removes. It is a precise surgery that leaves but a small scar on some. That was Kargin. You needed a microscope to see his scar because his soul was minuscule to begin with.

I would know. I trained him. Him and hundreds of others.

After the typing pool, I was a physical conditioning instructor. Then, a weapons instructor, both standard weapons and the special ones created by the Operations and Technology Directorate. Eventually, I trained certain recruits to be assassins, ones whose psychological profiles indicated their affinity for the work. Ultimately, I received only those recruits who showed the most promise to train. I ran the training division for all operational recruits, oversaw the curriculum of every recruit's classroom training, and developed the exercises to test every recruit's physical and operational development.

But, my personal, dedicated attention went only to those "special" candidates.

When I joined the KGB as a typist in the training division, I was like all the other young women in the typing pool. I joined the KGB to spy for my country, to conduct intelligence operations in foreign countries to benefit my country. However, even in an "egalitarian" socialist society, women learn their place. Operational spying was for men, and the women could type their reports.

Unless, of course, you were a beautiful woman. Then, you were trained to use your looks and your bodies to compromise specific targets. As well as their looks, these women had to show an affinity for sex in their psychological assessments. I have been told I was beautiful, but my psychological profile indicated I would not have been a good swallow.

Of course, there were exceptionally beautiful women recruits who, perhaps, fit the type of woman a specific target preferred, and they were forced to use their bodies for the state. Some of the women liked this work, even looked forward to such assignments, especially when it involved an older man. One "swallow" once told me, "I like it, Comrade, because Western men are better lovers than Russian men. No 'wham-bam-thank-you-ma'am' from Westerners. And they have stamina."

It turns out the least favorite assignment for a "swallow" was the young U.S. embassy guards, usually Marines. No finesse and no stamina is what I was told.

A few handsome men also did this same work. The "ravens" seduced women or men. The prime target was a female embassy secretary, far away from home, lonely and lacking male attention, someone who would respond to a man who treated her, above all, like a queen.

I trained both swallows and ravens—classroom instruction only, not physical instruction. I developed the curriculum and had the more experienced swallows and ravens teach the newer ones— all under my observation.

Why did I not do "hands-on" training in this area? Again, my desire to have no encumbrances, though I understood only many years later why physical intimacy with men had no appeal for me.

I progressed higher in positions of authority and responsibility because of my work ethic, not because I kowtowed to or slept with influential men in the Party. Three years after joining the KGB, I was training its elite operatives. Some might call it a meteoric rise, but I had no complaints against me. I was in charge of operational training for thirty-one years, and the next logical step would have been head of the KGB. That was the Red Circle's plan for me, but the non-Red Circle head of the KGB decided to try to overthrow Mikhail Gorbachev.

But I have digressed.

I have researched the writing of memoirs since I began this exercise, and I am of the school where I write about whatever memory enters my head. Still, time to get back on topic.

7

PART OF THE PLAN

ENTRY 4

1958

KGB Headquarters
First Directorate (Training Unit)
Moscow, USSR

Masha Vashnikova's prediction on my first day in the typing pool had been right. I soon progressed to the front row, a perfect spot from which to learn much about Captain Mikhailovna.

For the better part of each day, Mikhailovna stood at the head of the room at parade rest, her eyes watching, her ears listening. If she determined someone's behavior required correction, she did so publicly and in the most humiliating manner possible. I had avoided such attention, but I had witnessed its bestowal on others.

One young woman, reduced to tears by Mikhailovna's humiliation, and whose tears engendered more humiliation from the captain, had slit her wrists with her own belt buckle during a toilet break. Everyone in line complained about how long she was taking to do her business—until the blood seeped from under the door. I kicked open the door and saw right away nothing could be done. When summoned, Mikhailovna had stared at the ghost-white body, the sad face streaked with tears.

"An inefficient way to deal with weakness," Mikhailovna had said, "but an effective one." She laughed at her own joke, a sound I never forgot.

Some weeks later, I paused my tape player and came to attention when Captain Mikhailovna appeared at my desk. According to the Red Circle's plan, or rather, my small part in it, I was due a promotion to captain and a reassignment out of the typing pool. Indeed, it should have happened two weeks ago, and I had wondered if Mikhailovna had deliberately held it up.

"Yes, Comrade Captain?" I said, raising my voice over the din of typists.

"How long before you finish your current reel?"

I gave the reel a quick glance. "Approximately a half hour, Comrade."

"When you finish, bring the reel, the transcription, your cover, and yourself into my office."

"Understood, Comrade Captain."

I stayed at attention. Mikhailovna seemed displeased, but she said, "Carry on, Comrade Lieutenant."

"Yes, Comrade Captain."

I resumed my seat and my transcription. Twenty-seven minutes later, I removed the reel and stacked the typed sheets neatly into an official folder. I picked up my hat and looked toward Masha, two rows behind me. Masha gave me a fleeting smile and a single nod.

Items in hand, I went to the closed door to Mikhailovna's office and knocked. No response, but Mikhailovna herself opened the door. I marched in and came to attention before her desk. The desk was a plain affair with no ornamentation. A ledger lay on one side of the desktop, a fountain pen atop it and a full bottle of ink beside it. A pristine blotter dead center. Nothing more.

Against the wall behind the desk, several file cabinets stood in a row, each file cabinet identical to its fellows. Above the cabinets hung three official photographs: Lenin, Felix Dzerzhinsky, and Khrushchev. I had been in here numerous times to deliver my transcriptions, and the room bore no surprises.

Except for a man who leaned against the wall in a corner of Mikhailovna's office.

He wore an ill-fitting black suit whose trousers were too long for him and bloused at his ankles; a white shirt yellowed from much laundering; a black bow tie. His hair was full on top and brushed back off his face. Thick eyebrows lay like caterpillars on his forehead, and his dark eyes were muddy and dull. He smoked a cigarette held at the top of the V of his index and middle fingers. Like a Westerner.

I took all this in with a brief twitch of my eyes toward him.

Mikhailovna took her usual stance behind her desk, her fingertips resting on the blotter. At Mikhailovna's nod, I placed the reel and the transcription file on the desk. Mikhailovna opened the ledger and found the entry with the reel's identification number. She unscrewed the cap to her fountain pen and made a mark next to that entry. She turned the ledger around to face me and handed me the pen. I signed my name next to the mark and handed back the pen. Mikhailovna double-checked the number on the file and the reel against the ledger entry again. I wondered if the more meticulous than usual attention to detail was for the strange man's benefit.

Satisfied, Mikhailovna opened the top righthand drawer of the desk and placed the reel inside. The file went into the corresponding lefthand drawer. Mikhailovna stared at me for an interval that would have made anyone else's nerves jumpy, but I remained quiet and still.

Mikhailovna opened the desk's center drawer and removed a file from it. I recognized the blue folder as being from the Human Assets Department. Mikhailovna did not hand the folder over.

"I have received the appropriate paperwork for your promotion to captain and your transfer within the training department to be a physical fitness and martial arts instructor," Mikhailovna recited, her inflection flat, her mouth turned down. "Effective immediately. Our comrade here . . ." She inclined her head toward the corner where the man stood. ". . . will escort you."

After more intense scrutiny of me, Mikhailovna turned to the man. "Comrade, I would like to speak to the lieutenant in private. To offer a word of advice."

The man's eyes went from Mikhailovna to me and back again, seeming to issue a warning to both of us. He pushed away from the wall and exited to the hallway via the office's private entrance.

"Comrade Lieutenant," Mikhailovna began, once he had left, "I can do nothing to stop either the transfer or the promotion, neither of which I believe you are ready for. Bearing that in mind, I have to ask, who in the Party are you sleeping with?"

"No one, Comrade Captain."

"Do not lie to me."

"I swear, Comrade Captain, no one."

"Are you a virgin?"

"Comrade, I do not see—"

"Answer me."

"No, Comrade. I dispensed with it when I was sixteen."

Mikhailovna's upper lip curled into a sneer. "Oh? Were you deeply in *love*?"

"No, Comrade, merely curious."

"I see. You will thank yourself for that curiosity and for the fact you are not a virgin in your new posting. You will be the only female instructor. The male instructors will establish their dominance immediately by disciplining you with rape."

"Respectfully, Comrade, they may try such crudity. Their success is unlikely."

"Do not overestimate your . . . talents, Lieutenant."

"Comrade Captain, I believe you said my promotion was effective immediately."

"You are a lieutenant until you leave this room. You have no mother, so I consider it my duty to warn you. Our socialist state touts its equality for women, but official policy and reality are two different things. When you walk through the doors of the training academy, the men there, from the instructors to the recruits, will not see you as a peer but only as a convenient means to satisfy their lust. I am not being hyperbolic. I speak from experience."

"Allow me to reassure you, Comrade Captain. They will discover I am not a pushover for their lust. They will have the bruised balls to show for it."

Mikhailovna laughed, the sound taking me back to the bloody toilet and the jagged cuts on the young typist's wrists.

"I wish you luck, Lieutenant . . . Captain Lubova. When you have reality thrust into your face, among other places, I will happily take you back here."

"Do not hold my desk for me, Comrade. Thank you for your advice. Am I dismissed?"

Another bout of staring and Mikhailovna hissed like the snake she was, "I hope they put you in the same gulag that killed your whore of a mother. Dismissed!"

8

MOI OTETS (MY FATHER)

ENTRY 5

Since I have mentioned him earlier, now I will write about my father. The fashionable thing to say about him would be that he and I had a "complicated" relationship. In truth, it was simple. All of Yevgeny Lubov's children knew exactly what he expected of them: to be the best at whatever we chose to be.

My father had been the best at whatever he did. What he did was spy on his own people, but there was none better.

When I joined the KGB and people recognized my patronymic, they would always speak of my father in glowing, patriotic terms, no doubt expecting me to tell him of their flattery. However, one person—about whom we shall learn more later—told me of a rumor that my father had been among the ones who shot the tsar and his family. I was not sure I wanted to know the truth and never confirmed it.

It was enough that he was the best at what he did, and he communicated clearly what he expected of us.

For my oldest brother Yevgeny Yevgenevitch that meant being

an elite athlete, a top weight-lifter in his case. Zhenya won a team gold medal in the 1964 Olympics. He was proud of that accomplishment, but I was sure my father expressed his disappointment that Zhenya did not receive the individual gold.

For my next brother, Boris Yevgenevitch, who, like me, favored our mother, it was acting. He never quite achieved our mother's fame, but he appeared in well-received Soviet films of the 1960s. Like our mother, his specialty was playing brave Red Army soldiers in the Great Patriotic War or in made-up conflicts with the Americans. He was quite handsome but decided he did not want to be associated with our mother too closely. He acted under the name Boris Smerdlov. He won several noted awards and received medals for his work in the arts but not the Order of Lenin he, and my father, coveted.

For brother Arkady Yevgenevitch, it was the Red Army. He advanced quickly through the ranks, no doubt to evade our father's criticism. When he was fifty and due to be a general, he died in Afghanistan with his officer staff when the Mujaheddin shot down his helicopter with an American RPG. Papa was not alive to witness what he would have characterized a failure, but Arkasha received a Hero of the Soviet Union medal posthumously —no promotion, though.

For my youngest brother, the one younger than me . . . Well, he never got a chance to receive my father's advice to be best. Alexander Yevgenevitch—Sasha—died when he was nine months old, but up to that point, he was energetic and curious. He particularly loved my father's borzois.

Papa had taken to breeding the Ukrainian line of borzois, and we all grew up with them, adult dogs and puppies of various ages all over the house. We fed them and washed them and watched Papa train them with a care and compassion he sometimes did not show us. They were magnificent animals.

Before the Revolution, only the tsar could gift one, usually only to other royalty or nobility. After the Revolution, the animals were considered too much a symbol of aristocratic decadence, bourgeois, even *nekulturny*. They fell out of favor and were often turned out of houses to fend for themselves.

In the 1940s, a Russian soldier noticed the borzois he found in Cossack villages and began to manage the breed, lest it suffer from too much inbreeding. That soldier was a friend of my father's and gave Papa his first breeding pair.

Commensurate with his desire to be the best at everything he did and to serve as an example of that to his children, he studied the history and behavior of the borzoi and became quite the expert. He eventually procured a dozen breeding pairs and would select the best puppies from the litters to gift to Party officials and friends. He also conducted hunting parties with the animals— they were originally hunting dogs. That made my father quite the popular figure.

But my brother Alexander . . . Little Sasha . . .

I said earlier I could not remember when I last cried, but now I do.

Sasha was born when I was six. I was seven when he died.

Papa's top borzoi sire was a beautiful, white dog named King of the Steppe. We children called him Stepi. Borzois are well-behaved, calm animals, even gentle. They can quickly resort to hunting behavior with animals smaller than they are, but, for example, if you introduce a borzoi to a smaller dog or a cat when the borzoi is a puppy and they grow up together, you have no problem. Even then, borzois are not aggressive toward humans unless humans trigger their hunting behavior.

One day, like any other day, Sasha played with Stepi, but for some reason this day, Sasha seemed determined to test his boundaries with the dog. All day long, I heard Papa say, "Sasha, leave

Stepi alone. Sasha, do not pull Stepi's tail. Do not crawl on Stepi, Sasha. Sasha, listen to me!"

Papa would put Sasha and Stepi in different rooms, but Sasha would find Stepi in no time. Once Sasha learned to crawl, nothing and no one could stop him from going anywhere. Even Stepi himself would get up from a nap and leave the room with Sasha in it, and Sasha would crawl after him.

Papa was about to take Stepi to his kennel—people in Russia at that time should have had such a roomy place to live—but a phone call interrupted him. Then, Papa went to his office to do his paperwork of tracking the breeding cycles of the bitches and which male should next be put with which bitch. He paid meticulous care to this to ensure no inbreeding, and he was likely too deep into this work to pay attention to Sasha's continued badgering of Stepi.

My brothers were playing outside that day, as they often did to escape Papa's lectures. Sasha was too young to play their rough games; he was a nonentity to them, much as I was, though I would push myself into their play. On this day, as I often did, I skulked about the house, from hiding place to hiding place, without my father seeing me, perhaps a portent of my future employment. I was outside Papa's office, listening to Sasha's incoherent babbling, Stepi's impatient sighs, and Papa turning the pages of his ledger.

I peeked through the gap between the door and the door jamb, watching Papa. His thick, dark hair was oiled and combed back off his face. He wore his home "uniform" of trousers, boots, and tunic. His brow furrowed as he studied the entries in the ledgers and made notes.

Though borzois are not frequent barkers, I heard Stepi give a short, deep bark. He did not growl. He barked as if in pain. I heard a wet sound I could not identify, followed by a thump, as if someone had thrown a book to the floor.

My father's head jerked up, and he paled, his face so white I though he had become a ghost. He leapt from the desk, hand on the gun he always wore at his side. He went out of my limited field of vision. I heard a shot, loud in the confined area. My ears rang from it. The burnt cordite (of course, then I did not know what it was) tickled my nose and made me sneeze.

I peeked around the door.

My father was on his knees, his back to me, and I heard him weeping, murmuring, *"Nyet, nyet, nyet,"* over and over. I saw Stepi's rear legs, unmoving.

I could not see Sasha.

I tiptoed into the room so quietly that my spy father did not hear me. At first, I thought Papa had shot Sasha. Papa's gun lay on the floor between him and Sasha. Stepi had a neat hole in his head, black against the white coat and right behind his right eye. There was blood on his muzzle and flesh in his mouth. Blood spread on the floor around his head.

Sasha was whiter than Stepi's coat and also in a pool of blood. From his chin to the esophageal notch, there was nothing but raw, torn skin and a hint of bone and cartilage.

Days later, after the funeral, where my mother screamed and cried—"Her best performance," Papa would say after—I did my usual skulking among the guests who had come to offer condolences. My mother was upstairs in her bed, sedated.

My father spoke to a man who had rested his hand on Papa's shoulder. The man's face was pock-marked, and he had a thick, graying mustache. I recognized him at once. His picture adorned almost every room and hallway in our house, hung in every public building in town.

Chairman Stalin.

Papa said, "It was so quick. Stepi shook him like a rag doll and slammed my baby boy against the floor. There was so much blood.

I . . . I had to shoot him. I had to shoot every one of his pups in the kennel and the bitch pregnant with his latest litter. I had to."

That was how I confirmed the King of the Steppe had killed Baby Sasha.

As did my mother, I blamed my father.

"Why did you not put the fucking dog in its pen?" my mother would wail every time she was in my father's presence.

I realized later, my father had acted from his extensive knowledge of the animals and their intrinsic behavior. Despite no doubt remembering the hours Sasha slept with Stepi curled protectively around him, how Stepi would guard Sasha from venturing into dangerous things, my father knew he could not predict the moment Stepi would lose patience and strike at Sasha in annoyance and frustration. My father had no choice but to do what he had done—avenge his child.

After witnessing my father's grief, I forgave him. My mother did not.

Papa was not the same after. He stooped when he stood or walked, and his hair seemed to gray overnight. He started to drink more vodka. His waist thickened, and his face grew fleshy and mottled. I had always thought him the handsomest of men but no more. He seemed a sad, old man, which made it easier for me to follow in his footsteps and be better than him.

I never had a dog of any breed ever again, until . . . Well, that is for later.

My father was drunk in 1949 when he denounced my mother as a traitor, counterrevolutionary, and anti-Stalinist. The authorities took his drunken word on it. He watched unmoving, unblinking when his own men led her from our house, to which she never returned. I was ten, and I worshipped Papa. Whatever he did was right in my eyes.

When the car had taken her away, he took down all her

pictures, gathered all her clothing and belongings, and started the bonfire from which I rescued that one picture of her. Olive, my wife, found that picture many years later and had it restored and framed for me. It rests beside a picture of Olive on my fireplace mantel, reminders of the two women I loved most in this world.

When you grow old yourself, you look back on your memories with a certain sentimentality. It took Olive's love to remind me my parents had loved each other. They'd had four of their five children in four years, after all. Before Sasha, my mother's eyes would shine on sight of my father, and he would always smile at her. Whenever she returned from making one of her propaganda movies, she would gather my brothers and me into her arms, but her eyes would be only for "*moy lyubov Genya.*"

Perhaps seeing my mother led away to prison and my father remaining stoic in his duty was the source of my distaste for encumbrances. Avoidance of encumbrances kept me from Papa in the last years of his life, as his vodka-infused liver failed, and the physically fit, handsome man became a bloated, jaundiced shadow of himself.

Perhaps I would have been a comfort to him in his last days, as daughters often are to fathers. I do not know.

One day in 1970, one of my staff told me I had a phone call from my brother Zhenya. I instructed the secretary to take a message. I focused on my task at hand, overseeing the training of my latest group of *ubiytsy*, assassins. When I finally went to my office to dictate the day's reports, which some up and coming lieutenant in the typing pool would transcribe, I did not read Zhenya's message until nearly midnight.

In her neat Cyrillic cursive, my assistant had written on a folded slip of paper: *Ot vashego brata: <Nash otets ymer. Zhenya.>*

From your brother: "Our father has died."

I did not go to the funeral. I had to conduct the final examinations of the *ubiytsy*. To this day, I do not know where the Party buried Papa.

Addendum:

Some days after writing this, I felt compelled to go through my box of the few items I brought out of the dying Soviet Union with me. One was a small portrait of my father, taken in his NKVD days, in his uniform. Ah, so handsome but unsmiling. He was the way I remembered him, the way he was before Sasha died, before Mama left. I realized that was how he should be remembered: strong, resilient, effective, a spy above all others, the man after whom I modeled my career.

I am glad I did not go see him at the end. No one should ever see their gods die.

9

ON MY OWN

ENTRY 6

1961

KGB Training Division
Moscow, USSR

The man who had escorted me from the typing pool to my new position and promotion went by a single name, Strakh. Any of the definitions of that word—fear, awe, fright, dread, anxiety—fit the man.

His position in the Training Directorate was never clear to anyone within it, but everyone knew when Comrade Strakh spoke, his words were to be heeded. He looked and dressed like any other bureaucrat, but he fought nastier and dirtier than anyone I had ever seen, and he taught me to do the same.

From the time I'd arrived at my new posting, Strakh would hover at the back of my fitness classes. Always dressed in workout clothing, also too big for him, he observed—not me but my students. If a student refused to follow my instructions or acted salaciously toward me, Strakh would single him out for "special" attention, which was to thrash the offending student senseless.

This happened often enough to compel me to request a conference with Strakh.

In his office, Strakh almost never sat at his desk but paced back and forth, like a caged lion, while the other person spoke. When Strakh was ready to answer or comment, he would stop before the speaker, almost nose to nose, and puff away on his ubiquitous *Belomorkanal* cigarettes.

I had been a frequent visitor to his office, where I received my assignments, discussed students, and occasionally listened to his lectures about the history of the various iterations of the Soviet intelligence services. His knowledge was as extensive as my father's, but where my father tended to focus on operational issues, Strakh imparted philosophy.

Before the revolution, my father had formed the group for Lenin that became the Cheka. My father's spies had spied on the tsar's spies and learned effective lessons from the Okhrana to use against them and to put to use after the Revolution. Indeed, the Cheka wasn't much different from the Okhrana. My father had been Lenin's trusted man. Surely Strakh knew this. But he supplemented the "what" my father provided with the "why."

Strakh stopped pacing and lit a fresh cigarette when I entered. I came to attention and said, "Comrade, if I may speak freely?"

"You may always speak freely here, Comrade Captain. You are aware of that."

I was, as I was also aware Strakh was Red Circle.

"Comrade Strakh, with respect, I ask that when a recruit is disrespecting me that you allow me to address it," I said.

"How would you address it, Captain?"

"I would make a single attempt to reason with the recruit. One only. After that, I will kick his ass. I am quite capable of that."

Strakh's smiles were rare and somewhat terrifying, but he smiled at me; I wasn't afraid. "Yes, Comrade, I remember your first day here when I asked you to demonstrate your skills for me."

The smile dropped away with an abruptness that made my heart race.

"Comrade Captain," he said. "I am simply assisting you in the handling of these . . . enthusiastic young men."

"And in the process, undermining my authority, Comrade."

He smoked, directing his exhalations away from my face, but he never broke eye contact.

"Very well," he said, "I will no longer observe your classes, but if you end up in a situation you cannot handle—either from one of your students or from another instructor—you will be on your own. Understood, Comrade?"

"Of course, sir."

"Now, we have addressed that. It is good you wanted to see me. I have something to discuss with you." He stepped closer to her. "'As long as I breathe, I shall fight for the future,'" he said, the Trotsky quote cuing me we were about to discuss Red Circle business. "Do you agree?"

"Of course, Comrade," I whispered.

"We are not bugged. They would not dare. Your performance has exceeded expectations, and it is time for your next step. In addition to your regular instructional duties, for the next six weeks I will train you in assassination techniques. Poison. Knives. Guns. Improvised weapons." He paused, eyes peering into mine, no doubt seeking a reaction. "By hand." He smiled, again fearsome, when he saw my reaction. "Excellent. Your pupils dilated in arousal and, therefore, showed your interest in this new aspect of your career."

"As my part in The Plan was explained to me, being an assassin was not mentioned. Has my role changed?"

"We do not expect you to be an assassin, unless a situation presents itself, and that will be your choice. You will continue to train recruits, including the hidden Red Circle recruits. Rather, you will be training not raw recruits but the most elite who have been identified as potential assassins—both Red Circle and regular KGB. Our expectations of you will be commensurately high, and after your training, you will be observed for some time to determine if you are suited to conducting this training. If you do not succeed—but you *will* succeed—you may resume your current duties here. I have full confidence, however, that you will end up training the most elite recruits for our most important work. For the Revolution." A slight pause. "And for The Plan."

At times like this, I wished I could turn to my father for advice. No, I thought, I am twenty-two years old, a grown woman. I will make my own decisions and handle the aftermath myself.

"I am ready, Comrade Strakh," I said. "I will never disappoint you."

"Disappointing me is not the issue, Olechka. It is disappointing *Rossii-matushki*, who has given you so much. Clear?"

Mother Russia.

I will do this for my country.

"Absolutely clear, Comrade. *Dlya Rossii-matushki.*"

10

MAYA MAT' (MY MOTHER)
ENTRY 7

My other complicated parental relationship was, of course, with my mother. During the war years, she was in constant demand for films, and her visits to our home or *dacha* were infrequent. I have a vague memory of a tall, beautiful woman swooping into the house and calling for "*moy mladentsy!*"—my babies. She would bring gifts for us, toys mostly. Sometimes chocolate. Mama learned fairly soon I was not one for dresses and dolls, and she stopped bringing them. She replaced them with other things—books, records, drawing paper and pencils—which I enjoyed more.

I remembered the smell of her perfume and always wondered what it was. When I first came to Moscow, I went to GUM to the fragrance counter and sampled the half-dozen or so Soviet brands there. None of them matched what I remembered. I shrugged it off to the fact it was a childhood memory and not reliable.

Years later, when I came to America to work for my friend Bukharin and his wealthy wife Mai Fisher, whom I have always called Maiya . . . She is not Russian; it is simply what I called her.

She has one of those unisex . . . No, pardon me. She has a gender neutral name, Maitland, but she has always been called Mai; hence, Maiya.

One day she came into the family room. She and Bukharin were not on a mission but going out to dinner, only the two of them, and she smelled like my mother.

"What is that perfume you wear?" I asked, trying to be nonchalant. "It is a lovely scent."

"Chanel No. 5," was her reply.

That was an expensive, French perfume. The only way my mother could have obtained it in the 1940s Soviet Union was via the black market, which Party members had used almost since the Revolution. Or someone, some admirer, gave it to her. Indeed, my father noted that in his report when he accused her of being a traitor to him and Mother Russia, of being an adulterer to him and the Party. So, my father was not the giver.

As a good operative, Maiya would not wear such an easily identifiable perfume on a mission, and one day when Natalia was at school and Bukharin and Maiya were away somewhere, I went into Maiya's dressing room and sprayed a handkerchief of mine with that perfume. I put the handkerchief in a plastic baggie. I would open the bag only a little, enough to catch a brief scent. That was the only way I could bring my mother's face to mind.

After so many openings, as careful as I was, the scent evaporated, and I dared not repeat my little theft for such a sentimental indulgence. For the Christmas holiday that year, my gift from Maiya was a bottle of Chanel No. 5. The perfume. Not the *eau de cologne*. How she knew, I do not know.

I probably do not want to know.

How, you ask, did any of this make my relationship with my mother complicated?

It was complicated because I barely knew her. I was six when the war ended and the demand for propaganda films ebbed. She was home for at least a year, during which time my little brother Sasha was born, and then the propaganda ministry wanted her to make films showing how decadent the West was. She played a number of parts as an American spy sent to Russia to seduce dedicated Soviets away from the Revolution—probably why people later called her a prostitute.

Then, Little Sasha died. My mother retreated into her anger and grief, shutting herself away in her room for weeks, refusing to see my father or us children, who needed her. She eventually went back to making films, this time as a director. Documentaries, all extolling the Soviet way of life. I will never know whether she truly believed this or was still playing a part.

When she was home, she and my father argued, and my father drank. My brothers, because they were boys, ignored this, but the harsh words my parents exchanged, my father's drinking, all of it bothered me.

Until I realized worrying about my family was an encumbrance. I, too, began to ignore them and took the easy way of blaming her.

Of course, with hindsight, I ask, was it really her fault?

Also, with hindsight, the answer is no. Rather, my life revolved around my father. He was the constant presence in his children's lives, good or bad. Even when Mama was away making her movies, he would tell us, "Your mother does important work for the State and the Party. It is our sacrifice, and we bear it for *Rodina*. Every citizen is expected to sacrifice for our great country."

My mother did come to grips with Sasha's death, how it happened, that it was an accident, but the arguments did not cease. Now, they were not about Sasha but my father's drinking. They were constant and increased in intensity until the day the men came to take Mama away. She did not fight them. She did not defend herself against the charges. My later training convinced me she did not because my father's accusations were correct. She did not fight because she knew she was guilty.

The men who took her away were my father's men from his unit in the Second Chief Directorate (internal security); they respected him. When my mother asked calmly and politely to say goodbye to her children, they did not refuse her. After all, she had held onto her beauty. Hers was the face these men had seen in cinemas when they were boys. They had probably had sexual fantasies about her then but would never admit that now.

I was ten and remember this quite well. She spoke to us together and individually. My brothers were confused but stoic. They nodded when she asked them to be good to Papa, to study hard, to do their best. She asked the same of me, and I would not look at her. She told us she loved us and that we were her reason for existence.

She left with the men. I never saw her again. Papa had us write letters, which he took and said he would post for us, but we never got a reply.

Two years after she left, Papa gathered us children to tell us Mama had become ill at her "rehabilitation center" and had died. When she left, he told us Mama was exhausted from all her work for the State, tired from her service to her country, and that she was going to a special resort to rest and recover. Again, my later training instructed me on what those "rehabilitation" or "reeducation" centers really were. Gulags.

I suspect she was dead not long after arriving at the gulag. My father put her there for treason and adultery. That was the official record. More likely, it was jealousy and vindictiveness. However, even at ten I understood how the system worked. Without anyone explaining this to me, I denied my mother, denounced her crimes, and told everyone who would listen that she had gotten the punishment she deserved. I did that to survive.

But that day when my mother said goodbye to me, when I would not look at her, she pressed one of her beautifully embroidered handkerchiefs into my palm, in case I needed to cry, she said. That was the handkerchief I sprayed with my employer's Chanel No. 5. I still have that handkerchief, and I refresh its scent when I need to.

A scorched photograph.

A handkerchief.

Vague memories.

Encumbrances all.

11

TEST

ENTRY 8

1961

Khimki Forest
Outside Moscow

Disguised with camouflage paint and with scrub and brush to hide from my quarry, I crept closer. I had only one weapon, the *chernyy nozh*, the "black knife" issued to every Soviet soldier. I held it almost casually, my eyes centered on the lone sentry, my target.

He rocked from foot to foot and blew on his hands. His Kalashnikov would be strapped in front of him, and I needed to be patient, to wait for something to occupy both his hands. I stayed still and quiet, modulating my breathing, mindful of my breath condensing in the cold air.

Waiting wasn't difficult for a Russian. For its entire existence, Russia had waited for something—peace, freedom, prosperity, all the things the Party said it had in abundance but which most Russians never experienced.

The sound of faint tapping reached my ears. The sentry had taken out his pack of cigarettes and tapped it against an index finger to free one. Once he had a cigarette in his mouth, with his lighter in one hand and the other shielding the flame from the breeze, I struck.

Head back to bare the neck. Stab. Drag.

One. Two. Three.

He fought, of course, trying to throw me off, but legs strengthened from my years of martial arts training held me steady. His struggles ceased, but I held him a bit longer. Patience, always patience.

When I released him, he didn't crumble to the ground but turned to face me as he rubbed a reddening scratch on his neck.

"You forgot this was a simulation," Strakh said. "I feared for a moment you had sharpened that training knife."

I looked at the facsimile of a Red Army combat knife. "I am sorry, Comrade," I murmured.

"Do not ever apologize to the victim, Olechka," Strakh said. "I know some assassins who do. They feel it is important, I suppose, to obtain some sort of forgiveness from their victims. That is bourgeois and self-indulgent, and I expect better of you. Because the victim is . . . ?" He raised an inquisitive eyebrow.

"Unimportant in death," I responded.

"Yes! The victim may have earned our disdain, even our anger, but once you have taken his or her life, the empty shell is of no importance. You did take me by surprise, by the way. Where were you hiding?"

I pointed to show him, and Strakh smiled. "I must have looked there a dozen times and never saw you. Excellent. Commendable. Now, divest yourself of the camouflage and let us head back to Moscow. I will explain for you the concluding operation of this training."

As Strakh drove his new Chaika along the tree-lined road, I sat quietly in the front seat, using cold cream and a man's handkerchief to remove the camouflage paint. I had a flash of memory of my mother sitting at her vanity in her bedroom, removing her makeup the same way. I pushed the memory away.

The setting sun strobed through the leafless trees, lulling me. Another flash of memory. A drive with my mother and brothers in a car gifted her by Chairman Stalin from his private collection.

"What is it the westerners say?" Strakh said, glancing at me. "A ruble for your thoughts?"

"The expression is 'A penny for your thoughts.' It would be more analogous to say, 'A kopek for your thoughts,'" I replied.

"Ah, ever the good instructor. What were you thinking about just now?"

"Nothing."

"I always know when you lie, Olechka."

"I was thinking about a day when my mother took my brothers and me for a drive. Not long before she went away."

"Not nothing but something. Something meaningful to you."

"It was merely an errant memory. It is not appropriate to dwell on her."

"You think I am some apparatchik who will run back to a political officer and report you? There is no harm to think of her. She was your mother."

"Do you think of yours, Comrade?"

"Of course not. She was a White Russian bitch. Yours was a credit to the arts in this country. Ah, how she could command the screen. When you saw her in whatever role she played, everything about her performance—the makeup, the costume, even the smallest gesture—all convinced you she was that character. The propaganda films brought her status and privilege, but she longed for more challenging roles. No other director would bother to ask for her in a film because the Propaganda Division would not allow it. Her films held the country together in time of war, and she was happy to do them. However, they were a waste of her talent."

"You speak as if you knew her."

"I did. Your father, too. I even met you when you were a child, but, now, let us discuss your final examination."

An abrupt change of subject and my training told me I needed to be wary and prepared. I wanted to ask him questions about my mother, but once that topic shift occurred, I knew it was best to stay quiet.

"You have excelled at every simulation and with every weapon," Strakh said. "However, there comes the time to test the practicality of your training. Do you understand?"

"You need to know if I can do this with a real weapon to a real person?"

He looked sidelong at me as he drove. "Can you?"

"Yes, Comrade, if that is what is expected of me."

"You are absolutely sure?"

"Yes, Comrade."

"You sound confident. I will give you that, but you will have to prove it. Not specifically to me." He glanced at me again, this time with a smile. "Having been your 'victim' several times now, your 'deceased' victim."

"How am I to prove myself?" I asked, dreading the thought that I might be ordered to kill him. If that were the case, I would not succeed.

"You have one week from today to select a target, conduct any research or surveillance as necessary, and then eliminate your target. I do not want to know who it is or the exact day, place, or time you will do it, but once you have done it, undetected by the way, you will report immediately to my residence and provide your report with sufficient detail for me to verify it—where, when, who, how. Any questions?"

"No, Comrade."

"You are certain you understand?"

"Of course, Comrade. You have explained it clearly."

"Excellent. Good hunting, Olechka."

Strakh dropped me off before the building housing my one-room apartment—a kitchen, bedroom, and living room all in the same space with a bathroom in a tiny alcove enclosing the smallest bathtub I had ever seen. I was glad for my flexibility.

After I watched Strakh drive away, I went up the four flights of stairs and filled the tub, happy that the building had hot water today. I undressed and soaked in the tub, planning as I washed. Within an hour, with the water now tepid, I had outlined the mission and concocted a plan. From the moment Strakh had told me about this special training, I suspected what the "final exam" might be.

I already had a target in mind.

12

CONFIRMED KILL

ENTRY 9

One week later

Moscow Metro

Padding and prosthetics from the technicians in the Seventh Directorate made me look like a thick-waisted babushka. Wisps of wiry gray hair peeked from beneath my faded, tattered red scarf, and my thick glasses made my rheumy eyes huge. Appliances made convincing warts and moles on my cheeks and neck. Special dentures showed discolored, crooked, cracked teeth. My overcoat was frayed at the cuffs and hem, almost worn through at the elbows. My stockings were laddered with runs, and the chunky shoes I wore were scuffed, a heel hanging on by only a nail or two.

I looked like one of many such women on the Metro, war widows living on meager pensions, making ends meet by sweeping streets or caring for children in one of the state daycare centers.

Ahead of me, standing though plenty seats were empty, was

my target. Fashionable shoes with a modest heel and a high polish; pristine stockings and a new wool coat—blessedly black; that color hid blood—with a sable collar. A multi-colored silk scarf adorned the neck, and a lovely, red leather purse rested in the crook of one arm.

I thought to myself, who in the Party are you sleeping with, Comrade Captain?

I edged closer and looked around. At the front of the subway car sat a Fourth Directorate transportation guard. He'd folded his arms across his chest, and his chin was tucked in. Sleeping. If I were close enough, I would note his badge number and report him, but I had other things to do. Everyone else in the car was absorbed with his or her own thoughts and paid a poor, old, ungainly woman no attention.

I had studied my target and learned the times she used the Metro. My rising status in the training directorate allowed me access to medical records. I also knew the woman's exact height and had even studied a chest x-ray from a recent physical to obtain the precise location of the woman's heart. I accounted for the average thickness of a winter coat plus a couple of layers of clothing and selected my weapon. I had practiced with it on a sawdust-filled mannequin made to the woman's measurements.

I didn't rush to my target because I knew she would get off the train four stops from now. I made my way forward with caution, closing in on her position as the train neared a stop. When I sensed the reduction in speed, I brushed against my target, as if I'd been jostled by the train's movement or perhaps too much vodka. I pressed an eight-inch long cylinder against a spot on the left side of the target's back and thumbed a button on the cylinder.

A spike slipped through coat, blouse, and brassiere and between the ribs anchored to the fifth and sixth thoracic vertebrae to pierce the heart.

How easy it was, like slicing soft butter. I had thought surely that heart was made of stone.

Another press of the button and the spike retracted. All done in two seconds. Maybe fewer.

A slight gasp from the target, nothing more. I eased the target to a seat and knew I should go. Now. However, I couldn't resist.

I leaned down and whispered, "An effective and efficient way to deal with weakness." The eye I could see blinked, the mouth hung open in surprise, but no sound emerged.

Louder, but not too loud, I said, "Thank you. Have a wonderful day, Comrade."

Strakh would not have approved of speaking to the target even if I did not apologize. I would leave that out of my report.

The train heaved to a stop, and the doors opened. I shuffled to them and exited. Merging with the crowd, I hid myself among them as I headed for the escalators.

Several blocks from the train station, I used a public toilet to divest myself of my disguise and to wash the "old woman" makeup from my face. From my shopping bag, I took a change of clothing then turned the shopping bag inside out, revealing a different color and pattern, and put all the items from the disguise and the weapon inside.

For the rest of the afternoon, I was a typical Muscovite woman going about my business, taking taxis, buses, and the Metro on a convoluted route around Moscow.

WALKING the final few blocks to Strakh's residence, I allowed myself to categorize my emotions: tension, apprehension, excitement, and something more, something indefinable but something that needed attention.

When Strakh opened the door to his personal apartment, I saw low lights, smelled delicious food, heard soft music, and that strange feeling somewhere below my navel intensified, spreading to every point of my body, a sensation so intense I almost shook.

Strakh closed the door behind me. "How?" he asked.

I extracted the weapon from the shopping bag and pressed the button again. The spring-loaded spike emerged with a soft snick. Even in the dim lighting, I could see the blood on it.

"Why not a knife?" Strakh asked.

"Too much effort to thrust. Too noticeable. Harder to hide."

I was almost panting now.

Strakh nodded, and I again retracted the spike, returning it to the bag. I removed the disguise to show him and got another nod of approval.

"Where?" he asked.

"The Metro. Between the Prospect Mira and Rizsnaya stops."

"Why there?"

"Because it was public. Easy to blend in. Easy to hide among the crowd."

"When?"

"Approximately 1300. The busiest time for the Metro."

"Who?"

"Captain Mikhailovna from the Training Unit typing pool."

A raised eyebrow. "Her reports on you were always glowing. Why her?"

"Because she was a cruel bitch."

"That is the emotional reason. What is the rational reason?"

"I have no logical reason. The choice of target was mine, you said. She is who I selected."

He stepped closer to me, and for the first time I let myself notice how beautiful his eyes were, how sensual his mouth.

"Think harder for the rational reason," he said.

"I researched the typing pool's error rate. Under Captain Mikhailovna, the error rate has increased an average of eleven percent. I also observed her demeanor as a commanding officer for more than a year and concluded her only means of motivating the typists was humiliation, which filled her need for position power. She was serving her ego not the Party. My rational reason is that the efficiency of the Training Unit typing pool would be improved by her removal."

"She humiliated someone close to you, did she not?"

"Not close to me, but I knew her. After constant and persistent humiliation by Captain Mikhailovna, a young woman slit her wrists in the toilet. Captain Mikhailovna found that amusing. I considered the woman's death a loss to our socialist republic."

"Would you say you have exacted your revenge?"

"I would say I contributed to the efficiency of a key department in the KGB."

A faint smile and another nod, but Strakh went to his phone and dialed a number. He murmured so softly I couldn't make out what he said. He hung up and returned to me.

"Your kill is confirmed. Captain Mikhailovna was thought to have had a heart attack, but the fatal injury was discovered by the police. I have instructed that the heart attack remain as cause of death. Less paperwork. Congratulations on the successful completion of your final exam and on your new position. Do you have a suggestion for Captain Mikhailovna's replacement?"

"Yes. Lieutenant Maria Vashnikovna, and could you make certain she knows the recommendation came from me?"

His smile broadened. "You have made her beholden to you. Excellent, and be assured, she will know."

"Was that part of the test?"

"What do you think?" He peered at me, again moving closer. "Are you hungry?"

"Ravenous."

"How do you feel?"

"I feel nothing."

"No, how do you feel inside?"

His voice, low and soft, was alluring, and the spreading warmth, the tingle of excitement flared again. His pupils dilated, and I remembered what that meant.

"Like I am on fire inside," I said.

"A fire that needs to be put out?"

"Yes."

"This is another kind of arousal, Olechka. Quite a normal sensation after what you have done. I can put that fire out. Do you want that?"

My mouth was so dry, I couldn't speak. All I could do was nod.

To my surprise, Strakh's official apartment had a whole separate room for a bedroom.

13

BRAT' (BROTHER)

ENTRY 10

1967

Metropol Hotel
Moscow

I wore my KGB major's uniform to dine at the Metropol. I did not want to be here, but after his constant pleading, I had given in and agreed to meet my brother for dinner. He would probably be vexed to be seen dining with a uniformed KGB officer, but that would teach him to pester me.

Indeed, the nervous, sweating host showed me obsequious deference when I informed him I was there to dine with the actor, Boris Smerdlov.

When the host walked me through the dining room to Boris' table, conversation ceased throughout the restaurant, and diners became interested in whatever was on their tables and looked nowhere else. A soldier in uniform would not have had such an effect. A high-ranking Party member would not. Not even

Brezhnev himself. Yet, a woman in a KGB uniform could render a room as silent as a tomb. Even waiters bearing trays stopped their activity, eyes on the floor.

As I passed each table and did not stop, I could hear the soft sighs of relief. By the time the host reached Boris' table, activity had returned to near-normal. The host gave a slight bow and hurried away. Boris stood with an effusive smile.

"*Mladshaya sestra*!" he exclaimed and kissed my cheeks.

We sat, and I placed my regulation purse on the floor beside my chair, my hat on a corner of the table.

"I hope you did not mind I called you little sister in public," Boris said, the broad smile with his perfect, white teeth emphasizing his movie-star good looks.

"You have done it. It cannot be undone," I replied.

He had the sense to lower his voice for what he said next. "*Boizhe moi, sestra*, you look like Mama. When you entered in that uniform . . . You reminded me of her in the film where she played the soldier."

"Which one? There were several."

Boris laughed and said, "There were. *Victorious Revolution*. That's the one. Remember?"

"I have seen none of her movies. In my position, I should not." A lie, of course. I had seen them all, noting that her name had been removed from the credits.

"I am allowed to use them for my classes," Boris said. "However, I cannot mention her name or that I am related to her. They are wonderful movies. I, for one, like seeing her. She is as I remember her."

"Boris, it is not that you are not allowed to say you are related to her. You do not, you never have, acknowledged her as your mother. Correct, *Gospodin Smerdlov*?"

"Do you?"

"If I am asked, I do not lie, but I point out she failed her country. Besides, I could not deny her if I tried. I kept the family name, and every morning when I look in the mirror, I know everyone of a certain age can see whose daughter I am."

Though many Soviet women did not take their husband's name upon marriage, my mother had. She had decided Svetlana Lubova sounded better for an actress than Svetlana Glikman.

"What do you want from me?" I asked Boris.

The smile returned but was a nervous twitch. "Why should I want anything other than seeing my own little sister?"

"Whom you have not bothered to contact since I left to serve my country."

"I serve country and Party, too. You do not have a monopoly on that. I do not have a war to promote like Mama, but I play roles that honor our Soviet way of life."

"That was defensive, Boris. What do you want?"

"No need to cut to the chase, Olechka. Let us order, enjoy a good meal, and have a good, long talk."

"Boris, I have neither the time nor inclination for that. Tell me what you want."

For a moment, I thought I had made him angry. The scowl, the curling of his fists on the red tablecloth. Instead, he leaned back in his chair with a sigh.

"It is my second wife, the actress Nadezhda Opanskaya," he said. "We have recently finished a movie together. She had a minor role only, suited to her single talent, which is the size of her breasts. One evening toward the end of shooting, after too much vodka and remembering why I had married her, namely, that she is a wild cat in bed, we had sex. Kinky and uninhibited sex, which, unknown to me, she filmed. Now, she threatens that if I do not recommend her to directors for more substantial roles and if I do not give her a teaching position at the drama school, she will see that the appropriate Party officials receive copies of the film."

"It is merely sex. Gift a copy to Brezhnev yourself. He enjoys that sort of thing. He would probably give you a medal."

"Well, there was, uh, there was some role-playing involved with Nadezhda dressed like Brezhnev's wife, and me . . ." He broke off with a shrug.

I held up a hand. "Do not embarrass us both with a detailed explanation. Still, I tell you he would like it."

"Except, you see, I might have said . . ." He cleared his throat and lowered his voice again. "Counterrevolutionary things. All egged on by Nadezhda, but still . . ."

"I see."

"If Nadezhda goes through with her threat, I will lose everything, including my current wife."

"Number four, is it not?"

"Yes, but what does that have to do with anything?"

"You will soon, no doubt, trade her for a younger one anyway. Why worry about what she will think?"

"Olechka, when did you become such a cold bitch?"

"I am Major Lubova to you. Not Olga. Definitely not Olechka. Tell me what you want from me or I am leaving."

Another sigh, and Boris said, "Is there anything you can do to persuade Nadezhda that she is being unreasonable?"

"You ask this of me because I am your sister?" He squirmed in his chair. "A sister you have not seen in over a decade," I added.

"Yes, but we are blood," Boris replied. "No matter how long since we have seen each other."

"Why do you not ask Papa for this? He still has more authority than I do."

Boris flushed and looked away. "Papa is..." He looked up at me, his face stony. "Papa is drunk most of the time. He keeps insisting Mama will be home from her latest movie any day now. Olga . . . Major Lubova, please, I will lose everything. I will be blacklisted from acting. I will lose the drama school. Quite possibly, I will never see any of my children again. I may have fallen out of love with their mothers, but I love my children. Granted, I may not have the right to ask this of you, but you are the only person I can turn to. As you well know, if this film were to be seen by certain Party members, there is always the possibility of forced labor or a gulag, and I do not want to end up like Mama. Help me, *sestra*, please."

"Do you call me sister because you expect me to gift this favor to you?"

"Olechka, I am a mid-level actor with a modicum of talent. I do not have the position or the power to do anything for you. It is the other way around."

"I only expect one thing from you."

"Yes?" he said, his eyes glittering with hope.

"I never want to hear from you again or see you except on the screen of a cinema, and I have a choice in that."

He paled, blinked, daubed sweat from his upper lip with a napkin. "Major . . . Olechka, what have I ever done to you that you would ask this?"

"You have done nothing. You kept Yevgeny and Arkady from bullying me, and for that I am grateful."

"Then, what is it?"

"Our father was respected, feared, in the NKVD and the KGB, but he never rose higher than a provincial officer. That was because his life was encumbered. With a wife who was never home. With children he had to raise alone. Even with those damned dogs he often preferred over us. I want to be more than that, to rise higher than Papa, higher than any woman in this organization. To achieve that, I can have no encumbrances, and right now, you are one, asking me to use my position to protect you from your own weakness. You encumber me with your foolish, reckless behavior. I am aware this is not the first time you have been caught with your trousers around your ankles. I doubt it will be the last."

Boris paled even more, a hand coming to his mouth, as though he might be sick. "How . . .?"

"I know. Leave it at that. Are we agreed?"

"Then, you will . . .? You will help your brother?"

"Agree to my terms and yes."

Tears came to his eyes. I had expected relief or joy, but I saw only infinite sadness. Of course, I thought, he is an actor; nothing about him is real, like our mother.

Boris nodded, unable to look at me. I gathered my purse and hat and rose. I strode from the dining room, silence again my bow-wave and wake.

I TOLD them to go in the middle of the night, as was often the case in these matters. They pulled the troublesome woman from her bed and almost dislodged her flimsy nightgown.

How did I know this?

Before I arranged the raid, I had the silly woman's apartment bugged for audio and video. I wanted to make sure my orders were carried out with discretion.

My former sister-in-law cringed on the floor, on her knees, begging for mercy as my Second Directorate men ransacked her small apartment. I had told them they could have anything valuable they found, and they followed those orders. Indeed, Opanskaya insisted they take anything they wanted, anything at all. She bared her voluminous breasts and offered them, too.

My two political officers in their black suits observed, smoking constantly, ignoring the weeping woman at their feet, even when she lay on her back and spread her legs, pleading for them to have her and leave her alone.

I knew they would have her, all of them here, but that would be in the vehicle on the way to Lubyanka or in her cell after their arrival, and, of course, during the obligatory interrogation.

One of the uniformed men emerged from the bedroom and handed a video reel case to one of the suited men.

"Is this the one?" the political officer asked.

"Yes, Comrade," was the smiling reply. "She labeled it with a date and the man's name. It is not the only one. She has dozens. All different names. Some Russian, some English or American. A few women."

"Very well," the political officer said, tucking the reel under his arm. "Confiscate them all. I am sure some of our comrades will enjoy them." He tapped the reel with my brother's name on it. "This will be on Major Lubova's desk first thing in the morning. I will mention your diligence to her."

The uniformed man frowned. "Comrade, I would rather the Major not know my name."

"Of course." He nodded to the half-naked woman groveling on the floor. "Take this sniveling bitch away. You and the others may have all the fun you want on the way to the Lubyanka, but save some for me."

"Of course, Comrade. Thank you."

After using the woman's pillowcases to hold all the videos she had, the uniformed men dragged the wailing woman away, and the second political officer turned to the first.

Unaware I watched, one political officer said to the other, "You know Lubova's orders about those men?" He nodded to where the uniformed men had exited.

"Of course. Underachievers all. They will not be missed, but why not let them have a final romp before their end?"

"Are there . . . Did she have orders about us?"

"She said nothing about us, but you know how she is about encumbrances. We know now about her brother, so there could be orders somewhere."

"So, what do we do?"

"There is nothing we can do, Comrade, except enjoy what is left of our lives."

I knew if I showed them mercy, I would have them beholden to me, but that, too, is an encumbrance. I am not a spy myself who needs to blackmail assets. I am a teacher of spies.

What is it I teach?

When an asset is no longer useful, you eliminate it before it becomes an encumbrance.

14

BRAT'YA (BROTHERS)

ENTRY 11

I have mentioned one of my brothers, Boris, but as I indicated earlier, I had three others. Yevgeny, Arkady, Little Sasha. All dead now, outlived by their "skinny little *sestra*."

Arkady, as I said, died in Afghanistan in 1983, coincidentally the same year my friend Bukharin lost his half-brother there. The details of Arkady's death are typical; I reviewed the reports, out of operational curiosity, I suppose, more than sisterly concern. The fact he received a significant medal for being in the wrong place at the wrong time never sat well with me, but disputing that would have encumbered my own service to my country. Arkady gave his life for his country. I cannot dispute that.

Because he was the third son, with Arkady, it was all about being first. First to fill his plate at meals, first to finish eating, first to rise in the morning, first to go to bed. First to take our father his afternoon tea. First in his class at the military academy. First to bed a particular woman.

On the day he died, he traveled by helicopter to inspect where his first field command base was to be, and, of course, he wanted to be the first to step out of the helicopter. Arkady was not the first Soviet officer killed by a shoulder-launched missile. That would have disappointed him. Perhaps he was the first Soviet officer killed because of his ego. Probably not likely either, but I will concede him that.

Yevgeny, the one who had called to tell me when our father died, lasted barely a decade longer than Papa. All the steroids the Sports Ministry gave him, all the experimental, undetectable performance-enhancing concoctions had weakened his heart. He was in constant training mode, working to build the strength and concentration to clean and jerk a record weight—260 kilograms, a bit under 580 pounds.

One particular day, he had already spent hours working at lifting until, at last, he succeeded. He cleaned, jerked, and held 265 kilograms for the prescribed seconds. A world record, but when he dropped the weight, he fell to the floor as well, slumped over the bar, dead of a heart attack. Probably dead before he hit the floor. Sad enough. Even sadder was the fact that because he died in the process, the record was never certified. I have never thought that was fair to him. He was alive long enough to know that he had done what no other weightlifter had.

Years later, a Georgian managed 264 kilograms for the world record, but Yevgeny died knowing he had done it first and at a higher weight.

I could have intervened, could have made a pointed suggestion to the governing body to count the effort as at least a Soviet record. Quite often, when the KGB asked for something, it was done, but doing a favor for a dead brother who had had little use for me? Too much of an encumbrance.

Boris was the brother I was closest to. As the middle of the first three boys, he was often ignored. Our father focused his attention on his namesake Yevgeny as the oldest and on Arkady, who was the baby boy until Sasha. On me, too, because I was the only girl. Boris was something of a loner, like me. Yevgeny and Arkady bullied me relentlessly, and until I learned to defend myself, Boris would intercede. I did not want his help or anyone else's, so I applied myself to martial arts. I became good quickly. Arkady and Yevgeny did their best to out-fight me. They did not succeed, and that made me even more determined to take care of myself.

Boris was tall like our mother and handsome, having, like me, her auburn hair. He and I would often be mistaken for fraternal twins. He was still alive in 1991 when I left the Soviet Union.

As I said, Boris had some success as an actor and ran a drama school for aspiring actors, state-controlled at first and then his own for-profit enterprise after Communism. He attracted students from all over Europe, even a few from the United States. One can be proud and remain unencumbered.

He also had a succession of wives, tending to exchange the current one for a much younger model. He had children with several of them, six in all, I believe. One of his daughters also pursued acting. When she learned of her grandmother's brief fame, she found copies of most of her films and studied them. As a result, she decided not to use Smerdlov, Boris' stage name, but Lubova. She took over the operation of the acting school when Boris died.

In America, I learned of Boris' death from a Russian-language newspaper. Under a cover name in the U.S., I taught Russian language courses for a local parks and recreation department. I encouraged the students to practice their skills by reading Russian newspapers. They were to select an article, translate it, and read it, in Russian first, to the class, followed by their translation. I would assess and critique their translations.

When one student read from the newspaper, "Noted Russian Actor Dies of Suicide," I thought nothing much of it. In post-

Communist Russia, there were plenty of suicides. As she read on, the details told me the truth.

On his seventieth birthday, Boris drove to our old *dacha* outside Moscow. He still owned it but had not visited it in some time. He shot himself. When he did not show up for a class the next day, his daughter engaged the police, who found him in short time. Thank goodness. No note. No indication of an illness. A shock to his family, including me, the sister he thought was dead.

By the time he died, I had "retired" from my au pair/body-guard work, and Olive and I had been married a few years. We had settled in Portland, Oregon, in a charming little house. We even had a dog. I was happier than I had ever been, but this news of Boris received in this way disturbed me for days. Of course, I could not contact his family. For them, their *tyotya* was dead.

When I came to America, I had staged my death in the Soviet Union, to keep Soviet intelligence from taking revenge and to not be a source of intelligence for the U.S. CIA. The U.N. Intelligence Directorate gave me a new identity, a new name, though my immediate "family" in America always called me Olga Lubova. At the time of my faked "death" in 1991, Boris and his various children were my only blood family. Because he was listed as my next of kin—he was my only kin by then—he was the one the KGB notified of my demise.

My staged death was also a suicide, using the corpse an unidentified drunk who had frozen to death one night on the street. A carefully placed shotgun blast to the face, redressing the corpse in my clothing, placing the body in my apartment . . . An easy conclusion that I, dismayed by my pending dismissal and possible imprisonment, had eluded justice with a shotgun from my own home arsenal.

I hope Boris' method of death was nothing more than coincidence, that he had not done it the way he thought I had.

That knowledge made me curious about Boris. I asked Bukharin if he could check into my family. Bukharin told me Boris had been "devastated" by my death, whatever that meant. He and his family attended my "funeral" in Moscow.

Boris died without ever learning I was still alive, happily married, and living in America. And gay.

At that time, I had learned that some encumbrances are to be embraced, and I think my disturbance I felt at learning of his death was how I mourned him.

I know my mother lies in an unmarked grave near the gulag where she died. I have no idea where Papa, Yevgeny, Arkady, and Boris are buried. Little Sasha rests in a cemetery in the town where we lived when Stepi killed him. Give me a moment, and I can bring the name to mind. I do know where "Olga Lubova" rests—well, the hapless, unclaimed corpse who was passed off as me.

I think I should have let Boris know I was not dead, that I was doing something that made me happy.

No. That is all water beneath *Krymsky Most*.

15

SPECIAL STUDENT

ENTRY 12

1963

KGB Training Directorate
Moscow

At least he is on time today, I thought, when my newest elite trainee entered the gymnasium. To date, he had brought to every lesson a disinterest I longed to beat out of him. Perhaps today was the time for that.

He had learned at least one lesson well: When he entered the room where I appeared to be the lone occupant, his blue eyes swept the room, looking for anyone who might be hiding, noting his escape points. Satisfied he'd found nothing, he looked at me. No respect shown, no deference offered. Some instructors would be insulted by that because it is all about their egos, but I was not. It was a necessary part of his training.

He wore the gray-olive colored gym shorts and a singlet, no

shoes, no protective padding. When training with me, padding was always omitted.

He stood before me, at attention, eyes on an indistinct point across the room, shoulders back, hands in loose fists at his side.

"Reporting for training, Comrade Captain," he said, voice devoid of inflection.

His head had been shaved, like all recruits, though he had been here long enough for some re-growth. The overhead lighting no longer reflected off his bald head, now covered with scant, blond peach fuzz.

"I will not mince words with you, Comrade," I said. "You are close to washing out."

Not even the flicker of an eyelid.

"Because of the sensitive nature of the training you have received so far, washing out is a death sentence," I continued.

Not even the twitch of a muscle.

Ah, but that was what he wanted, was it not? He wanted to die but did not have the guts to do it himself. He expected me to do it for him, personally or by order. I suspected if I gave the order, he would not resist his death but welcome it.

Time for the rebuilding to start.

"I understand you," I said, "better than you do yourself. You want to die. You want me to kill you."

His mouth pursed into a thin line. I had scored a point.

"Today, I will grant your wish, except I will not do it."

From behind my back, I produced a handgun, holding it out to him grip-first.

"Here is the means. Take it."

His fingers uncurled; his left hand twitched, but the muscles of that arm stiffened to keep his hand at his side.

"What is wrong, Comrade? Have you no stomach to do it yourself? Do you not want to join that pretty little wife? Though, she was not so pretty at the end. Scalding steam and boiling water. Not pretty at all."

His eyes shifted to look at me, the dark irises lightening.

"Why was she in that place, Comrade, in that job that put her life in danger? Because of *you*. Because of *your* foolishness, *your* stubbornness. Because *you* thought with the wrong head and wanted *your* way, not the Party's way."

His head dipped, but he caught himself and looked at me again, jaws clenched.

"I do not even know why they sent you to me. I only train the top, the best recruits, the ones worthy of my attention, but they sent you to me, Ukrainian trash."

His eyes narrowed at me before looking away again.

"Ah, you did not like that," I said.

"If I am here to be insulted, do not waste your time or mine," he said. "Comrade," he added, an afterthought. "I have been through *Spetsnaz* training. Nothing can be more humiliating."

Without warning, I scored a kick to his chest, one that knocked the breath from him and sent him staggering backward. I advanced, landing kick after kick, to his chest, his stomach, his groin, fending off his half-hearted defensive blows.

"Attack!" I ordered. "Attack!"

He stayed in defensive mode, hunching to take the blows from my powerful legs. I seized an arm he'd raised in defense, twisting it into a grip that would shear tendons if he tried to disengage. Now, with him immobile, I kicked again, left leg then right, over and over until I heard a crack in his rib cage. I released his arm, and, grunting, he went to one knee.

Before he could react, I was behind him, head and neck in a kill grip. He understood what that was; he did not relax, but he stayed still, breathing in shallow pants.

Lips at his ear, I said, "Your wife died from management incompetence. Are you angry?"

"There is no point in that now," he said, his jaw tight.

I pressed a knee against the side I had injured. He hissed in pain before he caught himself.

"Are you angry?" I asked again. "The truth or you die."

"Yes."

"Angry enough to kill?"

"Yes."

"Angry enough to kill me?"

A head-shake.

"Why not?"

"You are a woman."

"No! That must not matter to you. Here and now, I am your enemy who holds your life in her hands. Ukrainian trash, are you angry enough to kill me?"

Another head-shake.

"Not only trash but dickless. Perhaps your pretty little wife had a better man than you on the side?"

"I told you. Do not waste the time."

"She was Ukrainian trash, too. A Ukrainian whore, and you unmanned yourself over her. How stupid you are. I should kill you here and now to protect the KGB from your Ukrainian backwardness. At least that exploding boiler spared Sofya Grigorevna of spending her life with a dullard."

The sound he made was inarticulate, almost a growl.

I eased my hold on his neck, embracing him instead. My voice soft and soothing, I said, "Have you mourned her?"

A nod.

"Have you wept for her?"

A head-shake.

"Why not?"

"Useless emotion. Does not change anything. Will not bring her back."

"Have you held onto your anger?"

"Yes."

"At the Party?"

"Yes."

"Are you angry enough to kill?"

"Yes. That is why I am here, is it not?"

I rocked him in my embrace. Almost one by one, his muscles relaxed, and he leaned into that embrace.

"I will teach you, my darling," I said. "So. Many. Ways to kill. Do you want that, my darling?"

"Yes," he murmured.

"Say it. Tell me."

"I want to learn how to kill."

"Who?"

"All of them. I want to kill them all."

"That is what I needed to hear, my darling. Now, weep for her. Weep for your beloved, but never, never give up your anger. Let it build. Let it fester. Let it guide your hands. Anger will help you kill. Anger will make you what I need you to be. Do you understand me?"

"Yes," he hissed.

I continued to rock him. "Go ahead, my darling, let it out. Grieve for her."

He struggled against it for close to a minute. A sob escaped, and his shoulders shook with silent weeping. Then, a long wail and another and another, continuing and echoing off the walls of the cavernous gymnasium. Exhausted and in pain from his rib, he fell silent, trembling. I continued to embrace him, stroked his fuzzy head, made soothing noises until his breathing calmed.

"I think I have cracked your rib, Comrade," I said. "Are you done now?"

He tried a deep breath, stopping short when it hurt. He nodded instead.

"Are you angry with me, my darling?"

Another nod.

"Good. Angry enough to kill me?"

A head-shake.

I almost sighed. All this for nothing. "We shall have to fix that, then."

I released him and straightened, kicking him in his injured side. A grunt of pain, but he leapt to his feet and lunged at me. I had never let go of the gun. I slammed the butt against his forehead, the edge of the magazine slicing his eyebrow open. Blood gushed, and he hit the mat, out cold.

I shoved the gun back in the waistband of my sweatpants. "Medic!" I called, and two men in white coats rushed in. "Stop this *Ukrainskiy musor* from bleeding on my exercise mats. Clean him up, stitch his head, wake him, and send him to my office."

❦ ❦

THE KNOCKS on my closed office door were more like pounding.

"Come!" I called and pretended to be busy with an open file on my desk.

My recruit entered, walking gingerly, the binding of his ribs forcing him to stay upright even though it had to hurt. I glanced at him. A line of four stitches bisected an eyebrow, and I admired my skill. I had struck him on an existing scar, which would now be more distinctive, not enough to rule him out as an operative, but enough to give him character, to add to his sinister expression. His eye was already blackening.

I stayed behind my desk, eyes back on the file. I made notes on it and let him stew for a while. Without looking up, I capped my pen, closed the folder, and returned it to a desk drawer.

"Only four stitches," I said, looking at him. "Next time, I will strike harder."

"You fight dirty. Comrade."

"Oh, does the big, bad soldier get upset that a mere woman fought dirty? Do you expect our enemies to fight clean?"

"Of course not."

"Of course not, what?"

His scowl deepened, his jaw clenching again. "Of course not, Comrade Captain."

"You needed to get the grief out of the way for two reasons. It blocks your anger, and it makes you weak. You know your importance. You need to be better than the best. No weaknesses. Grief. Love. Those are encumbrances. They will prevent you from fulfilling your missions. Remove them from your repertoire, but remember how to fake them when needed. If you do not do this, you will fail. If you fail, The Plan fails."

"I am not that important, Comrade."

"Do not interrupt me, Ukrainian trash. The Plan is a chain with a wrecking ball at one end. One weak link anywhere on the chain leaves it vulnerable to failure, and the wrecking ball will not be able to do its work. That cannot happen. Too much is at stake. Lives have already been given for The Plan. If your commitment falters, you dishonor them. If I do not see that commitment starting right now, I will send you to the basement of the Lubyanka and shoot you myself. We still have your cousin, after all. You can be replaced if that becomes necessary, but we had our reasons in choosing you for the mission instead of him. Am I clear?"

His lips pinched even tighter. He said, "Yes, Comrade, I understand completely."

"Good. Purge yourself of every useless emotion except your anger. Except your commitment to The Plan. Every time you look into a mirror and see that scar I gave you, remember your anger with me. Remember your anger at the Party's incompetence that caused your wife's death. Be angry that I beat you unconscious and cracked a rib."

"Three ribs, Comrade."

"Even better. Use your anger when you need the balls to kill." As I had spoken, his irises had become a pale blue, almost translucent, like glacier ice. "One day, Comrade," I said, "you will thank me for kicking your ass. Now, are you ready to learn?"

His fingers closed into fists, and if he clenched his jaw any tighter, his teeth might break.

"Yes, Comrade Captain."

"Who knows, Comrade? You may end up in love with me."

"Never, *sooka*."

My smile faded. "Bitch what?"

"Never, Comrade *Sooka*."

"Excellent. Your ribs are only cracked?"

"Yes, Comrade."

"Lesson number one: working through a little pain. Run four miles around the track and report back here. You are dismissed, Comrade Trainee."

He about-faced and tossed me a sullen look over his shoulder, slamming the door shut.

I smiled again. An auspicious start. At last.

16

___

OTHER INSTRUMENTS

ENTRY 13

I wrote that entry about my stubborn trainee yesterday, and I see no better time than now to talk about this most special student, the one who would play a key part in The Plan. Recruited at fifteen, like many Red Circle members in the 1950s —an age where they tend to rebel and where they have learned to reason somewhat—he was a top scholar, a strong athlete, and an award-winning pianist.

His mother was his first piano teacher, but even at three years old, he needed someone far more advanced than she. The best pianists in the Party made the trip to the collective outside Kyiv to spend weeks or months at a time teaching him. Had he not become Red Circle, he would have attained sufficient renown and position in the Party because his talent with that instrument was boundless and still is. His music reflects his moods, though lately he has not played sad music, and that is a good thing.

Eventually, I gave him other "instruments," and he played them as well, perhaps better.

I cannot begin to describe the intelligence of this man,

though he was barely a man when he came to me for training. His mind then and now, even at his age, is quick, discerning. He can read another's emotions from the slightest flick of an eye, the tiniest twitch of a muscle. I taught him how to do that as Strakh had taught me. He can formulate a plan of action or improvise within seconds. Few secrets escape his scrutiny, though I managed to learn a few of his and hide most of mine from him. His partner and wife can read him almost as well as I can, but I suspect he lets her read him only when he wants to. With me, he has no choice.

He was and is a spectacular physical specimen, of particular note now because he is in his seventies. He had grown up on a collective where hard work had developed his body while his mother developed his mind. A remarkably perfect body and the face of a god. Yes, I can appreciate male beauty even if I have little use for it.

I knew right away he should use that body in his work. Not as a raven. He was beyond that and destined for bigger things anyway. I was the one who taught him women could and should be exploited for the purpose of a mission. For him, only women. I could see he would never succeed in seducing men. He was the epitome of heterosexuality, or as is said now, a "cis het male." Oh, he would have followed that order had I given it, but his orientation would mean he could never be one hundred percent convincing as a homosexual. That meant he would fail.

This is not to say he was or is a homophobe. I suspect he had the typical Russian reaction to homosexuality, the same as I did, that it was a weakness that left one open to exploitation and extortion by the enemy. Like all in intelligence occupations, his attitude evolved on this matter. Having a much younger and more tolerant wife and raising a granddaughter of her generation—Millennial, Gen-X, I cannot keep them straight—aided his evolution. He is now the most tolerant of people, though, like many of us, he has occasional relapses into bias.

That was the thing about this man. He could adapt. He evolved, he improvised. All the skills a spy needs.

He may have been a perfect physical specimen, but he came to me a broken man, not yet twenty years old, a young father, and a widower. He had accepted his role in the Red Circle's plan, but he was a young man with a young man's physical desires. He married against the Party's wishes, a young woman he'd grown up with on the collective. They both lost standing. His wife, Sofya, was removed from Moscow University. He was dismissed from a high-level military unit. Only the intervention of some well-placed Red Circle members in the Party kept the two of them from being sent to a gulag.

Sofya went to work in a plant that made rations for the Red Army and its allied services in Warsaw Pact countries. He returned to be a grunt in the army. They lived in a one-room apartment in a residential block in Moscow, but they had each other and their baby. That was all that mattered to them.

When their son was six months old, an ancient boiler exploded in the food-processing plant, killing thirty-two workers, among them Sofya. My special student was left with an infant son and a broken heart, a hurt that I believe sometimes still pains him. He left his son with his own mother and the child's maternal grandparents to come to me for his special training. Before the Red Circle lost him completely, they had moved up the schedule for that training.

For a while, he was my only student, but my first glimpse of him led me to believe he was untrainable. He was sullen, unresponsive, and completed his tasks and exercises with the least enthusiasm. It was obvious to me he wanted to die but had not the mettle to take his own life. I suspect he thought if he enraged me enough, I would kill him. That, however, was not part of The Plan. No matter how much he angered me, I would never give him the satisfaction of death.

At one point, I did report to Strakh that he was untrainable, that his emotions were too much in command, and that his grief had ruined him. Strakh reminded me that the goal of a KGB trainer is to divest a recruit of all emotion anyway and to focus on the one emotion that would make him the perfect KGB officer.

Easier said than done.

As I now know, grief is never over and done with; you learn to manage it, but it will never be gone. So, I had to break him down completely, wipe his mind of emotion, and rebuild him, using his grief and, yes, his anger as motivation.

I was barely four years older than he and was not sure I was up to the task, given his physical prowess. I learned later, he was a further test of my abilities as a KGB training instructor. I am glad I did not know that then. I might not have applied myself with such dedication.

I succeeded. I created the perfect operative, the perfect spy, the perfect killer. At the same time, I created a life-long friend, a man more my brother than the brothers who shared my blood. To this day, I cannot explain our bond nor can he, but it is there.

Perhaps it was because I understood him better than his mother, his wife—either of his wives—or his closest friend. I know who he is because I made him who he is. His second wife assumed we had been lovers, but that was not the case. I taught him the mechanics of intercourse . . . No, not so; he already knew that, obviously. He had a child. I refined intercourse for him—not physically but with suggestions to improve his seduction techniques so that he understood how to put a woman in a state of such ecstasy she would do anything for him.

Yes, that was sexist exploitation, and I also taught him when to walk away when the exploitation was no longer fruitful, with no qualms and no thought to the chaos he may have wrought in another's heart. I will never be sure if either he or his wife will forgive that.

All that mattered at the time was I had taken a broken piece of State equipment and transformed it into a smooth-operating, precise machine, ready to fulfill his assignments without question and with prejudice, extreme or otherwise.

As had been done to me, I gave him a final test of his assassin abilities: a selected target to be dispatched. Also like me, he used his test for revenge. When I learned of his target and his method of elimination, I approved, though not with his methodology.

I had imbued in him a preference for the knife. Combined with his skills as a *Spetsnaz* "interpreter," he was a force to be reckoned with. The other recruits feared him; on occasion that look of his, those soulless, empty eyes, sent a shiver up my spine. He was efficient and cognizant of the importance of the details.

Now that I think on it, he was much like the assassin in Fleming's book, *From Russia with Love,* as portrayed in the movie by Robert Shaw.

I suppose that makes me Rosa Klebb. As they say, I will own it.

Back to his final test. Unlike my quick dispatch of Captain Mikhailovna, he captured his target and toyed with him a while. I had to punish him and deduct points for that. Had I not done that, he would have been the highest scoring among his class of assassins. I understood his need, but I could not condone his behavior.

The target was the food- processing plant manager who had ignored the warnings about the defective boiler.

The special student?

Alexei Nicholaivitch Bukharin.

17

STRAKH

ENTRY 14

1968

"The Tsar's Village"
Kuntsevo, Moscow

Rare were the occasions when Strakh wore his KGB uniform, but today was one of them. I was still of a rank and position where the uniform (and the blasted girdle) was mandatory, so this was normal dress for me. Today, when he asked me to come with him, he drove us in his personal Chaika, tailed by his bodyguards in a stolid, state Volga.

When I realized we were headed toward Kuntsevo, a Moscow suburb where many of the *nomenclatura* lived, I wondered if Strakh had earned himself housing there.

No, that was not the reason for the trip.

He had a residence where his wife and children enjoyed the privileges of his status. I had only ever been to his apartment near the training academy where he spent most of his time.

"My wife does not come here," he had once told me as we lay in bed talking after intercourse. "Too low for her."

You must be thinking, this Lubova is having a great deal of hetero-sex for a lesbian. Remember, this was long before I understood who I am now. I felt my only option was sex with a man, and Strakh taught me things I could pass on to my trainees.

The suburb of Kuntsevo was called The Tsar's Village because in imperial days most of the tsar's relatives and ministers lived there. It was almost like a world away from the rest of Moscow. Here were well-maintained houses with fresh paint and no crumbling bricks or stones. The sidewalks and streets were in peak condition and pristine—no litter, no cracks, no frost-heave craters. No lines formed at the stores whose shelves were never empty, and the cars all seemed new and clean.

Some houses had soldiers for security; others had guards from the Fifteenth Directorate. The residential buildings on occasion took up an entire block and rose four, five, or six stories. The Party had probably divided them into apartments now, all far bigger than mine. These houses had previously belonged to nobility, aristocracy, and tsarist ministers, and their size and sumptuousness would be antithetical to a proletariat state.

Strakh stopped before the entrance of a stolid five-story building. The two bodyguards left the Volga and came to stand at the doors of the Chaika. I peered up at the building from my seat in the car. Likely three or four, maybe five apartments per floor. The building itself was white-washed stone with crenelated adornments on the roof. Either all the trappings of wealth had been removed, or this had not been the home of any high royalty.

The guards opened my and Strakh's doors, and we emerged, both settling our regulation hats on our heads. A man in an old Red Army greatcoat, replete with medals, and a military *shapka* stood at attention outside a set of brass double-doors. Above the entrance on each floor were sizable bay windows stacked to the top floor, and a pointed cap on the highest gave the impression of a half turret.

The top floor had plenty of windows, in contrast to the lower floors. A more modern apartment must have been added there. A penthouse, I believed it was called in the West. The views of Moscow from there must be beautiful, I thought. Yes, that had to be the candidate for Strakh's new apartment. Would he get that whole top floor, or was it divided into two apartments? Even if it were three apartments up there, any one of them would be two or three times the size of his current one, which made mine seem like a cubbyhole.

Strakh came around the car to my side and addressed one of the guards. "We will be perhaps an hour. You both stay with the cars. We are in no danger here."

"Yes, Comrade," they replied. The two of them leaned against the Volga and lit cigarettes.

To me, in an all-business voice, Strakh said, "Come with me, Comrade Lubova."

He never made me walk behind him, though he was of a higher rank. Side-by-side, we approached the entrance where the doorman saluted and opened a door for us.

The lobby was like nothing I had ever seen; probably the reception hall for the original residence. The black and white marble tiles gleamed beneath a crystal chandelier. A woman in a crisp, utilitarian suit stood up from behind an ornate desk, and Strakh went up to her.

"General Strakh and Major Lubova," he said. "The keys."

"Yes, Comrade, of course." She opened a drawer and removed a brass ring with three keys on it. She placed that in Strakh's outstretched hand. "The smallest key is for the elevator," she said. "And, um, all the previous occupant's personal belongings have been removed. Except for the books. He had a great many."

"Not a problem, Comrade. The books will serve as reference material for identifying subversive ideas. They can always be disposed of later. Thank you, Comrade."

The elevator was tucked into an alcove off the lobby, and the small key unlocked a door that Strakh slid easily to one side. I saw the evidence that the door had once borne an appliqué of some kind, perhaps a family's coat of arms, but it had been chiseled off and the chisel marks buffed in an attempt to hide them.

Next, Strakh pulled aside the sliding scissor gate and motioned for me to enter. The interior of the elevator car was highly polished brass, to the point that I could check my appearance. I had removed my hat upon entering the building, but not a hair was out of place, not a wrinkle in my uniform from the car ride.

Strakh closed the brass door and the scissor gate. The elevator car had two buttons: a Cyrillic F and P. F for *foyye* or lobby and P for . . .? *Pyat*, five, fifth floor, or P for *pentkhayus* or penthouse? Strakh pressed P.

"A private elevator?" I asked.

"A necessary evil, Comrade. This was once some minister's residence. This entire building for one man and his family and their servants. A gift to that family from Tsar Alexander III. The top floor has been renovated from the former servants' quarters into a single residence. The other floors have three apartments each," Strakh explained, a smile on his lips.

The elevator came to a smooth stop, and he opened the doors again. We stepped into a vestibule with more marble flooring, wainscoting, and crown moldings. An ornate brass door across from the elevator bore a brass plaque with black lettering: 5A. Strakh unlocked that door and walked inside, holding the door open for me.

I walked into a small reception area open to the rest of the main expanse of the apartment. The furnishings were new, excellent quality German furniture—*West* German furniture: settees, plush chairs, tables with vases of silk flowers. I stepped to the left into a sitting area with floor-to-ceiling windows. I was right; the view of Kuntsevo and Moscow was breathtaking.

As if he were an estate agent seeking to sell the place, Strakh said, "Further left down that hallway, a master suite with dressing room, private bath, and its own sitting room. To the right, the kitchen with all the latest and newest appliances, the library the concierge mentioned, two guest rooms, and an entertainment room with a new television. It is also equipped to show movies. The whole place is fully furnished in a modern, European style."

When I looked at Strakh, I saw his proud smile. Well, why not? This was a perfect, fitting place for him.

"There is only one bedroom on that side?" I asked, pointing to the left.

"Yes, for privacy if there are guests."

I gave him a knowing smile. "Comrade General, have you brought me here for sex?"

He laughed, a pleasant sound. "That was not my original plan, but if you would like . . ."

"Comrade Strakh, is this your new residence?"

His smile broadened, lighting up his eyes. "No, Olechka. This is all yours."

I shook my head. "All right, you have had your joke. Who will live here?"

His smile faded. "Olechka, I am not joking. You are a major now, in a prestigious position in the KGB with added responsibilities. Your performance of your duties is exceptional, and your trained officers excel in their missions. This your residence."

"But how? Why? I have not requested new quarters. My apartment is suitable and convenient to my work."

"You will also have your own car and a driver now," he continued, ignoring my questions.

I blinked rapidly, surprised that he had not answered me. "How did this come about?"

He hesitated to answer, and that spoke volumes. His eyes, when he looked at me, were soft and yielding. "I requested it."

"Without asking me?"

Again, he ignored my question.

"There are people who owe me, and this was something they could provide," he said.

I pressed on. "The concierge mentioned removing the belongings of the previous occupant. Was he removed for me to live here? And, please, do not ignore my question."

"Yes, he was. That is how it works. You know that."

"Where is he?"

Strakh shrugged. "Who knows? Perhaps in even better quarters. It does not matter."

I walked to the window and took in the view. To see this beauty every morning . . .

No, I must not dwell on that. I turned back to Strakh.

"This is too much, too soon. People will talk."

"No, it is not. You deserve this. You have come far, but you will go further. This befits your new position. The Interior Ministry agrees."

"So, I have you to thank for this? This is you, rewarding your mistress for her performance?"

"Olechka, do not call yourself that. You know that is not what you are to me."

"What else is a woman sleeping with a married man?"

"You are my lover. That is what you are to me. What anyone else may think is inconsequential."

"It is not inconsequential. You know my position on taking favors from you."

"Olechka, this is yours not because of me but because of your merit and your performance as a training officer. Your promotion made you eligible for better housing, and you have received it based on merit."

"With your assistance?"

"Again, I only made a suggestion. The decision was the Interior Ministry's."

"No, you said people owed you."

Yet another shrug and a smile. "Yes, but they were people in the Interior Ministry. Again, I would never have suggested it if you did not deserve it."

"Am I now one of the people who owe you something?"

He came closer to me. "Of course not, Olechka. You owe me nothing other than your continued remarkable performance, and you would do that even if I were not in the picture."

I turned my back to him again. This had been coming for months. Not the apartment, bigger than the house where my father had raised four children and his damned dogs. I had let this relationship go on far too long, and now it was encumbering me. Only I could rectify that.

I faced Strakh again. "You are aware of my philosophy on encumbrances," I said, not a question.

Strakh looked away, again blinking fast. He sniffed, cleared his throat. "I am," he replied. "I am surprised you did not do what you are about to do long ago."

"Understand, I am grateful for everything I learned from you, but by arranging this apartment for me, you are an encumbrance now. You say you expect nothing more of me than my usual performance, but you are a man, a normal, human man. You will want more, eventually, and when you do, you will hold me back."

He sighed and looked at me, his eyes sad now. "That I do not want. The apartment is still yours, Olech—Comrade Lubova. That cannot be changed. No strings attached. I promise. I will remain the monitor of your work. You will continue to provide reports to me."

I did not understand why my throat seemed tight, why the words were difficult to say. "Of course, Comrade General. I welcome your observations and mentoring, as always."

Strakh cleared his throat again, as if nervous. "Your belongings are being packed while we are here. They should arrive within the hour. The Chaika is now assigned to . . . this apartment, and Konstantin will be your driver. You may trust him because I trust him, and he knows the consequences if he betrays my trust. He will be back for you in the morning to bring you to the office. The refrigerator and pantries are stocked with the foods I know you like. You are set, Comrade, and now I will leave you to become acquainted with your new quarters." He was halfway to the door when he stopped and turned back to me. "Olechka, I cannot go without telling you—"

I held up a hand. "No, please. That would be another, bigger encumbrance. Let us part as comrades and *druz'ya*."

"Friends," he murmured. "Friends. As you wish, Comrade."

He lay the key ring on a table near the door and left me alone.

I stared at the closed door for a long time, resisting the urge to open it and call to him. No, this was for the best, and I recognized what I felt as relief.

I set my purse and hat aside and headed first for the library.

18

DEDICATION
ENTRY 15

More than once have I debated with myself whether to continue this *memuary*, this memoir. The reflections I engage in have made me remember things I would rather forget. How I ignored and neglected my father. How I went along with the denouncement of my mother. How I treated Boris the last time I saw him. Pushing Strakh away.

Ah, well, then, perhaps it is time to write about something I do not and will not ever regret.

Strakh.

The whole time I worked with him, I never learned his real name. I did not want to know it; that would have detracted from the mystery of the man. Strakh was who he was—feared, respected, admired.

Did I fear him?

If I had refused him that evening after my first kill, would he have sabotaged my career?

Low-level apparatchiks would have, but he would not. He and I were both members of the Red Circle. We were both dedicated to the accomplishment of The Plan. We both needed to succeed in our positions.

Strakh and I were lovers for seven years. In bed, he instructed me on many things, including the arts of seduction and satisfying a partner. He had the benefit of the latter, but I could use both to instruct my trainees. It was a satisfying relationship on several levels, conducted in secret when we were both off duty. It was a comfortable relationship; I could discuss anything with him. His advice was always exactly what I needed. He did not, however, offer advice unless I asked for it.

As I said, it was a secret relationship. It had to be. He was married to a high-ranking commissar's daughter and had children. I wanted my career to be free of favoritism or even the hint of it. Strakh concurred with my wishes, and he was an excellent mentor.

Remember, I was very young when the relationship started. I often wanted to know more about him. When I felt comfortable enough to ask, he would answer. However, he developed my ability to read body language well enough that I could tell he held back some things. I suspected that was other women. It was no matter to me if he had other women. The only significance I attached to the relationship beyond the physical was what I learned from him.

He did tell me he was born in Moscow not long after the Revolution. He was a few days old when his mother fled the country with her rich, bourgeoisie parents, leaving her husband, Strakh's father, behind. They fled to Paris, as did many counter-revolutionaries, to keep Strakh's father from indoctrinating the child in Marxism. His father, though bourgeoisie himself, was an ardent Bolshevik.

Using a connection in the Cheka, Strakh's father had him kidnapped from Paris when he was a year old. This happened to many White Russian families who fled after the Revolution. The authorities kidnapped children and handed them over to "good" Communist parents, and the new judicial system would never agree to return them to counterrevolutionaries. Hence, none of his mother's attempts to have him returned to her succeeded. His father allowed her to write to him, and his father would refute her White Russian arguments line by line. When Strakh was thirteen, he wrote to his mother and told her not to write him anymore and that he would not read her letters if she did. I was in his office the day a messenger arrived to tell him, "Tatiana Fedorovna has died, according to our spies in Paris."

"How did she die?" Strakh asked.

"They say of a broken heart."

With a smirk, Strakh thanked the messenger, dismissed him, and said to me, "Well, that is one tsarist we will not have to waste resources to kill."

Strakh's father raised him with the intent he enter the Cheka, and when Strakh was seventeen, he joined what the Cheka had become, the OGPU, which was part of the NKVD.

Stalin purged the father but not the son in the 1930s. Strakh's father had become too vocal in praising the memory of Lenin instead of worshipping at the altar of Stalin. That was when the Red Circle recruited Strakh with the promise he could work to avenge his father's death.

Like his father, Strakh was an admirer of Trotsky, though he was more adept than his father at hiding that. Trotsky, Strakh thought, was the perfect combination of ardent Bolshevik and military strategist. He told me often of his admiration for Trotsky and how the Red Circle's use of Trotsky's words as code phrases had appealed to him.

Strakh was also a devoted Leninist, but the Red Circle had taught him how to make himself appear to be something else while retaining his true nature and personal philosophy. This, he taught me, too. Strakh told me that the day he learned Trotsky had been murdered was one of the saddest of his life, almost as sad as the day his father was executed in the Lubyanka basement while Strakh worked in an office floors above.

You will think it perverse when I say our post-intercourse talk often revolved around the best way to kill someone in a particular situation. Strakh himself was fond of the knife, and I absorbed that from him and passed it on. Our fabrications department came up with unusual and interesting weapons for assassins, weapons designed to look like everyday objects, but there is nothing quite like the result of wielding a good knife.

Some people are suited for knife work; others not, usually those who do not like to be close to their targets for the kill. I could easily determine who would be a good sniper and who would excel with the knife. I was never wrong. My friend Bukharin excelled at knife work but became too dependent on his guns. I cannot take full credit for him, though; the Spetsnaz had already taught him how to kill. I merely refined his skills.

In all the time Strakh and I were lovers, I refused to be referred to as Strakh's mistress, even if the nomenclature fit. I regret having used that description the day I ended our personal relationship. We were comrades, colleagues, and equals; he never treated me otherwise. That is not to say we were dispassionate. Far from it. The relationship between my friend Bukharin and his wife, Maiya, is also one between colleagues and equals, but also between them is love. With the exception of the latter, they remind me of Strakh and me—minus the contention, which they often fall into.

Strakh upset me only that one time, but that was enough for me to end the relationship. He meant well, but the apartment he gave me was something that I knew would cause gossip about my status in the KGB. He had always respected my desire never to seem to be sleeping my way to the top and was as careful as I was in keeping our liaisons secret. From the moment the unlamented Captain Mikhailovna had asked me with whom I slept, I was determined not to indulge that sort of encumbrance.

I accepted my physical relationship with Strakh because I learned much from him, and it neither hastened nor impeded my career. No, not quite accurate. It never impeded my career, but the lessons he taught me helped me progress further than anyone expected. That is, anyone except myself.

Again, this was not merely physical pleasure, though he was adept at that, nor was it the mechanics of assassination. From him, I learned how to read people, how to handle and manipulate people, how to find their weaknesses, and how to use their weaknesses to convince them to do what I wanted them to do. I used this knowledge on our KGB recruits and taught them how to do so as well. Those beyond the KGB noticed my successes, and I also trained officers in other KGB and GRU directorates in the fine "art" of interrogation.

Observing Strakh conducting an interrogation was a rare but educational occurrence. Strakh could merely enter a room and stare at a subject a certain way: eyes never wavering, a slight incline to his head, drumming his fingers on a table. A few moments of this and words would pour from the subject's throat like a dam had burst. Frankly, this could be attributable to Strakh's reputation; remember that his name means terror.

People feared Strakh, but that was not the source of his name. He chose that name for himself and made it fit him; rather, he made himself fit it.

With practice, I became as good as Strakh. As did Bukharin. Bukharin had size and his cold demeanor to his advantage. (After he defected, I received the information that his colleagues called him Ice Man or Ice, not because he was Soviet but because he was emotionless.) My advantage was my gender.

Subjects did not think a woman would hurt anyone. How wrong they were.

People feared me, too, but for a different reason. It was within my authority to dispatch people to prisons if they were mere common criminals, to labor camps to work on building roads and bridges, or to gulags where the labor was designed only to kill them spiritually and then physically. I could even send them to a basement cell in the Lubyanka for a quick execution. Most deserved what they received; some did not. Some were sacrifices, necessary to further the Red Circle's plan or to protect it from being revealed. Those deaths can weigh on a person, but Strakh taught me how to bury them in my memory and not dwell on the injustice. I felt that my actions, my "official" operations in pursuit of The Plan more than made up for that injustice.

How easy for me to absolve myself. No one else can, since I do not believe in some *dedushka* in the sky with a long beard and a vindictive nature. It was Comrade Trotsky himself who said:

"The end may justify the means as long as there is something that justifies the end."

I trust history to pass judgement on my actions and justify those necessary sacrifices. However, I also trust that there is no afterlife, especially no hell where my victims wait to "welcome" me. I am sure they would not be interested in my excuse: I did this for my country.

Strakh would laugh to hear me express such nonsense. It would, however, be good to hear his laugh again. His public demeanor was always so dour and serious. In private with me, beneath the covers and heads on pillows—pillow talk as they say in the West—he was jovial, even joking. His laugh was robust, and he had a teasing nature.

Was I happy with him?

I was content. Until he became an encumbrance.

Did I love him?

No.

I respected him, I admired him; I was grateful to him for all he taught me, a gratitude that is immeasurable. As good a lover as he was, though, I always felt as though something was missing. For me, that was definitely not a declaration of love. I neither wanted nor needed that. He may have engendered orgasms, excellent ones, but something was always "off," not quite right. Something incomplete. After the act of sex with him, even though it was pleasurable, I often felt I should feel something more. At the time, I concluded it was simply my need for dispassion.

I did not realize I was gay until I was in my sixties. That was when I understood what Strakh lacked. He was not a woman. He was a man who, yes, played a meaningful role in my life. I could not have been who I was without him. I likely would not have survived my enemies in the KGB without what he had taught me. He was not my life, but he assured my life.

By 1975, all those *Belomorkanal* cigarettes caught up to him, and the lung cancer was too advanced once the doctors discovered it. I was told he opted for the "dignified" way to deal with his mortal illness.

At his state funeral and his burial in the Kremlin Wall, I finally learned his real name, which I have never spoken to anyone, not even Bukharin, who knew him.

Strakh left a letter for me, delivered to me discretely by his secretary the day after the funeral. I have never read it.

Should I now?

19

MAIYA

ENTRY 16

Whether I can write with accuracy about Mai Fisher, the wife of my friend Bukharin, is questionable. She is complex but also more than that. She almost has multiple personalities. She can turn from being an affectionate spouse and parent to a soulless cold op to a raving harridan with whiplash-inducing speed. Some of this is attributable to PTSD. Most of it is. The other part is that, simply, she is a bitch, which she accepts and even revels in.

One thing (of many) I admire about her is that she could have let her capitalist, classist privilege poison her into living a useless, crass life. She chose the opposite. She chose to make a difference, to use her money and her title for a greater good than herself. Sometimes, her "making a difference" risked her life, which often put up a barrier between her and my friend Bukharin. On many occasions, I did not understand why he remained married to her.

Then, I found love, and it became crystal clear.

When Mai Fisher and I first met, she did not trust me. Would you, after four days of torture by the Stasi, trust a strange woman in a KGB uniform who comes into your cell and tells you, "I am here to rescue you?"

I think not.

I would not have believed me either, but two years later, at Bukharin's word, she trusted me enough to accept me as Natalia's au pair/bodyguard. As the old KGB would tell you, I am a loyal employee and was the same for Maiya. She paid me extraordinarily well, including educational benefits, health insurance, a pension plan, and my own apartment. Not as wonderful as my Kuntsevo apartment. It was in the basement of the massive house she built in America, but it was a bright and airy place I came to think of as home. The house I shared with Olive was not as big as either apartment, but it, too, became my home. Our home.

What Mai Fisher thinks of me, I do not know. I can only make inferences. Each time I thought we had trust between us, she showed me how manipulative she could be. That should not have shocked me, given who I was, but that charming, uppercrust, British aristocratic persona of hers can lure you into a state of comfort and acceptance. The moment you realize she now holds your existence in her hands, you are shocked and cannot help but admire her deftness.

I wish at times she had been my pupil. I could have made her into something far more formidable than Bukharin ever was, and she would have embraced it. Bukharin fought against the inevitable at times and retained his encumbrances—Maiya being one of them. Mai Fisher would have cast every emotion aside without a thought for anyone, and she often did.

I believe she respected me even if, on occasion, she blamed me for certain of Bukharin's proclivities. I know when she sought my help and I provided it—without question because I knew justice was always her motivation—she was grateful but quick to remind me what would happen if I ever spoke of it. Of course, on these occasions, she paid me bonuses that were more than generous.

I "came out" to her first, after Olive, of course. Knowing who I was did not upset Maiya. She accepted me, no questions asked.

I said to her, "If you wish to fire me from being Natalia's bodyguard, I will understand."

"Why would I do that?" she replied.

"In case you fear that I molested her."

"Olga, you're gay not a paedophile."

When Olive and I married, it was on the lawn at Maiya's Virginia house, next to the Potomac River. A beautiful location for the happiest event of my life, and Maiya had insisted the wedding be there.

Of course, I knew of Mai Fisher long before I met her in that Stasi cell. The first mention of her in a KGB file was her birth to parents who had been spies during the Great Patriotic War and who went on to be some of the first operatives for the U.N. Intelligence Directorate. The next was noting the death of her parents when she was five and that she had become the ward of another spy, Sir John Stone. In the Red Circle, there was some discussion of recruiting her when she was older, but that went nowhere.

Never in a thousand years would I have connected her to Bukharin, though he told me later he first met her when she was sixteen years old, after a brush-drop gone wrong (no fault of hers), and he and his partner Nelson rescued her from the Paris Ritz. He was attracted to her, but she was sixteen. He was thirty-one. He put her out of mind.

Obviously not.

Even when I learned he was her training officer, I never dreamed they would become partners, much less lovers, but Bukharin is a highly sexed man. Still, I thought he would use sex to mold her, make her into a good operative. I never would have believed a relationship would have come out of it nor that it would have lasted this long, more than forty years now.

In the years I spent in proximity to her and Bukharin, I observed her indifference to him, though never to Natalia. I saw her dismiss his affection, but sometimes that was his fault. It took him some time to commit to her alone, and on occasion, he faltered at that. But the way she would sometimes treat him . . . Many times I lost respect for her because of that, but he never did.

He almost died in the Kansas City Bombing some twenty-five years ago, and I saw how that affected her, how devastated she would have been had he died, her fear that she would lose him. That made me realize that relationships evolve and develop. Now, the two of them are strong together.

I am sure it is not all rainbows and unicorns. Olive and I had our share of disagreements, but we would cool off and discuss them. Bukharin, as always, hides his feelings, but you know they are there, ready to erupt. With Maiya, it is too easy to assume any feelings she expresses are faked.

She is a good actress. Like me. Like my mother.

She might not appreciate that comparison.

Recently, I have seen her with their new son, Ivan, the Russian orphan she and Bukharin adopted when the child was five. When he calls her "mama," I see something in her eyes, something like gratitude and awe. Natalia called her "Mums," but that was not the same as "mama" or having your name on official forms under "Mother's Name."

Sometimes, with Natalia, particularly in her teen years, Maiya's patience would disappear, and she would often try to have me deal with what she called Natalia's "adolescent angst."

"I am her bodyguard not her mother," I had to remind her more than once.

With Ivan, she is different. She relishes the role, and perhaps she is settled in the role because she took it on so late in life. She even has, as the British say, "an heir and a spare." Natalia and her half-brother Sergei will inherit half of her business in Ireland. Ivan the other half, including the properties in England. Otherwise, EuroEnterprises would be broken up among a number of second and third cousins.

Our little Ivan, born in a Russia that reclaimed the Tsar and his family as royals, because he is Maiya's legal son and carries British citizenship through her, will someday become the Earl of Uxfield. The little charmer that he is, he will have us all bowing and curtsying to him.

However, Bukharin and Maiya raise the child without privilege. They are good parents, and I am glad they have the chance. Yes, they raised Natalia, but she was always more her own than theirs. It is different when you have your own child—so they tell me—no matter if it is by adoption rather than birth.

Bukharin told me how before the first Christmas after they received custody of Ivan from his dead grandmother, Mai had discovered the child enthralled by the lights on a Christmas tree where he waited for Grandfather Frost. Ivan told Maiya he was sad for the way he had had to leave Russia so quickly and that he did not even have a picture of his grandmother to remember her by. Though it was Christmas Eve, Mai had her people find a surveillance photo of the child's Russian grandmother, Alekseevna, to frame and give to the child on Christmas Day.

"That is a mother's love," Bukharin said to me.

Maiya is now head of the U.N. Directorate, something else I did not foresee. I thought she would never leave field work, but after some period of adjustment, she has become quite the spymaster. I will take some responsibility for that. I taught Bukharin. Bukharin taught her. She is my creature as much as he was.

Except I taught Bukharin to control his ruthlessness. He either did not bother to teach her that or he quickly saw that aspect of her could not be controlled. She has done things as cold-blooded as Stalin and dismissed the aftermath; yet, she made certain a little boy who had lost the only family he knew had another to sustain and love him.

Yes, she is complex, but she is consummately human.

Do I count her among my friends?

That may go a bit far, but I do count her among the people I can rely on in times of trouble. She has never proven me wrong.

20

SURPRISED

When someone knocked on my door, I looked up from my typing to see it was dark outside. I had written through dinner. Again. Likely, Natalia had come to get me, but she would use the connecting door to her house, not the front entrance.

An assassin, perhaps one of my old pupils, come for me? If that were the case, I am too old to relish the exercise of resisting.

I saved my document and closed the laptop. This project Natalia had encouraged me to do was still something I wanted to remain private.

On my way to the door, I took a mask from a box and donned it. Next, I removed a folding knife from a drawer in the small table near the door. I might not be able to fight like I used to, but if this were an assassin, I would make him regret taking the job.

I opened the front door, frowned, and said, "Oh. It is you."

Mai Fisher returned the frown. "Why, yes, it is. You sound disappointed," she said.

"I thought perhaps you were an assassin."

"And if I were, what were you going to do? Let me in?"

I held up the unfolded knife, its eight-inch blade obvious.

Mai raised an eyebrow. "Good thing I'm not an assassin."

"It has been a while since you have come here."

"Yes, well, global espionage organization to run, people and governments to spy on."

Over recent years, Maiya's British accent had grown more cultured, refined, possibly because she used it more in dealing with heads of state, directors of other intelligence organizations, and U.N. bureaucracy. To my ears, she sounded much like that Lady Mary from Downton Abbey.

Her appearance on the same day I had written about her raised my suspicions. Had she bugged my apartment? I will sweep later for cameras and listening devices.

Mai cleared her throat, interrupting my thoughts. "May I come in?"

"Of course. I was simply . . . surprised by your visit." I looked over her shoulder. "Bukharin is not with you?"

"No. He has homework and bedtime duty tonight," Mai said as she stepped inside, eyes above her mask casting about, looking for danger. She removed her gloves but left her mask on. There was a pandemic going on, after all. As she unbuttoned her coat, I closed the door.

"Would you like tea?" I asked.

"Lubova, I'm British. Do you have to ask?"

To my surprise, Maiya followed me to the kitchen, keeping the appropriate social distancing gap between us. I gathered what I needed for tea and settled the kettle of water on the gas burner.

"How are you doing?" Maiya asked.

"I am fine. Why do you ask?"

"Natalia told Alexei and me about finding you down on the dock looking as if you were about to take a leap."

"Natalia may be grown woman, but she still exaggerates."

"Hardly."

"Then, she was mistaken."

"She also told me about your memoir project," Maiya said. "How is that going?"

"Why do you ask? What is your concern?"

"No concern at all. Merely curiosity."

"No, you are trying to worm out of me if you are in it."

"You've been part of the family for thirty years. I assume I'm in it. I hope you're being brutally honest about me."

"I know no other way."

"So, how *is* it going?"

"I am . . . remembering things. Things I think perhaps should have stayed out of sight, out of mind."

The tea kettle whistled, and I paused talking to pour the hot water over the tea ball in the pot and arrange cups, spoons, sugar, and cream on a tray.

"Let us sit at the table at the window," I said and led the way.

Mai shed her coat and laid it on the sofa. Once we settled at the table with the inky blackness of Lake Geneva below us and the brightly lit skyline of Geneva beyond, Maiya tugged her neck gaiter down and removed a shamrock covered mask she'd worn beneath it. I set my mask aside and poured tea.

I stirred a generous amount of sugar into mine, and Maiya took only a splash of cream. Maiya sampled her tea, but her eyes stayed on the view.

"That view is wonderful," she said. "A different angle from what we have up at the house. You can see more of the city."

"It and the lake are quite calming."

Maiya looked at me. "Did you know I can see the house from my office?"

"No. I have only been in the security forces building, as you know," I replied.

"Sometimes, I take a break—I know, hard to believe, but I do. I go to the windows in my office and look at the house. On occasion, I can make out Natalia's children and Ivan playing on the grounds. Alexei watching over them."

"Is that a comfort?"

Maiya frowned briefly then smiled. "Yes, it is. He hasn't worked with me in a long time, but catching that occasional glimpse of him reassures me that I know what I'm doing."

"You still have the . . . What is it called? Imposter syndrome?"

"I suppose that's apt. I suspect right about the time I'll actually be a decent manager of people, I'll likely retire. When I see Alexei and the family from across the lake, I want to be there with them." Her smile broadened. "Though keeping up with the little tornado can be daunting."

Ivan Alexeivitch had two speeds: motionless and running. Maiya had started calling him the "little tornado" almost from his arrival here.

"I must say, such sentimentality surprises me," I said.

Maiya's smile finally connected with her eyes. "Well, well, you take a walk down memory lane, and you think you're back in the First Directorate Training Unit admonishing your trainees about those pesky encumbrances?"

"Today, in fact, I was reminiscing that you would have been an excellent KGB officer."

"After being trained by your protege, I sometimes felt like one. Are you saying I was cold-blooded enough for the KGB?"

"More than enough."

"All these years, I thought you disapproved of me."

I shrugged and refreshed our teacups. "Not of your operational acumen," I replied. "On occasion, I was not fond of how you treated Bukharin."

"I was only nasty to him when he was being a bastard," was the reply. "You know, at times he deserved the cold shoulder I gave him. He was far from a perfect husband, and you know that. He was a perfect operative, yes, thanks to you, but a human being? He struggled with that. Of course, he'd probably tell you the same thing about me and likely has."

If Maiya interpreted my silence as concurrence with her last statement, I had no issue with it.

"Now that the American election is over and we have a new president, will you set aside your obsession with Kermit Harlan?" I asked.

"See, you *have* talked to Alexei. He's the only one who calls that my obsession, and, no, I will dog Kermit Harlan to the end of his miserable existence or my retirement. Whichever comes first."

I peered over my teacup at Maiya and raised my own eyebrow. "You control both those options."

She gave me an icy smile. "Yes, I do. Believe me, that temptation was difficult to resist."

"Why did you not hasten the 'end of his miserable existence'?"

"Well, one vengeful assassination was enough for me. So, I wouldn't have been a good KGB officer after all. I retained a principle or two."

"Because you are British, not Russian."

"A distinction for which I'm grateful. No offense. All right, we've done the obligatory Russian small-talk thing. Whether you were really contemplating a leap into Lake Geneva or not, understand this. You are family. I lament that you lost your wife in an horrific way, and, yes, the temptation to pack it all in and seek oblivion is strong. Twenty years ago, I thought Alexei had drowned in the Danube during that Belgrade mission. I decided that once the police found the body, I'd blow my own brains out. Not the first time I'd thought of that. Wasn't the last, but I remembered how he'd trained me, like you'd trained him. Mission first, above all else. If I hadn't finished that mission, I'd have dishonored him, and he'd have probably haunted me."

"He survived."

Mai laughed. "Because he's too fucking stubborn to die, thankfully. What I'm trying to say is you think you're alone, but you're not. It took me a long time to realize that for myself. You and I have three generations of Bukharins who need us, and you have one Englishwoman who needs you, too. Plus, you see, you're only four years older than Alexei, and since I want him to be immortal, you can't die and show him how it's done. Not for a long, long time. Don't give him any ideas about . . ."

Maiya's voice faltered, and her eyes grew shiny with excess moisture. I had never seen such a thing from her and struggled not to drop my jaw. However, it did not surprise me that she echoed Natalia about Bukharin's mortality. Those two women are more alike than they know.

"Do not give him any ideas about shuffling off the mortal coil?" I said.

"Yes, and the Shakespeare, very appropriate."

Mai drained her tea and rose, gathering the tea supplies back onto the tray.

"Now, I'll put these in the kitchen," she said. "You get your coat and a mask on. You're coming up to the main house for dinner. Alexei has made honey cake for afters."

Like the woman accustomed to giving orders she was, Maiya went to the kitchen. I catalogued my own emotions. I have been loyal to this woman not out of obligation, not because she had assured I had a comfortable life, but because Maiya loved Bukharin. She always had.

I put on my mask and rose. "Honey cake? How can I pass that up?"

21

NATALIA
ENTRY 17

When I was trying to save my life the year the Soviet Union ended, I do not know why I decided my best option was to fake my death and go half the world away to be the bodyguard for an eleven-year-old American girl.

The Red Circle's plan had been achieved, though not the way they'd intended. They had wanted a return to Leninism, but it and Communism died with the USSR. The Red Circle never planned to abandon its members, to let them survive or not in the post-Soviet world simply because they were no longer needed. However, they had placed me in a position where I had made a great many enemies—inside the Circle and out.

As I told Bukharin when I proposed my solution to his child-care issues, I knew the KGB's replacements, the FSB and the SVR, were not for me. I did not want to be some oligarch's head of security. I did not want to throw my lot in with the *mafiya*. I wanted out of Russia and to be free of spy organizations. I wanted to do something so different from what I had done my entire career, something that would never be associated with me.

I had one condition. I would never betray the secrets I knew, and I knew plenty, ones beyond the Red Circle. Also, I would never betray my country. All of what I had done my entire professional life was for my country. I knew if I defected to the CIA, I would pay a high price for a new identity and a government stipend. I would have to tell them everything I knew, and that debriefing would go on for years. The only organization . . . No, the only person who would not require that of me was Bukharin, and he happened to need me.

In the spring of 1989, Bukharin's son Pyotor, along with Pyotor's pregnant wife Rachael Langley, and nine-year-old Natalia Petrovna were involved in a serious automobile accident, their car struck by a drunk driver on a rainy night. Rachael and her unborn child were killed instantly. Pyotor was driving and suffered shattered legs and pelvis. For a while, it appeared he might not walk again. Buckled in the rear of the sturdy Volvo, Natalia suffered only bruises.

Facing many operations and a long rehabilitation of his legs, Pyotor made his father and Mai Fisher Natalia's legal guardians.

This is how Alexei Bukharin and Mai Fisher became parents of someone else's child. The first time.

Of course, they were both unprepared for this. Pyotor made his father promise not to place Natalia in the boarding school where Pyotor had gone when Bukharin brought him out of the Soviet Union. This was a private military school in Virginia, established by CIA and NSA employees, many of them single parents, who wanted their children to be in a secure situation when the parents were out of the country. It had an excellent academic reputation and did not teach these children to be spies. Still, Pyotor Bukharin, who called himself Peter Burke, likened its structured and regimented life to being back in the Soviet Union. He did not want that for his daughter.

Bukharin and Maiya were professional partners, but with Pyotor's condition and the hiring of nannies problematic, they faced a serious issue. They opted to put their partnership on hold and conduct solo missions, with one of them at home. A reasonable compromise, you would surmise, but Bukharin was convinced Natalia needed a mother figure more than a father figure. He played on his longtime friendship with Nelson, the head of The Directorate, and Bukharin got most of the missions.

I know that Maiya was as loving to and protective of Natalia as if she were a child she had birthed, but Maiya was at that time a woman not destined to be a mother. Being nothing more than an analyst at work and a housewife at home "threatened my bloody sanity." Her words.

On the occasions when she had a solo mission, it was not much better on Bukharin. Though he was the greatest believer in her capabilities and knew he'd taught her to take care of herself, he always imagined the worst-case scenario. Indeed, a few months before the fall of the Berlin wall, Maiya was rolled up by the East Berlin police, who turned her over to the Stasi—if you recall, this is how she and I first met.

Bukharin ended up owing me twice: Years before, I had helped to facilitate his son's escape from the Soviet Union, and I rescued his wife from what would have been certain death. He had no choice but to help me survive.

As I have explained several entries ago, I faked my death. Why? The KGB, following Gorbachev's orders, had rounded up the coup plotters, and Gorbachev conducted a purge of the organization. I was by then the second-ranking officer after the head of the KGB, who was the leader of the coup attempt. Gorbachev could have appointed me acting head of the KGB and made that appointment permanent some time later, but he and I both read the writing on the wall. I would never be trusted in or out of the KGB. Best to cut ties and start a new life.

Of course, a former trainee of mine, a member of the Red Circle who used his position in it for his own means and then abandoned it, found out I was alive and that I had defected. Who is that? The current ruler of Russia, Dmitri Kargin. Thirty years after my defection, Kargin sent assassins to kill me, but my wife died in my place because, well, one old lesbian looks the same as any other to homophobic eyes.

That was off-subject. My apologies.

So, I convinced my friend Bukharin I would be the perfect companion for his granddaughter while he and his wife resumed their partnership. I was a good cook. I had received an excellent education. I could make certain no enemy of theirs would gain access to Natalia. She could live a normal child's life: school, riding lessons, soccer, shop with her friends, sleepovers, and so on, and Bukharin and Maiya would not have to worry and be distracted from their missions.

Bukharin agreed, and I won over Mai Fisher. That took a bit longer, but I regaled her with stories about Bukharin during his training, including the time I kicked his ass.

Those obstacles overcome, the final person I had to convince was Natalia Bukharina. To my surprise, I did.

22

INTERVIEW

ENTRY 18

1991

Bukharin-Fisher Residence
Mount Vernon, Virginia

I insisted that my "interview" with the child I would be body-guarding be conducted in private. That did not sit well with either Alexei Bukharin or Mai Fisher, because they were, in effect, her parents. After all, my previous experience was teaching people how to be assassins. However, I knew children quite often would say in the presence of their parents what they thought the parents wanted to hear, rather than their true feelings.

"Remember what I said to you about recruiting her?" Bukharin said to me.

"Of course, and that is not the point of this, is it?" I replied.

"What is the point of it?" Maiya had asked.

"For the two of you to be able to work together again. That is what you want, is it not?"

Bukharin's assent was obvious; he seemed relieved more than anything. Maiya's was another matter, and I recognized what it was. A few missions worked on her own, and she enjoyed the independence and the ability to assess a situation and react according to her instincts, not her partner's. Not even the Stasi interlude had altered that.

I wanted this new life, but if the child did not want me, it would be pointless to live it. It would be pointless to try.

They chose the library for my chat with Natalia, that most English of rooms. This one was no exception. The presence of Bukharin's baby grand piano only made it seem more English than England itself.

After Bukharin had closed Natalia Petrovna and me inside the room, I went over to the piano and admired its mirror polish.

"Ah, I see your *dedushka* still plays, does he?" I asked.

"Yeah," came the reply, bordering on sullen. "I don't call him *dedushka*. I call him Popi. I, like, started that when I was little, and I, you know, kept it."

Two years from officially being a teenager, Natalia was tall for eleven and had her thick, red hair pulled into a single ponytail high on one side of her head. She wore a long-sleeved pink pullover beneath what I believed were called bib overalls in denim. She had rolled the cuffs of the overalls above her ankles and donned white tennis shoes with pink socks.

"You speak really good English," Natalia said.

"Thank you. Your *dedush* . . .Your Popi told me you speak decent Russian."

"My mom and dad—my real mom and dad—wanted me to be, you know, bilingual."

"An excellent choice. What grade are you in?"

"Sixth. I skipped fifth. You're, like, going to be my babysitter or something?"

"Something like that, but only if you agree."

"You'll live here?"

"Yes. In the apartment downstairs."

"So, three adults telling me what to do. That totally sucks."

"I only carry out the instructions of Bukharin and Maiya, and I will enforce their rules."

"Because they'll pay you to like me? Big whoop."

I frowned, remembering this was not a recruit I could beat senseless for insubordination. Also, the child was only two years past losing her mother.

"Natalia, let us sit by the fireplace and talk."

The girl put one hand on her hip, cocking that to one side, her face in that universal expression of boredom teens employed that was somehow skeptical and defiant simultaneously.

I went to a chair before the fireplace and sat, waiting. After a moment, Natalia sat in the matching chair, facing me. Natalia sat crossways in the chair, one leg dangling over a chair arm, the other bent at the knee, the sneaker on the chair's cushion.

"Does Maiya let you sit that way, slouched and feet on furniture?" I asked her.

"Sure. This is my house, too."

"You understand I can confirm that with her."

After several seconds of contemplation, Natalia swung both legs to the floor and sat straight in the chair, hands folded on her lap.

I kept my smile to myself. I liked that the girl pushed boundaries but also knew when to step back.

"Natalia Petrovna, you are interviewing me for a job. Please, ask me any questions you like," I said.

"*I'm*, like, interviewing *you*?"

"Yes. Now, do not misinterpret. I would not work for you. I

would be Maiya's employee, but you have the say over whether I work here or not."

"How so?"

"Your grandfather and Maiya want this, but you have to agree. Before you automatically disagree, ask your questions."

"Okay," Natalia said, drawing the word out. "How do you know Popi?"

"He and I knew each other way back in the Soviet Union. We were . . . in school together."

"Oh. Were you one of his girlfriends? Because that really, you know, pisses Mums off."

"No. He and I are friends only. I am a few years older than he is. He was a student in some of my classes."

Natalia's forehead scrunched as she contemplated this. I made a mental note to tell Bukharin the questions and my answers so our stories would match.

"Did you know Mums before right now?" Natalia asked.

"I met Maiya a few years ago at a meeting in Germany."

It was in a Stasi cell, and her "Mums" had been tortured, but I managed truth in my answer.

"They work for the U.N., you know, a refugee relief organization," Natalia said. "Is that where you worked?"

"No, but I knew them from that work, when my country would provide supplies and assistance for refugees."

"The Soviet Union?" A snort of disbelief. "Seriously?"

"The Soviet Union has always tried to make itself look good in the eyes of the world."

"Are you one of those defectors we see in the movies?"

"No. You might say I am now a refugee. The Soviet Union will likely end soon, and the situation there could become dangerous. I want to live somewhere safe. I contacted my old school friend, Bukharin, and he helped me come to the United States."

More disbelief. "To babysit me?"

"Bukharin explained his and Maiya's work situation and told me they need help. For me to stay here in this country, I would need a job, and they offered me this. And I would not exactly be your babysitter."

Another snort. "What else would it be?"

"You know Maiya is wealthy . . ."

"Duh. Look around."

I allowed myself to smile. "Yes. It is obvious. She is wealthy, and wealthy people receive all sorts of threats. Your grandfather and Maiya are concerned someone might kidnap you for money. In the Soviet Union, I worked in security, so I will protect you."

"You mean, like, be my bodyguard?"

"Something like that, but the key is for the bad people not to know I am a bodyguard, so you should call me your au pair. Do you do know what that is?"

"Yeah, a couple of my friends have au pairs, but they're, like, young girls."

"Ah, but since I am also bodyguard, it is better to have the experience of age."

"So, I could tell my friends that you're my bodyguard, right? I mean, that would be totally cool."

"No, because it would have to be a family secret. You see, your friends might tell a parent, and one of them might accidentally say something to someone, and . . ." I shrugged.

"Do you carry a gun?"

"No."

"A knife?"

"On occasion."

An eye roll. "How are you supposed to protect me, then?"

"I have a black belt in five martial arts."

"So, what about boys?"

"What about them?"

"When I have a boyfriend, will you have to be around?"

"Let us worry about that when you are old enough for a boyfriend. You are eleven, and boys are limiting."

"Yeah, Mums says that, too. Do you have a husband or a boyfriend? Will he come live here?"

"Husband, no. I have never been married. Boyfriend for a brief time, but that was long ago. My focus was on my career, on serving my country."

"You don't have kids?"

"No. I never had the time, but I was a teacher. I thought of all my students as my children." Though they did not think of me as their mother, I thought.

Natalia nodded, her face scrunching again as she thought. "So, if you're here, Popi and Mums will go do their refugee work together again?"

"Yes."

"I wouldn't get to see them as much."

That wasn't a question, more like musing.

"Is that good thing or bad thing?" I asked, my voice soft.

"Well, like, it's both. They've argued a lot lately, especially before and after Mums goes away, and Popi's left here with me. I mean he's not mad at me or really at her, just the fact they're not working together. When it's him gone away to work, she's mad because she's not with him. So, they argue. They don't think I can hear it. They mostly argue in their office, but not always, and they forget I can hear them. That's the bad thing. If you were here, they'd work together again and wouldn't argue. That's the good thing, but then, they'd both be gone instead of only one of them, and that's another bad thing."

Bukharin had said the girl was smart beyond her years, and she was. She had examined this from all angles and had presented her arguments. Time for some adult logic.

"Natalia Petrovna, if you wish to treat this like a balance sheet to keep score of the good and bad things, yes, the bad things might outnumber the good. This is a situation where you must look at what is called the big picture. Your Popi and Mums do important work that helps many people, and working together they are happy. That makes their work more productive and efficient, meaning they would finish their work and come home sooner than expected. Yes, it would also mean both of them would be away at the same time, but I would do my very best to make certain you are safe and secure and have a life much as you have right now, with your riding of horses, your soccer, and your friends. That would also make you happy, and Popi and Maiya happy, too."

What nonsense, I thought; surely, she is smart enough to see through the *vraki*, the bullshit.

Natalia looked around the library, as if seeking someone hiding in the shadows. She leaned toward me and lowered her voice. "So, Mums says no TV, like, ever. When they're not here, would you let me watch TV?"

"If that is one of her rules, I would have to enforce it or risk losing my job." I echoed Natalia looking around and leaning forward, also lowering my voice. "Of course, you know, sometimes I will be busy, perhaps planning meals or cooking, and my back would be turned." I shrugged. "What I do not see . . ."

Natalia grinned, her eyes amused and shining with a deep intelligence I had seen before—in Natalia's grandfather.

"I bet you have stories about Popi," Natalia said.

"I do, but they may have to wait until you are older."

Eyes gleaming, Natalia said, "Really?"

Another shrug from me, but Natalia wasn't finished.

"What happens if you don't like me?" she asked.

"I would sell you to gypsies or kidnappers."

Natalia's eyes widened, but when I winked at her, her grin returned, and she burst out laughing.

"Mums threatens to give me to the Tinkers all the time. It's, like, a standing joke between us."

"You are intelligent girl, much more mature than I expected, and you have good sense of humor. I can see we will get along well." I dropped into the tone that had made my trainees take notice. "Provided you do as you are told, *devushka*."

Another grin. "Popi calls me that."

"It can mean girlfriend or sweetheart, depending on who is speaking."

"What do I call you?"

"Olga. You may call me Olga."

"Okay. Olga. Mums is probably, like, right outside the door, trying to listen to what we're saying. I think she has the house bugged because she knows everything that goes on here."

"Shall we go put her out of her misery, then?"

Natalia laughed again, a beautiful sound of innocent joy. She would soon transition to adult reality. What a shame. I decided that laughter would be a sound I would look forward to hearing for a long time.

23

OLIVE

ENTRY 19

If you remember early in this memoir I wrote of a young woman also in the KGB Training Unit typing pool with me. This was the one the captain constantly humiliated—for her typing skills, for having the tiniest of wrinkles in her uniform, for having a stray hair out of place. Any small thing that would reduce the young woman to tears, which compounded Captain Mikhailovna's desire to humiliate her further. As I said, that young woman killed herself during the morning toilet break, and Captain Mikhailovna laughed.

That young woman's death affected me deeply, though she and I had barely exchanged a half-dozen words. And, of course, she was the reason I selected Mikhailovna as my target for my "final exam."

Now, I understand it was because I was attracted to the young woman. At the time, I told myself it was the injustice of it that bothered me, but it was a lost opportunity. Even if I had recognized what my feelings were, I knew to keep them to myself. Even today in Russia, as other nations become more tolerant and accepting, there is no tolerance or acceptance of homosexuality. Bigotry has been enshrined in law.

Indeed, that intolerance was so indoctrinated into me I not only did not recognize my true nature until the later stages of my life, but when I did, I made myself deny it.

Yes, Strakh was my lover, but I believe now that was because I knew in my society if I, as a woman, were to have a lover, it had to be a man. This is not to say the experience with him was not pleasurable. He had sufficient technique in creating pleasure, but as I have said, something about the act with him left me unsatisfied.

Did he force me to have intercourse with him? No. I went into the relationship willingly, and I continued the relationship because he not only instructed me in the techniques of physical love, which I used to train my swallows and ravens, but he also gave me the benefit of his vast knowledge of human psychology and human behavior. I learned more from our pillow talk about how to read people and manipulate them than I had in any KGB training room.

Even after I concluded our physical relationship, he continued to mentor me and was always available to assist me in working through any work-related problem. This was until his death.

Between Strakh and Olive, I had no other lovers. Several Party members and members of the Red Circle wanted to be my lover, but I worked on developing a reputation of being so dedicated to serving my country that I had no time for non-Revolutionary diversions. When these propositions waned, I didn't miss them.

Besides, I knew how to take care of my own sexual needs.

When I met Olive, I immediately liked her—merely as a friend, I told myself. She was almost a decade younger than me, but we shared an interest in music and theater. The excitement I felt at seeing her was for a friend only. You see, even homosexuals can be homophobic, especially those of us in denial. Later, Olive would explain to me that this was "internalized homophobia." Even when Olive confronted me with her suspicions about me, I denied it. I thought if I acknowledged what I felt for Olive, if I accepted my true sexual orientation even to myself, the people who mattered to me would reject me for my vile perversion. Yes, that is what I believed then.

My greatest fear was that Bukharin would believe I had molested Natalia or exposed her to a deviant lifestyle. I feared disappointing my oldest friend.

So, to me, Olive was my friend first. When she admitted to me that she was gay and told me she was attracted to me, my own self-loathing of what I might be made me reject her with harsh words.

I am thankful she was persistent. She saw something in me I could not accept in myself. For the life of my career, homosexuality was nothing more than a way to compromise a potential asset or to extort government secrets from that asset. Homosexuals were detested as human beings but recognized as useful in espionage. The thought of acknowledging such perverted behavior in myself was anathema to me.

Yes, I have used the words "deviant" and "perverted." For most of my life, I knew no other way to think of homosexuals, given Party protocols on this. After the fall of the Party and the Soviet Union, the newly powerful Russian Orthodox Church preached that it was wrong and sinful behavior. Even though I had left the Soviet Union before the rejuvenation of the church and I did not undergo some sudden conversion to superstition, all that I had learned my whole life was to pity or hate or persecute, even kill, homosexuals. I could not possibly be one.

American attitudes were changing when I came there, but some religions still have too much sway over secular life. Though homosexual rights have been affirmed as human rights, there is still talk of keeping "the gays" from jobs, even talk of killing them, plus the accusations that we were too perverted to be allowed around children because we would "recruit" them or "groom" them.

I love Natalia Bukharina as a grandmother or an aunt loves a child, but after Olive was my "catalyst" as it is called, my self-loathing, my indoctrination made me believe even that those purest of feelings for a child were wrong, disgusting.

Once Olive and I became more than friends, when I realized my true nature, I felt I had to tell Bukharin and Maiya and face the consequences of their disappointment in me. In the end, I was too much of a coward to tell Bukharin myself. As I have said, he was never my lover, but he was more a brother to me than my own brothers. He was and is my friend. Once he found out about me, I feared he would no longer be either. Maiya has always called me part of the family, and I was fearful of losing that, too.

I was even afraid he would harm me, fearing that I had perverted his granddaughter. Self-loathing, remember.

I told Maiya first, a good choice because she is somewhat of a social justice warrior, as they say. Though she is a most tolerant person, she has her prejudices; however, intolerance of homosexuals is not one of them. Even so, I assured her that nothing improper had ever happened between me and Natalia.

"You're gay, Olga," Maiya said, "not a paedophile."

She told Bukharin by mistake, and he was upset. Not because I was gay, but because I had not come out to him first.

When I told Natalia, she shrugged it off, but she was of that generation raised in the first wave of change toward the LGBTQ+ community. She had friends from childhood who were gay and out; she accepted them without question and defended anyone who spoke ill of them.

Olive's journey was much different from mine. She recognized her orientation and accepted it in her teens, but she also knew her family and the small town she lived in would not be so accepting.

She left for college in Berkeley, California, and was active in the gay rights movement there. It was in those groups she met her husband. He was bisexual, or so he thought at the time, but was uncomfortable coming out as that because he was a police officer. They became close friends, and mostly to quiet their families' nagging about marriage and grandchildren, they married. Again, to satisfy their families, they had one child together, whom they both adored.

After a certain amount of time, they divorced amiably and remained friends until . . .

Until Olive was mistaken for me and murdered.

Her husband eventually accepted he was gay and not bisexual. He married a fellow police officer. Olive went to his wedding, and he came to ours. Their son, Rick, told me his father wept when he learned of Olive's death. They truly loved each other as friends and had long been a part of each other's lives. I should have spoken to him after, but my grief, my anger, was too fresh. I did not want to comfort others when I could not be comforted.

Olive and I met in 2002 because Natalia was dating Alex Terrell. Rick was a member of Alex's Ranger unit. After graduating from Harvard, Natalia wanted to be closer to where Alex was based in Georgia and leased an apartment there. Bukharin would only "allow" it if I continued to provide protection, so much as we had done in Cambridge, Massachusetts, we rented two connected apartments.

Olive, too, had wanted to be closer to her only son and had, coincidentally, rented an apartment in the same complex. That was how we met—at the complex's pool.

It began as any relationship does—talk about books and movies, the things we liked to cook, politics. She had lunch on occasion at my apartment and me at hers. We met for coffee. We went to the theatre or to concerts. We took long walks, went shopping, watched television in each other's apartments.

It was in her apartment one evening she told me she was gay and that she was attracted to me. More than that, she said, "I have feelings for you, deep feelings."

Of course, still in my denial and still wary of encumbrances, I was appalled. I was offended. I insisted I was not "that kind" of person.

"I think you are, Linda," she said—at that time, she knew only my American name. "My gay-dar is pretty good."

Then, I was by choice and design unaware of the language surrounding homosexuality, and she explained "gay-dar" to me. I still insisted she was wrong, and I left immediately. I went weeks without seeing her, not accepting her calls or texts. I avoided encountering her at the apartment complex, denied to Natalia there was anything wrong.

I was more miserable than I had ever been in my life.

Oh, you simply miss her friendship, I told myself, but a flood of memories came back: my attraction for the lieutenant who had killed herself; Masha, also in the typing pool and a member of Red Circle; other women I had encountered over the years; the dissatisfaction with intercourse with Strakh. I realized I had always looked at women the way straight men look at them. I realized Olive was right about me, but I was terrified. I did not know how to be gay.

To my surprise, when I knocked on Olive's door, she let me in as if nothing had happened and I had not spoken so harshly to her. With Olive's guidance and love, I understood for the first time who I was.

She taught me that some encumbrances I should embrace.

24

COMING OUT
ENTRY 20

2002

Mount Vernon, Virginia

The French doors from the library opened, and, cup of coffee in hand, Bukharin stepped out onto the multi-level deck on the rear of his and Maiya's house, a deck he had built himself. He walked past me to the railing where he could look down the long lawn to the Potomac River. The moving water, he once told me, had a calming effect on him, as it did on most humans.

I could see he was disturbed by something. I had known him since he was twenty years old. I knew his moods. I knew better than to ask what was wrong. He would come to it in his own time. I did suspect what it was: Maiya had likely told him what I had confessed to her. That I was gay.

After several minutes of contemplating the water, he turned to face me, his scowl intimidating but not to me.

"Why did you tell Mai and not me first that you're gay?" he asked. Before I could answer, he continued, "You and she were never that close. You're no more than employer and employee."

"Unless that is what we want people to believe," I replied, fighting not to smile.

"You and Mai? No. Impossible. Mai perhaps surpasses me in her unfaltering heterosexuality. You and I, we are comrades, *tovarishchi*. Colleagues and contemporaries. Friends. I could not be trusted with this momentous secret?"

"Sit," I said to him. "We will discuss this."

For a few seconds, I thought he would walk away, but he sat on the chaise next to mine, separated only by the width of a small beverage table.

"How much exactly did Maiya drink in your apartment last night?" he asked, switching to Russian.

"By my standards or yours, not much at all. However, enough for her display of, ahem, public affection toward you last night. *Ochen' zabavnoy*."

"Yes, definitely amusing. She should drink vodka more often. It put her in a good mood. Jameson makes her surly."

"Ah, the opposite of you. I have never seen her quite that demonstrative. Natalia could not stop laughing. Did you and she have good time last night?"

"She passed out, unfortunately, and snored most unattractively all night. Why was she drinking vodka?"

"She had questions."

"What questions?"

I gave him my most displeased side-eye. "I think that is between her and me. If she wants you to know . . ." I shrugged and sipped my coffee. "Why do you ask?"

He returned the side-eye. "Maybe I am jealous."

"Ah, I see. She told you herself, after insisting I 'man up' and tell you."

"In her defense, she was rather hung-over this morning and would never pass up an opportunity to one-up me."

"I am not attracted to her. I never have been, and I am seeing someone who is important to me."

"So she said."

"Besides, given how strongly she resisted your earliest attempts to seduce her, Bukharin, you should have no doubt about, even if I had tried."

Bukharin's mouth tipped in a brief smile, no doubt at the memory. "She did not resist me all that much."

"We remember things how we want to remember them," I said, smiling as well. "The reports said differently."

"What reports?"

"Come now, that is not what you are here to discuss."

"What reports?"

I sighed, even though this had always been a possibility. "All right, if you will not let it go. Before Nelson became Director, Sir Nigel Hume fulfilled The Directorate's part of the bargain with the Red Circle. He sent us regular reports on you. Detailed reports. Even more so when you became Maiya's training officer, and in one report he mentioned his instructions to you to seduce her to make her more compliant." I rolled my eyes. "As if that were ever possible."

Bukharin laughed. "Nothing short of death will ever make her compliant. Even then, she will fight death tooth and nail."

"Agreed. So, Hume detailed all your failed attempts and your ultimate success. Does Maiya know you were ordered to become her lover?"

"I have never confirmed it, but I think she has suspected it."

"Enough small talk. Ask me what you came out here to ask."

Bukharin finished his coffee and set the cup on the table. He swung his legs off the chaise and sat on its edge, facing me.

"Again, why did you feel you could not confide this new revelation about yourself to me?" he asked.

I nodded and sipped more coffee. "I see. Your jealousy is not because of some imagined sexual attraction between your wife and me. By the way, she once asked me if you and I were lovers. I told her no."

"Because we were not."

"You are jealous because I trusted this personal revelation to her and not you."

"You know me better than she does."

"Yes, because I made you who you are. That never meant you knew me to the same depth. You do not. I would never have allowed that."

"You, Olga Yevgenyevna, are my oldest friend."

"And you, Alexei Nicholaivitch, are mine."

"But you could not tell me first?"

"I had to convince myself it was true. Tell me, Bukharin, from your upbringing, from the lessons I taught you in the KGB, what was the prevailing attitude about homosexuality?"

"That it is a perversion we could exploit. And I have done so. In the past."

"The operative word is 'perversion.' You and I were raised and indoctrinated in a system that imbued us with the belief that people like me are disgusting, abnormal, revolting."

"People do learn to manage their prejudices, Olga. I have. Part of that was Nelson bringing The Directorate into modern times. Now, it is far more diverse than you can imagine. However, the first gay analyst or operative I worked with, I had to overcome that indoctrination, as you called it, but I soon realized they were no different from me in their dedication to the work, for me to understand love is love." His fleeting smile came again. "Besides, you know Maiya and Natasha. Do you think they'd let me get away with being a bigot?"

"Good for you, but I still struggle with my own bigotry," I said. "As much as my . . . See, I do not even know what to call her. My girlfriend? I am not a teenager. My partner? That is too cold and sounds like a business arrangement. My friend? That is inaccurate because she is more than that."

"She is your lover."

"Yes, but . . ."

"But what?"

"That implies it is merely sex. It is not. Let me finish my thought. As much as Olive has helped me accept who I am, I am still troubled by that knowledge. I need to shed my self-loathing before I can accept what I have learned about myself."

"Are you disgusted with yourself?"

"No. Yes."

"Does Olive disgust you?"

"No! Never!"

"And I seem to recall hearing you say, 'Comrade, the KGB will divest you of all your useless emotions.'"

I had to laugh at that. "You are one to talk," I said. "And do not use my own words against me."

"I am only doing what you taught me to do. Be honest with me for once."

"All right. I do not want anyone who matters to me to struggle with accepting me as what I have realized I am."

"That I do understand. That I can relate to," Bukharin said. "You know how I struggled to accept my feelings for Maiya, how long it took me. I admitted to myself and to her that I loved her almost too late. I came close to losing her over that. Now, does Olive make you happy?"

"I have never known such happiness."

"That is why I stayed with Maiya through it all. Because when I was with her, in the good times and the bad, was the only time I felt truly happy, as happy as my brief time with Sofya Grigorevna. But my pushing Maiya away when we would get too close broke her trust to the point where she could not believe me when I told her I did love her. Every time I say it to her, even now, I read the hesitation in her eyes. I see the doubt she has before she responds in kind. That is like a knife in my chest. Every time. Do not do that to yourself. Or to Olive."

He stretched out on the chaise, arms folded over his chest. "You should have told me before you told her," he murmured.

I shook my head. "Such pettiness does not become you, Bukharin, and this behavior will make your wife think I lied about being your lover," she said.

"Let her wonder a while more," he said. "I would not want her to become complacent in our relationship."

I adopted the same position in my lounger, glad my friend had not stayed as I had trained him.

25

GORBACHEV

ENTRY 21

Another person I have mentioned more than once and should write about—as if not enough has not already been written—is Mikhail Sergeivitch Gorbachev. People in the West know him as the originator of *glasnost* and *pere-stroika*, openness and restructuring, respectively. I knew him of course as a key member, eventually the top member of the Red Circle. Of course, he was the first Red Circle member to become head of the Soviet Union.

In 1986, when Gorbachev spoke to the annual meeting of the Communist Party Congress about being more transparent, as it is said today, only a few in the audience knew what he meant. For members of the Red Circle, those were the code words to indicate The Plan was coming to fruition. Gorbachev, the de facto leader of the Red Circle, was the leader now of the Soviet Union, in the perfect position to assure a return to the original socialist goals of Lenin and the Revolution.

People now try to label him a social democrat, but it was only a few years ago he said in an interview for a documentary that the

Soviet Union could have and should have been restructured—under socialism. That is why he refused to sign his resignation and inaugurate the Russian Federation on television, because the Revolution had been set aside, not what the Red Circle intended.

People too often think of him as affable, grandfatherly, and he is a good man. However, he could be as ruthless as any KGB officer when he needed to be, as the KGB leadership found out after their attempted coup. Gorbachev's revenge—though he would not call it that, ever being the politician—was not for what they had done to him. They held him captive in his own *dacha* while they reported to the world he had had a heart attack and discussed, where he could hear, how they should kill him. No, he could not bear the effect this had on his beloved wife, Raisa. He avenged her.

He followed through with *glasnost*, surprising the world when he admitted that Chernobyl had happened, and with *perestroika*, by reforming how the Soviet economy was handled. He is a man of his word.

Gorbachev was a young man when he recruited Bukharin to the Red Circle. He was not my recruiter (that was an old veteran of the Revolution and a former advisor to Stalin, a surprise to me), but Gorbachev did recruit key people for placement in various government and military positions. One of those recruits was Boris Yeltsin, who fulfilled his requirement in convincing the Army not to support the 1991 attempted coup. The Red Circle knew that at some point, one of them would lead Russia and would enact The Plan's final stages and that either the intelligence community or the military in the Soviet Union would try to stop it.

Gorbachev was not a "power hog" within or outside the Red Circle, though he did establish what role each recruit would play. He gave me broad guidelines on training my recruits, those "special students" who were also Red Circle. But it was Gorbachev's idea that the best way to hide their true purpose from the KGB was to train them as KGB officers. That was my part in The Plan. Gorbachev had a way of making even the smallest cog think he or she was a "big wheel."

I have always suspected the Red Circle had a mole because as the KGB bigwigs were planning the coup, they were careful to compartmentalize it. Not a single Red Circle member in the KGB was aware of it. Misha and I discussed it afterward, and I gave him the benefit of my thoughts on who such a mole might be. I could never prove it. I have since told Maiya, and she has found nothing to prove it either. Sometimes, though, all you need is the feeling in your gut.

No one was more surprised than Gorbachev at how abruptly the Soviet Union ended. Yes, that was essentially the Red Circle's plan, but it did not turn out the way they wanted. I suspect that was because they simply relaxed too much and let events overtake them. Gorbachev and I were shocked at how quickly the loss of the single-party system and a taste of democracy would make people want to shed every vestige of socialism, even the good parts, including him.

To this day, he is unpopular among a portion of the population. Some blame him for the loss of all the protections the Soviet State gave them: free education, free health care, a guaranteed job, and so forth. Others say he led Russia down the path to oligarchy, but I believe if he had remained in power, there would be no Dmitri Kargin today. Gorbachev would have found a reason, a good one, to have him killed.

Some of the world followed the lead of the United States. To one particular U.S. political party, no one and nothing from the Soviet Union could be trusted. (My, how the Republicans have changed, but I will not digress.) The political leaders criticized everything about Gorbachev: his height, his weight, his birthmark. His wife. That hurt him the most, especially when the Western media focused on the fact that Raisa Titarenko went by her own family name. Americans cannot shake the religious nonsense that a woman is a man's property and must take his name.

Also overblown was the fact Raisa and the American First Lady Nancy Reagan did not get along. Putting those two women in the same room would be like putting Einstein in the same room as a first grader and expecting the two of them to come up with the unified field theory. Raisa was a well-educated, working woman, and Mrs. Reagan consulted astrologers.

But Gorbachev himself had little use for President Reagan. Gorbachev was an intelligent, erudite man confronted by a B-movie actor who liked to spout one-liners that appealed to his sophomoric base. Gorbachev would have torn down that wall; it was part of The Plan. It was not because Reagan demanded it. And the "trust but verify" negated any trust the two men could hope to build. Plus, the Americans made untenable demands. They wanted to neuter the Soviet Union's defense capabilities while bloating their own. A partnership of equals could not be created in such distrust.

As Gorbachev has also said, "America won the Cold War, and it went to their head."

No truer words.

Gorbachev was a seminal figure in my life and work, especially toward the end of the Soviet Union when he often used me as a sounding board. To this day, I would do anything he asked of me.

26

MAYA SMERT' (MY DEATH)

ENTRY 22

November 1991

The Kremlin
Moscow

As I had advised, President Gorbachev had extra security now at his offices in The Kremlin. I selected them myself from among my staff I trusted. Though the coup attempt was three months in the past, it was better to be cautious than repentant.

Because the increased security knew me, I passed through every checkpoint without an issue, but they were thorough in checking identification and examining my briefcase.

"Do not wear your uniform," Gorbachev had told me when he had requested the meeting. "If Raisa is here, it will make her too nervous."

I settled for a pair of slacks and a matching belted jacket that was uniform-like, but my rank and service insignia, my medals and decorations, and the prim hat were gone. The damned girdle, however, remained. I did have an image to uphold.

Despite the several examinations of my briefcase, not even my own officers found the case's false bottom. After running the gauntlet of my own design, Gorbachev's assistant escorted me into the private office he now used more often.

He looked tired. His face was thinner, his eyes haunted and ringed by dark circles. The port-wine birthmark seemed more prominent against his pale skin. I suspected it was all from worry about his wife. The coup had caused Raisa to have a nervous breakdown, even costing her temporarily the ability to speak.

Gorbachev did not like leaving her at home because she worried so about his safety. He had started bringing her to the Kremlin with a doctor watching over her. To keep her calm, she saw her husband at least once an hour.

Mindful I was not in uniform, I forced myself not to salute and accepted Gorbachev's offered handshake.

"Olga," he murmured. "Olechka, as always, good to see you. Please have a seat."

"Thank you, Mr. President. May I inquire about the health of your wife?" I didn't ask because I didn't know; I did. Rather, it was polite, and Gorbachev needed to know some people cared for Raisa's well-being.

His eyes became sad and rheumy. "Good days and bad days. She still goes days without speaking. Sometimes, her legs will not hold her up. The doctors have said it is like the effects of a stroke without having a stroke. She has nightmares and is afraid to sleep. So, I do not sleep either."

"I am terribly sorry to hear this."

While we made the small talk, I opened my briefcase and passed Gorbachev some files in classified folders. They were fake but provided an excuse for me to be in his office. I raised the false bottom, revealing some electronic equipment. I activated the device, closed the briefcase, and set it on the floor by my chair.

"That is jamming any eavesdropping devices I might not know about," I explained. "We should have at least a half-hour before someone figures that out and neutralizes the jamming. Even so, I suggest we keep our business to no more than twenty minutes in case a brilliant technician is on duty today."

A smile got started but faded fast. He said, "I have asked you here to explain some things. Let me begin by saying what I am about to tell you displeases me, but I am as subject to the Council's decisions as you are."

I stayed quiet. The council he referred to was the group of decision-makers for the Red Circle.

"But first," he said, "give me a report on the progress of the investigation."

"The Gang of Eight have been removed from their positions, as have their staffs," I began. "Of the people responsible for the coup attempt, all have been dealt with or transferred."

"All except for you," he said.

I struggled to maintain self-control. The thought that he might be ordering my death made me light-headed. I took deep breaths. "I was not involved, as you are aware," I managed to say with calm.

"I am aware," he said with a sigh. "Logically and by seniority, you should be head of the KGB now, but that cannot be."

I swallowed my disappointment. "I never expected it."

"Why not?"

"I am a woman."

"That should not have mattered."

"May I ask, Mr. President, why I am to be sacrificed?"

"*Boizhe moi*, Olga, I am not pronouncing a death sentence."

The knot in my stomach relaxed.

"No, I was convinced from the beginning you were not complicit in the coup, but the Red Circle Council cannot accept the fact you did not warn of it."

"Because I knew nothing of it!" I said, aware of the defensiveness in my voice. "The Gang of Eight had never trusted me and so did not include me in their traitorous plans. Kruchkov himself admitted this."

"Under interrogation."

"Yes, and I know that under interrogation, people generally lie or give up the names of uninvolved people hoping to save themselves. But you know Kruchkov told the truth about me."

"I do, yes. I have no doubt of it. I assure you of that, but you have to go. The purge of conspirators has to appear complete to the public's eye, and the public would not understand that someone so highly placed as you would not know of the plans for the coup. You are a 'loose end,' as the Americans say, and I am sincerely sorry for it."

"I see, and despite your reassurance, am I to be taken to my own prison and shot by one of my own men?"

"Of course not! I would never allow that."

"Then what is it you want of me?"

"You must either resign or set a retirement date. However, I suspect that in a very short time—this is all I can say—there will be no Soviet Union for me to be in charge of. Whoever succeeds me may not have a soft spot for you."

"Agreed."

"However, if you were to arrange your death as a cover for defection, you could be gone before the inevitable happens when I can no longer protect you."

"Comrade, I would never defect and have what I know cajoled from me with the offer of money and a good life. I would rather die in reality than that."

"I know. I have made an overture to the United Nations Intelligence Directorate. Its operational head is Nelson, who is a friend of *your* friend. Nelson has guaranteed you a new identity and a new life, with no strings attached."

"Per our profile of Nelson, I doubt that."

"Hear me out. As you know, Alexei Bukharin and his wife have guardianship over Bukharin's granddaughter for two years now. This means Nelson has the use of his top operatives only one at a time. Nelson has suggested that you contact Bukharin and tell him it is important that you see him in person. When the two of you meet, you will pitch to him your services as a companion for that granddaughter."

"First, it is still dangerous for Bukharin to come to Moscow. Kyiv can be overlooked, but not here. And second—"

He held up a hand for silence, and I obeyed. "First, *I* can make certain Bukharin is unmolested if he uses a cover identity," Gorbachev said, "and second, Nelson wants his two best operatives working together again. Moreover, Bukharin wants it. Whether the wife does is another matter."

"Bukharin does not know Nelson is involved?"

"No, and Nelson prefers it that way. Comrade . . . Olechka, this is your best choice, in some ways your only choice. You can start a new life in America, and you will not have to compromise your loyalty and service to the country of your birth."

"By becoming a nanny."

"I believe Mr. Nelson suggested 'au pair/bodyguard.' Well, what do you say?"

"I honestly cannot believe what I am hearing, but you are correct. My choices are few. I can likely convince Bukharin easily. He owes me for his son and his wife's escape from the Stasi. Convincing her, however, is questionable."

Gorbachev smiled with affection at me. "You will have to be

your most charming with *Gospodina* Bukharina." Gorbachev looked at his watch. "How long will you need to set things up?"

"A week to ten days. When I stage my death, I want to be assured nothing will happen to the people who have been loyal to me," I said.

"I will do what I can as long as I have power."

"No, you will assure it because I can and would sneak back into this country and avenge them."

We stared at each other in silence, Gorbachev's face flushed with anger, mine set in determination. Gorbachev picked up the fake file folders and handed them to me.

"Thank you for making me aware of these issues, Comrade Lubova," he said with an abrupt nod. "You have done your usual thorough job. Is there anything else today?"

"No, Comrade, except for this: Let us not forget that revolutions are accomplished through people, though they be nameless." A final quote from Trotsky to tell Gorbachev the Red Circle had gotten what it wanted. "I must go back to work, Comrade," I continued. "My regards to *Gospodina* Gorbachevna. Good day."

I was at the door when Gorbachev called to me. "Olechka? Good luck to you. I mean that with all sincerity. An army cannot be built without reprisals."

I looked back over my shoulder. How many times had Strakh said that to me?

And how did Gorbachev know that?

I nodded and left.

27

BUKHARIN AGAIN

ENTRY 23

As I have been writing this, some 40,000 words now, I have given a great deal of thought to why Bukharin and I became as close as we were, we are. I am not saying I had affection for him. Never. Rather, I envied the power he had as a man and used that in a surrogate manner.

Despite my skills, my knowledge, my abilities, and my dedication to my service, I was still a *prostaya zhenshchina* to the men around me, a "mere woman."

Not to Bukharin, but he had the example of a powerful, strong mother. Once he got over the fact a "mere woman" had beaten him senseless, he accepted my authority. He listened to me without wavering, he accepted my training, and on occasion I managed to wrench a smile from him.

I knew, of course, from his Red Circle dossier, of the father, brother, and sister killed in Stalingrad and that his mother had appointed him to assure revenge for that. I knew his surviving older brother and sister ignored him. I knew his younger half-brother Bukharin felt protective of even though he thought of him as a pest. I knew he loved Sofya Krasnovskaya even though he was not supposed to, and I knew he loved their son.

I knew, as well, that when it came time for him to do his part for The Plan, he would defect as required. I suspected he would only do what was necessary and nothing more for that plan. It would be easy to say a man would leave his son behind for love of country, but Bukharin did not love the Soviet Union. Oh, he had a mission, his mother's mission as well as his own personal one. He wanted to die.

Now, he is an American, but he always points out when someone calls him Russian that he is Ukrainian. He accepted his service to the Soviet Union, to Rodina, to Mother Russia, but in his heart he remained Ukrainian.

Of course, I exploited that to fuel his anger and make him the perfect instrument to be played by spymasters. I reminded him of the "inferiority" of his heritage and that there was no Ukraine, only the Ukrainian Soviet Social Republic. I called him "stupid Ukrainian trash" at every opportunity, and he took it from me because he understood why I did it. I needed his anger. He needed his anger.

If a fellow trainee used such language toward him, Bukharin had my permission to deal with it his own way. The other trainees soon learned to mind their bigotry around him.

Was I proud of him?

I was proud I had succeeded in making him the Red Circle's committed, efficient, unrelenting instrument. I was proud that what I had created would do the work to restore the Revolution in my country.

I was proud of him.

And the other one, the other Bukharin? More on him in a bit.

I am sure you would ask, "Did you love Bukharin?"

He did have the body and looks that can reduce women to

servile parodies of themselves, but of course, I did not love him. I loved no one. I wanted to love no one, or so I thought until I met Olive. Through Olive's love I understood I loved my mother and father and those annoying brothers, but I had never learned how to accept it. Because love was an encumbrance, as were the people I loved.

Yes, my admiration of and my pride in Bukharin were likely encumbrances, too, but I accepted them because they were a means to an end.

We have always called each other friends, though he was the one to start that. Not long before his time to defect, he said to me, "Comrade, you have been my trainer, but you are also my friend because you saw in me some part you wanted to live on." I was the last person he saw before that defection, not his mother or his son; me.

I believe he sought my blessing for the work he was leaving to do, and I willingly gave it.

Do I love Bukharin now?

Now, I can admit it. Of course, I do. He is my little brother, my replacement for Little Sasha, if you will, though he is only four years my junior. He never faltered in his missions—the Red Circle's, his Nazi hunts, or his Directorate operations—though he did decide he no longer wanted to die. I take the credit for the mission success. I would like to take credit that he chose to live, but that belongs to Maiya.

I was not happy about his obsession with his much younger wife, but that is what it is. I will admit she saved him.

All my blood family is gone. Mama, Papa, *moya brat'ya*. Olive, who was more than blood family to me.

But Bukharin remains.

Now, I should talk about the other one, the cousin who looked so much like Bukharin people assumed they were twins.

He, too, had a role in The Plan, a role he knew could mean his life, and it ultimately did.

Nicholai Bukharin and Alexei Bukharin were the sons of twin brothers, only a few months apart in age, and more like brothers to each other.

The cousin was mine to train, too, but he came to me a whole man, no grief, unbroken. He received the same specialized training, but his demeanor was so carefree I could not break him down and rebuild him. I did not consider this as a failure because I taught him how to use his personality for The Plan. Nicholai accepted his role in The Plan because he loved his country and his cousin Alexei.

They had bonded as children, and Gorbachev himself recruited them into the Red Circle. They were alike physically and yet different.

Nicholai was gregarious, outgoing, playful, a contrast to the ever-serious Alexei. So, instead of anger, I used love to train Nicholai, so he would draw on his love of his cousin/brother to fulfill his role. I exploited that as I would have any other weakness.

That was then, this is now, you say. In truth, if given the opportunity to train spies again, I would do it the same way.

As Alexei impressed me with his intelligence, his strength, and his commitment to a cause (even if it wasn't the Red Circle's), so did Nicholai. He was as smart, as strong, as committed as his cousin. Perhaps more committed since he was the one who had to be willing to give his life for his cousin.

The Red Circle's plan was deliberately obtuse, and I believe perhaps only two or three people knew the entirety of it. That was for security. Each of us knew our part in it, and if we were ever questioned, the whole plan would never be revealed. Alexei and Nicholai had but a small part, but they had key tasks in The Plan. Bukharin was to pretend to be a defector and to pretend to be a double and feed intel to the KGB. A secondary aspect of his task was to eliminate Red Circle members who were either suspected of collaborating with the Soviet government or whom the Soviet intelligence agencies suspected of disloyalty.

Yes, each of us only knew a small part of The Plan, but if enough of us had been captured and interrogated, the KGB could have put it together. Despite portrayals in the West's movies and novels, the KGB was not stupid.

I did express to Strakh my only concern about using the two Bukharins. The Bukharin family had lost so much in Stalin's purges and in the Great Patriotic War.

"They know and accept what needs to be done," Strakh replied. "The Bukharins will continue to sacrifice much for our Glorious Revolution."

Alexei fulfilled his part of The Plan, as did Nicholai. The irony is this was less than three years from the dissolution of the Soviet Union. Suppose Alexei and Nicholai had not been betrayed by a member of the Czech secret police hoping to curry favor with Moscow. Were that the case, Nicholai might be here now, enjoying his grown children and his grandchildren.

But that is not my story to tell. I leave that to a better writer than I.

28

THE OTHER BUKHARIN

ENTRY 24

1964

KGB Training Directorate
Moscow

I studied the file on the trainee who had asked for a private audience. I'd written most of the entries myself. The request for a meeting in itself was unusual. I did the summoning of my trainees, not the other way around.

All of his ratings were excellent, above average, almost as high as his cousin's. This trainee wasn't designated to be an assassin but a regular KGB officer, and I granted his request for a meeting because of his part in The Plan.

As I checked my watch, a movement in the doorway had me look up. The trainee stood at attention in his training uniform of olive-gray trousers and tunic but with no insignia.

Precisely on time. Good.

"Come in, Comrade," I said, again startled as always by how much he resembled his cousin. The eyes were slightly different. The same piercing blue color but without the oriental touch. Close up, clearly a distinguishing characteristic that could present a problem; from a distance, however, no problem at all. That was what mattered.

"Trainee 259 reporting, Comrade Captain," he said, still at attention after taking two steps inside.

Even the voice was similar, though heavy with a Moscow accent. I'd had to teach that to the Ukrainian cousin.

"I am busy, Comrade Trainee. What do you want?" I asked.

"Comrade Captain, may we speak in private?" he asked, almost whispering. "I need clarification on whether we think alike in many things."

I nodded to him and activated a switch beneath my desktop. The trainee closed the door and resumed his stiff posture.

"The code phrase was not necessary, Comrade Trainee. I suspect the purpose of your visit," I said. "You may speak freely. Sit if you like. I understand you sprained an ankle yesterday on the obstacle course."

"I was stupid and clumsy, Comrade Captain. I will stand."

"Yes, Comrade, push through the pain. What are the matters we need to discuss?"

"I respectfully request that you make a change in assignments for Operation Janus."

That I had not anticipated.

"Explain," I said.

"Since I cannot have contact with my cousin," he said, "I have not been able to consult with him about this. He knows nothing about what I am asking."

"I require details, Comrade Trainee, for this request. Explain. Do not make me ask again."

"I am not married and therefore have no children. I should be the one to defect, and my cousin should take my role here, assume what was to be my part of the operation."

"Why?"

"So he can be a father to his son. He and I both know what it is like to grow up without a father. His son should not have to know that. All my instructors, including yourself, have given me top ratings. So as not to delay the timetable, I will work additional hours on the required specialized training."

"Your request tells me you do not fully understand Operation Janus," I said. "Relate to me what you know of it."

He frowned, both eyebrows pristine. Should I scar him, too? No. Again, from a distance, that small difference would not be a problem for him.

"My pardon, Comrade Captain. I thought you knew all about—"

"I do know, Comrade, obviously. I am questioning your understanding of it."

"Yes, Comrade Captain, of course. My cousin is to defect to the West, ostensibly as a double agent, to work for Western intelligence interests while funneling their secrets to us. In reality, he is a conduit for the status of Red Circle plans and operations so those Western intelligence services can perform their parts in The Plan."

"That is his part. What is yours?"

"I am to be available when summoned in a case of extreme danger to my cousin, to substitute myself for him so he can return to the West and further The Plan."

"A somewhat simplistic explanation but essentially correct."

"Thank you, Comrade Captain. What I am suggesting is that he and I switch roles. Let me defect and let my cousin remain here to be a father to his baby son. A child should know his father."

"You make this request from emotion, Comrade Trainee."

"Yes, but I also speak from experience. As I indicated, growing up fatherless is an experience my cousin and I share, and we suffered from it, my cousin more so than I. I had my father for six years. He never knew his. Why should baby Pyotor Alexeivitch go through the same?"

"There was never supposed to be a Pyotor Alexeivitch," I said. "You and your cousin received the same instructions: Have as many women as you want but no marriages. No encumbrances. Your cousin did not follow his orders."

"He was in love, Comrade Captain."

"A bourgeois affectation."

"For which he was punished, yes?"

"What are you suggesting?"

"The first thing you teach us in our training is that there is no such thing as coincidence. I do not believe Sofya Grigorevna's death was an accident. It was too coincidental."

"Keep that opinion to yourself."

"Why, Comrade? Because I am right?"

"No. Because if you say this to the wrong person, it will get you killed. If you die before Operation Janus starts, there can be no Operation Janus."

"Operation Janus is one which, at some point, may require me to give my life. What is the difference?"

"You are as stupid as your Ukrainian trash cousin," I said, noting the paling of the trainee's irises, like his cousin when he was angry. "Without the both of you, there is no Operation Janus."

"I understand that, but there should be no issue with switching me for him now."

"The issue, Comrade Trainee, is that our glorious Socialist state has invested a great deal of time and money into your cousin's preparation for his designated role. On a whim, you are demanding we simply throw that investment away and spend more time and money to train you to do what we have already trained him to do."

"I will work hard, Comrade, extra hours to assure the expenditures are minimal."

This one seemed to have an answer for everything.

When I stood behind my desk, he came to attention again. "Comrade Trainee, are you certain no one has planted this suggestion in your head?"

"I swear, Comrade Captain. I am not compromised."

"And you arrived at this idea all of a sudden, magically, with no prompting?"

"There was no magic involved, Comrade Captain. It was . . . "

"Go on."

"It was something else. Last week marked the thirteenth anniversary of my father's heart attack. I am always introspective on that anniversary, remembering the milestones in my life that he has missed, how he is not here to advise and guide me, and yes, I understand I have the State for that, but does not the father reinforce the state? I will never know if he would be proud of me. I do not want my cousin's son to be deprived of that."

"Comrade Trainee, as the quaint American expression goes, you are blowing smoke up my skirt. Were he alive, your father would never be aware of your role in Operation Janus. That was a decision made after his death anyway."

"But I will be a KGB officer, yes?"

"Yes, but you are not one yet. Given this display of emotion, you may not be one after all."

The slightest of smiles moved his lips. "Respectfully, if that were the case, Comrade, Operation Janus would not happen."

Pursing my lips to keep from smiling, I gave him a steely stare. "Comrade Trainee, you are too glib for your own good."

"Thank you, Comrade Captain. All I ask is that you take this suggestion to the Red Circle. I suspect many of them are fathers or mothers. Perhaps they will . . ."

He trailed off when I held up a hand.

"Whereas your dedication to the mission, and your cousin, are admirable, albeit misguided in the latter case, what you request is now impossible."

"May I ask why, Comrade Captain?"

"You may, and I will answer. Nicholai . . . Kolya, your cousin Alexei is already in Cairo, ready to meet his contact from the United Nations Intelligence Directorate. Operation Janus has begun. From now on, your focus needs to be on your training so that you will be ready should your cousin need you. Understand?"

His eyes dipped to the floor momentarily, and he blinked rapidly. With a sniff, his head came up again. If anything, his posture stiffened even more.

"Understood, Comrade Captain! Thank you for your time."

"You are welcome, Comrade Trainee. At 0500 tomorrow, report to me at the training gymnasium for disciplinary action."

His control faltered, and he looked me in the eye. He'd gone a bit pale.

"Disciplinary . . . But why? What have I done, Comrade Captain?" he asked.

"Because I have decided you require it. If you ask more questions, and I will have to assume you are questioning my judgement and authority."

"No, Comrade Captain, of course not. I only want to understand why."

"Because you ask too many questions, Comrade Trainee. You are dismissed."

"But—"

"Dismissed, Comrade!"

Nicholai Bukharin snapped to attention again, saluted me, executed a flawless about-face, and marched from my office.

Moy droog Alexei, I thought, you need to be careful; I do not want to lose this one.

29

AN IMAGE OF AMERICA

ENTRY 25

In the Soviet Union, we were all provided an image of America, the United States, as a decadent society of nothing except rich people with their feet on the necks of the poor. Some of us were skeptical of that characterization, but naturally, we kept that to ourselves. The U.S. citizens I encountered—mostly spies disguised as embassy employees—were as dedicated to their country as my officers were to the Soviet Union. Most of them were honorable and challenging opponents. Each side won some and lost some. A good balance in the long run.

But when I arrived in the United States not long before Christmas 1991, I found little to dispute that original image indoctrinated into me by the Socialist State. The income gap between rich and poor was wide then and has since grown wider. Race relations had more downs than ups, and that is still the case, with policemen kneeling on black men's necks until they suffocate. Yes, I have softened in my old age.

Now, of course, the United States, for four years, has toyed with authoritarianism from a man who models himself after

Dmitri Kargin. I will say despite his mediocrity, Kargin always did a good job in finding weaknesses to exploit to turn an asset. The American president is no different from any low-level bureaucrat we caught in a scandal and used for our own purposes.

However, when I first came to America, I was overwhelmed by everything: the different stores, the choices among brands, and the colorful diversity of the people. I was given an apartment almost the size of the one I had left in Moscow, one that could have housed a half-dozen workers' families. I was even overwhelmed by the responsibility of assuring the safety of a young child.

Of course, I primarily came to the U.S. to guard Natalia Petrovna and to save my life. I never expected the job or her to matter to me. Believe me, no one else would have expected that either, and it was not simply because she was the grandchild of Bukharin. I found a bright, curious girl and was able to see her become a caring woman focused on achieving justice for all her clients. The work she does as a human rights lawyer will leave a mark on the world far greater than anything I have ever done because she will improve the lives and safety of women and children who do not have the opportunities she did growing up.

In that way, she is much like her mother. Not her birth mother, who died so tragically, but the woman who was destined to become her mother, Mai Fisher.

Bukharin and Maiya made the United States my home, and I grew to enjoy the routine this offered: wake Natalia, feed Natalia, take Natalia to school, pick her up, oversee homework, supervise the watching of television (only when Maiya was away), and enforce bath and bed times. I know some women chafe at this unending routine, and I do not disparage them. If I had had the misfortune to become a mother early in my career, I would have hated the routine and my child for it. But I came to America at the end of my career, and my previous life, with its routine and strict schedule, was behind me. Still, the Natalia routine was comforting to me, and I did not often have to look over my shoulder. Though Americans are perceived by the world as "laid back," they are slaves to their chosen routines. They complain and wish it was not so but repeat it every day until they die from it.

As young Natalia would say, "You are weird." I am, perhaps, but I prefer routine.

Perhaps that is why I am so troubled now, almost two years after Olive's death. She and I had a routine, a relaxed one but a routine nonetheless, and we both reveled in the sameness of each day. Here, I have no routine other than the staring at four walls and occasionally out a window.

Until the writing of this memoir.

As a routine, this will have a short life. A day will come when I will no longer have anything to write about.

I did eventually become a United States citizen, like Bukharin. Of course, not as Olga Lubova but under the name given me when I came here, my cover name, Linda Collins. A plain, unexciting name, but I understand the need not to draw attention to oneself. But within my "family" of Bukharin, Maiya, and Natalia, then Olive, her son, and Alex, I have always been Olga Yevgenyevna Lubova.

Still, becoming a citizen opened many opportunities. At the proper age, I received Social Security and Medicare, those socialist-based conventions Americans do not mind having even as they declare they need nothing from the "govmint."

Voting is the highest responsibility of a U.S. citizen, one I do not understand why so many do not exercise. I was proud to cast my first vote in the election year of 1998. That year Natalia Petrovna turned eighteen and cast her first vote as well. Three of us went to the polling place: Bukharin, Natalia, and me. Maiya, of course, is a dual citizen of England and Ireland and votes in

England. She stayed home. I felt immense pride at participating in choosing the government of my new country.

Of course, I voted in the Soviet Union. Voting in the Soviet Union was mandatory. Voting, however, implies a choice between or among candidates, more than one candidate for an office. In the Soviet Union, there was one party, always a single name for whatever office, and that was whom everyone voted for. The candidate was picked by the Party, not the people. We had no real choice.

In America, I have choices, even if, as I have seen, some citizens do not always make the best choice. In America, the power comes from the people, all the people, not a single class or individual. That was what our Revolution in 1917 intended. In retrospect, and despite the fact I fought hard to restore its principles, I do not know if that equality was ever the case.

This might be a cliche, but in America, I found everything brighter, from the color of clothing to the color of houses to the color of cars. Every task had a certain convenience and efficiency, for the most part.

And everyone smiled. I was so unaccustomed to that because of my entire life in the Soviet Union that I initially found it, as young Natalia would say, creepy. I have still not quite mastered smiling on cue. Neither has Bukharin.

As I said, in America, I never had to constantly look over my shoulder for danger, for someone following me, for being spied upon by my neighbors. No listening for the sound of jackboots on the stairs at night. That possibility of that in America is changing, but I believe Americans will reject becoming an authoritarian state. At least, I hope so. America is still a young country, Russia a very old one. In Russia, we have never been blessed with enlightened rulers. I trust what is happening in America now is an aberration not a trend. I hope so, for I have lived in the aberration.

I never expected America to become my sanctuary, like some

defectors who had been stationed here and did not want to leave that convenience, that freedom. If not for that failed coup against Gorbachev, I might have come here only as a tourist. But once in the United States, after I became a citizen, and especially after meeting Olive, I wanted to be no other place.

The last two years in Switzerland have made me miss America, but I have been with my family, the one that welcomed me so long ago. That was the balm I needed at the time. But Olive is dead. Olive will never be again. Unlike Bukharin, I only had one love in my life, and she is gone.

That is my fault. I was not home. I was sticking to my exercise routine. Had I been home, perhaps I could have saved her. Or at least we would have died together.

Had that been the case, we would have been buried in America, side by side, something denied my parents.

30

AMERICA

ENTRY 26

1991

Springfield Mall
Northern Virginia

Natalia Petrovna hopped and skipped along the wide aisles of Springfield Mall, explaining the purpose of each store to me. It did not take me long to be overwhelmed by the differences between shopping in America and shopping in Moscow.

Here, there was a separate store for almost anything: shoes, men's clothes, women's clothes, jewelry, hats, and even women's sexy undergarments. I observed a food court that offered extensive choices of cuisine types. Bukharin steered Natalia away from there despite her pleas for something called Sbarro, which I have since learned is pizza.

Natalia chattered on and on, a constant stream of words that seemed to require her to take in no oxygen and made me wonder if this new position was the right choice for me. Bukharin walked beside me, essentially interpreting the eleven-year-old girl's pre-teen slang. To me, it sounded somewhat like the English I had learned well enough to teach others to speak, and I had studied American slang from the recordings from the taps on U.S. Embassy phones and other bugs. But Natalia's speech contained a curious mixture of interjections: "okay," "like," "you know," "really," and "seriously." Perhaps a few more I did not catch.

"What do you think of all this?" Bukharin asked me.

"The Party was right about one thing. America is decadent," I replied in Russian. "Should I not speak Russian? Would that be too suspicious?"

"Not suspicious at all in Northern Virginia. You'll find almost any language you can think of spoken here. Do whatever makes you feel comfortable."

"Your Russian is still good, though you have let your Moscow accent slip back into your Ukrainian one. Even Maiya and Natalia sound like Ukrainians."

"Well, Natalia learned from her father, and Mai came to me speaking schoolroom Russian. When I tutored her further, she picked up my Ukrainian accent. So, this is a suburban mall. If you think this is decadent, we'll have to take you to a 'luxury' mall."

"I cannot wait," I said in English. "And she comes here a lot?"

"She would live here if we would allow it. Most of the time, she meets school friends here, but Mai and I require that an adult has to be present. No being a mall rat without supervision."

"There are rats in American malls?"

Bukharin's mouth formed a stingy smile. "It's an expression. The teens and pre-teens who hang out in malls on weekends and school holidays are called mall rats because they swarm everywhere, usually at a run, make a tremendous amount of noise, and occasionally leave destruction in their wake."

"*Boizhe moi*," I murmured.

"It's holiday shopping season right now, which makes it worse," Bukharin said. "After that, it won't be so bad."

"You sound as if you speak from experience."

"I was the supervising adult only once for one of the mall rat swarmings. I told Mai a man has his limits and that I had encountered mine. I'll bring Natasha here when it's her and me but not with her friends along. I'd rather have a running gun battle with the *Stasi* than experience that again. Of course, Natalia and her friends like coming here with Mai because she can be, as you might guess, generous. However, she also has them all marching to her tune."

"Popi!" Natalia broke in, bouncing on her toes in front of her grandfather. "If we can't have Sbarro, can we please, please, please, pretty please have lunch at Bennigan's?"

"I was going to fix lunch when we got home."

"Please, Popi. Please, please, please. I'm asking politely, and I'm remembering to say please. So, can we, please?"

"We are quite able," he replied, surprising me with a joking tone. Bukharin had never been one to joke.

Natalia rolled her eyes and said in a perfect imitation of Mai, "Dearest Grandfather, may we please have luncheon at Bennigan's wonderful establishment?"

Again, to my surprise, Bukharin smiled fully. "Since you asked so nicely, yes."

"Yay!"

After more bouncing, she resumed her monologue about shopping choices.

"This Bennigan's is a fancy place? My outfit is all right?"

"Oh, no. It's about as one-star as you can get, but the food is decent enough," Bukharin said. "In my opinion, the only thing worth eating on the menu is a deep-fried sandwich called the

Monte Cristo."

"What is deep-fried?"

"They make a two-layer sandwich with whole wheat bread. One layer has turkey and Swiss cheese. The other has ham and American cheese—a cheese product, quite unappetizing, but there is something about it on this sandwich. Then, the whole sandwich is dipped in a batter, dropped into a vat of hot vegetable oil until it is golden brown, then served cut in quarters. It is accompanied with a dish of raspberry jam. You dip the sandwich in the jam and take a bite. It is delicious. I have tried to deconstruct it and make it at home, but *malyishka* here says it does not taste quite right. I agree."

"I shall try this American sandwich with a European name."

"It's a bastardized version of a *Croque Monsieur*, but I find it quite tasty. Right now, Natalia is in a burgers-and-fries phase, which she won't eat at home. Apparently, the way I make burgers is too fancy." He leaned closer and murmured, "I hope your KGB training prepared you for pre-adolescent hormones."

"Did yours?"

"No, it was woefully inadequate in that regard. Luckily, I'm a quick learner. Even so, it seems she takes it as a challenge to test my ability to adapt."

"Good for her. Does she have her menstrual cycle yet?"

"Not yet. Mai has discussed this with her, *slava bogu*, and has all the necessary, uh, equipment packed in a small bag which Natalia carries to school with her. I hope, I actually pray, it won't occur on my watch."

"It is a biological function, Bukharin. I have never understood why men fear it."

"As a man, I've usually been more concerned when it doesn't show up."

I allowed myself a smile. I studied him for a while. Despite a brief smile or two for his granddaughter, he was stone-faced as ever. "Do you have regrets?"

"About what?" he asked with a slight frown.

"Anything, any of your choices."

"No, you ripped that emotion from me, remember?"

He became thoughtful again, glancing toward Natalia.

He continued, "I would wish the car accident hadn't happened, that Rachael hadn't died, and that Peter hadn't been crippled physically and emotionally by his grief. But having Natalia in our lives has been positive. For both Mai and me. I see the potential in Mai to be an incredible mother, if that were to happen for us again. Watching her be a mother to Natalia only makes me love Mai more. She didn't have to be involved, but she is more than that."

Bukharin indicated a right turn down a short hallway that was not as crowded and was quieter. The restaurant he indicated was on our left, near an exit to a parking lot packed with cars.

Within minutes, we sat at a table for four with a view of that parking lot. I could see some mid-rise buildings, a hotel, and a knot of highway overpasses with clogged traffic. America, I thought, too many people, too many cars, too many choices.

A young black woman came to the table and made me almost do a double-take. The woman's hair was in a mass of coiled tendrils, not braids. Ah, yes, dreadlocks I believe they are called. Mixed-race Russians were numerous in some areas, the results of Soviet Army incursions in Africa or Cuba, but fully black people were rare in the Soviet Union. Rather than let it put me off, I relished this experience in diversity.

The young woman took our orders with genuine cheer, quickly and efficiently. Natalia had not ceased her endless chatter, now relating stories about her previous trips to other malls.

"I really, really like Tyson's Corner. It's, like, way bigger than this one. A lot more stores. It's totally, like, amazingly awesome," Natalia said.

Bukharin spoke to her softly, without reproach. "That's enough about shopping. Lubova will think you're spoiled."

"Pope, I thought we're supposed to call her Linda," Natalia whispered to him.

"That is her new, American name, but among us—you, me, Mums, and Olga—you can call her Olga."

"Why do you call her Lubova?"

"Same reason I call him Bukharin," I said. "It shows we are friends but somewhat formal. A Russian thing."

Natalia looked at her grandfather. "Did you get a new name when you came to America?"

"Somewhat. You know I go by Alex Burke for business, and your papa goes by Peter Burke. It is easier for Americans to pronounce. You see, when I came to America, people didn't trust someone with a Russian-sounding name."

"But I go by Natalia Bukharin."

"You were born here. You don't have an accent like me, your Papa, and Lubova. People think nothing of it when you have a foreign name but speak like an American."

Natalia grinned at her grandfather, and I was reminded of the girl's grandmother, Sofya, in that smile.

"Popi, you barely, like, have an accent until you're, like, pissed at Mums." She looked at me. "It's hilarious, totally. Mums' accent gets all posh, and Popi, like, sounds like Boris Badenov."

I decided I would ask Bukharin privately who this Boris Badenov was, since I did not recognize the name.

"Tell me about your school," I said to Natalia. "I will be taking you and picking you up, yes?"

Bukharin nodded, and Natalia replied with a sigh, "It's school. It's boring. They have, like, way too many rules and restrictions on the girls and not on the boys. Oh, Popi, I forgot to tell you, unless Mums did. My P.E. teacher asked for Mums to come see her while you were gone to bring Olga here. I got, like, called out of class to attend their meeting, and it was totally embarrassing and the whole thing was like totally bogus."

"She didn't mention it," Bukharin said. "What happened?"

"So, like—"

"Explain it clearly and without 'so' and 'like' as every other word," he added.

Another sigh. "Fine. The P.E. teacher is a literal blond, and she tells Mums I play soccer too aggressively and that I, oh my God, play like a boy and it's not ladylike."

Bukharin's smile was wry. "Oh, to have been a fly on the wall for that," he said. "How did that end?"

"Well, you know how I said her accent gets all posh when she's pissed . . . Uh, angry, but this was all Queen Elizabeth. She said, 'Is this not physical education?'" Natalia said, again imitating Mai. "'Does one not get physical in physical education? And I believe soccer is a gender-neutral sport, is it not? The ball doesn't know the gender of the handler, true? Much like my jet doesn't know whether a man or I am at the controls. Do you have some rule about not allowing girls to play competitively? If so, lose it.' She went on and on, and the teacher couldn't get a word in. It was so totally awesome."

"What an ignorant teacher," Bukharin said. "How did Mai resolve it?"

"Popi, it was great. Mums got the teacher to apologize to me, and when we left Mums looked at the teacher in that way she has and says, 'I will be monitoring this situation and trust there will not be a repetition of this sexist behavior.' I thought the teacher might pee her pants. Totally laugh-worthy, but I managed not to because that teacher will totally take it out on me in class."

"Keep me apprised, too," Bukharin said and thickened his accent. "Perhaps I will go be Boris Badenov with this *plokhoy uchitel*." He winked at Natalia, and she laughed.

The food arrived then, and the cheerful waitress placed a plate with a hamburger the size of the girl's head in front of Natalia. The mound of French Fries would have easily fed two people. Bukharin and I had ordered the Monte Cristo.

It was a large sandwich, cut into quarters, and dusted with powdered sugar. A good sized dish of the jam was also on the elliptical plate with another gargantuan serving of fries.

"Do y'all need some ketchup?" the waitress asked.

"Yes, please," Natalia said.

"Not for me," from Bukharin.

"I will try this catch up," I declared.

"It's totally yummy," Natalia said.

"My homemade version is much better," Bukharin said.

Yet another eye roll. "Duh, Popi, but unless you, like, go into the kitchen here and make it, we'll have to make do with Heinz."

"What an astute observation, *malyishka*," he replied.

"Ugh! I'm not little anymore."

Another wink. "You will always be my little girl."

She rolled her eyes and cut her burger in half.

I observed Bukharin take a quarter of the sandwich in his hand and dip it into the jam. Wanting to make certain I looked no different from anyone else, I followed suit and took a bite. The sugar, the jam, the fried batter with a hint of sweetness, too, was a good contrast to the savory bread, meat, and cheese. It was a mouth-watering combination; my first American restaurant food.

"*Khorosho, da?*" Bukharin asked.

"*Ochen' khorosho.* When you made it at home, did you put sugar in the batter?"

"No, I didn't. You can taste sugar in the batter?"

"Yes, only a little, but it might make a difference."

"Olga," Natalia began. "Oops. Linda, you said you cooked, right? Do you like it?"

"Yes, I like cooking, so when your parents are away, you will not starve."

"Can you make pizza?" Natalia asked.

"I can learn."

"Cool." She leaned toward me and, in a stage whisper, said, "I'll tell you all the foods they won't let me have, and you can make them for me."

"She will not," Bukharin said.

Natalia stuck out her tongue at him, laughed, and continued eating her lunch.

To my amazement, Natalia downed her entire burger and all of her fries. I finished the tasty, delightful sandwich but left most of my fries. Too greasy for me.

"Your first American restaurant meal," Bukharin said. "What do you think?"

"I like it. I believe I can make this Monte Cristo, and it will taste similar to this one," I said.

"Cool!" Natalia declared. "Popi, can we . . . Excuse me, may we have Cinnabon for dessert?"

"What is a sin ah bawn?" I asked.

"You think America is decadent so far, wait until you taste this," Bukharin said.

"And we'll have to take one home to Mums or she'll be upset," Natalia said.

Bukharin took a credit card from his wallet and handed it off to the waitress.

"And we would never want that," he replied.

31

KARGIN

ENTRY 27

Because he has been such a headline-grabber for two decades, now I suppose it is time for me to talk about Russian President Dmitri Kargin. He was one of my trainees, yes, and he was ostensibly a Red Circle trainee. I suspected him of not being totally committed, but that was a hunch only, a feeling I got when interacting with him, as a trainee and a colleague.

He is at best mediocre, but sometimes a spymaster prefers the mediocre operative. Kargin was no-drama, predictable, efficient in his own way. He never recruited anyone "big" or important, but he was consistent in meeting requirements. He was far too much into creature comforts to be spectacular.

For example, his shoes.

Boizhe moi, the man and his shoes.

Whenever he found a pair that elevated his height without being obvious, he became obsessed with that particular brand and style. Whenever he had a position in the west, he would have dozens of pairs made for himself.

Now, you ask, how does the average KGB officer pay for such luxury items? Of course, coercion and threats are a possibility, but a supervisory officer in a foreign country had a discretionary budget, for informants, for paying assets, etc. If Kargin used government money for his personal indulgences, he covered his tracks well. We could never catch him; his accounts were "clean," his expenses somehow all accounted for. Many officers would use this discretionary fund to buy extravagant gifts for wives and/or mistresses, and if Kargin did this, he was extremely careful to hide it.

Or, he was in the pay of some other intelligence organization. We suspected that, too, but again, we could never prove it. Of all the possible explanations for his comfortable lifestyle, that is the most plausible. He was routinely questioned, as was any officer who served abroad, to determine if he had been compromised, with inconclusive results. However, they never had me question him. The outcome would have been different, I assure you.

Boris Yeltsin was also Red Circle, but we recognized his shortcomings, namely he drank like a fish and spoke too freely when he was drunk. We assigned Kargin to keep him on track. We did not expect Yeltsin to resign his presidency for "health reasons" and have Kargin replace him.

Of course, many men in Soviet leadership positions over the years departed because of their "health problems," an uncountable number, but again, my suspicion was Kargin had something significant on Yeltsin and coerced Yeltsin to resign in his favor. This gave Kargin a heady dose of power and prestige, something he would never have received as a *rezidant,* the top KGB officer in a foreign embassy. You might say, he became addicted and has continued to get his fixes for twenty-plus years.

And he will not give up power as long as he lives.

If the West or the people of Russia want him gone, I have given them an obvious hint how they can achieve that.

He has been consistent as well in his accumulation of power, personal and state, in his hands alone, and he has the support of the oligarchs and the *mafiya* bosses, who really control the economy. Were he to ever exit the scene, he would leave a tremendous power vacuum, and Russia could be left with someone worse. Kargin's suppression of any opposition to him and his failure to groom a successor means the transition from Kargin's Russia to a post-Kargin Russia would not be smooth.

Furthermore, he would never leave of his own will and lose access to a treasury he can plunder and the protection of his security detail. He has made plenty of enemies, and I doubt he would last long out of power.

He is a petty, little man, concerned only for himself, in love with the power he can wield, with the knowledge he can issue an order to be rid of a pesky journalist or politician, and it will happen. If you think he has any qualms about the people he has had killed—the defectors, the media, the opposition—do not delude yourselves. He feels nothing except the need for revenge.

Why bother killing defectors long after they have done their damage? Simple revenge. An affront against the national security of Russia is a personal insult to him.

The opposition? He has the image of a strongman to maintain, and the opposition dares to question his ability to govern.

The media? That is obvious. The light they shine on his abuses, his corruption, his venality is too bright, too public.

In reality, all of it is because he is a little man, in stature, in intellect, in vision.

When I trained him, I never foresaw him as anything more than a man who would be assigned to mediocre posts and would achieve only mediocre results, who would serve only long enough to earn his government pension and nothing more. I did not misread him, but I think he learned over the years how to position himself for opportunities. You can be both cunning and stupid if you cultivate the proper relationships.

Though his only assignment in monitoring Yeltsin was to make certain Boris did not blurt "Red Circle" at an inappropriate time, Kargin watched as Yeltsin built popular support, as well as the support of the military. During the coup attempt against Gorbachev, it was Yeltsin whose appeal to the soldiers' patriotism that cut the coup off, and Yeltsin was at the height of his popularity. He was the star to whom Kargin hitched his wagon.

However, I am confident the deal for Yeltsin's resignation and Kargin's succession was sealed under the influence of copious amounts of vodka.

I am, after all, one of those defectors Kargin had his odious "butler" send assassins for. They missed me and killed my wife and our dog, Dolly. I have ample reason to despise the man, but I disliked him even before he became an autocrat and long before I met Olive.

He has made my country both his personal bank account and his personal toilet. Understand, do not call him a Communist. He does not want a return to Communism, where the state controls everything. He wants to be the State. He wants to control everything. That is why under Kargin, Stalin came back into favor. That is why the last Tsar's family has been restored to their place in Russian history and made saints.

Kargin thinks of himself as Russia's tsar.

How do I know this?

I will give you a history lesson.

Whenever a tsar sent Russians off to war, the soldiers would receive his blessing, often in person. Long lines of soldiers would file past the tsar, who would touch them and give them a gift, usually an icon of a saint or a picture of the tsar himself, small enough to be carried in a pocket in battle. The implication was that the tsar, the Little Father, the divine sovereign, would protect them with his divinity.

Immediately after taking over from Yeltsin, Kargin went to Chechnya, to the Russian lines. The officers brought every soldier before him—not because they wanted to be there but because they were ordered. Kargin shook each man's hand and gave him a hunting knife. The message and the symbolism were clear: I am your new tsar, and you will kill for me.

As I have said, Kargin is a good opportunist, so when a rich American could no longer get loans from American banks for his business deals because of bad credit and bankruptcies, Kargin told his oligarch friends to step in and make that rich American beholden to them and through them to Kargin.

Did Kargin know that rich American would become president of the United States? No, but I believe he manipulated events to make that happen. Russia having an agent in the American Oval Office is no mere coincidence.

The Soviet Union always saw America as its major capitalist enemy. Since the Revolution, the goal of our intelligence agencies has been to bring down that "capitalist cesspool." Everyone in the KGB knew that was the goal. I knew it. I taught this to my trainees. But the U.S. CIA and British Intelligence worked as hard to destroy the "Red Peril."

After the fall of Communism, America was still the enemy because that richest country in the world gloried in its victory but offered no hand of help in teaching Russia how to be a democracy. America was still the enemy because it was what Russians thought was their destiny: to be the greatest, most significant world power.

Kargin used President Kermit Harlan like any other asset he

had ever run so he could ruin America from within. His plan is working well.

Why did Kargin order his GRU hackers to undermine Mrs. Renee Randolph's campaign four years ago? Because of his encounters with her when she was Secretary of State. She stood up to Russia, to Kargin's interference in world hotspots. He knew if she were president, sanctions against Russia would be crippling and that the U.S. would provide more assistance to Ukraine's fight against Russia.

Trust me. I know how he works. I taught him to work that way. I taught him how to manage assets. I am not exaggerating when I say the U.S. President Harlan is a Russian agent. It is obvious to anyone who understands counterintelligence. Every decision rendered by President Harlan regarding foreign policy works to benefit Russia.

Pull American troops out of Syria? Russia steps in.

Pull American troops out of Iraq and Afghanistan? Russia steps in.

Russia becomes the "world power" to rely on, with influence over a large source of middle eastern oil fields and reserves, not to mention oil refineries and billions and billions of dollars' worth of mineral assets. As the U.S. leaves the world stage, as President Harlan is doing, Russia declares itself the world's only superpower with Kargin as a world leader.

Nikita Khrushchev once pounded his shoe on a desk and swore that the Soviet Union would bury the United States. He never meant it literally, of course, but by subterfuge, by manipulation of its well-placed assets, by *desinformatsya*, by interfering with the elections.

Khrushchev was right. This has come to pass, but Kargin buried you; and you did nothing about it.

32

GRIEF

ENTRY 28

2018

Cologny, Switzerland

I wondered if Maiya felt odd knocking on a door inside her own house, but she was the one who said guests had the right to privacy, too. I managed to murmur, "Come in."

Once inside, she closed the door behind her.

I sat in a chair by the window, a chair I had stirred from only to address biological needs. Since I had fled the scene of my wife's murder for sanctuary here, I had little reason to do anything except grieve. That was a week ago. Perhaps ten days ago. Time has no meaning now.

I turned only my head toward my visitor. "You are not usually home so early," I said.

"True, but I had some news for you I thought would be best delivered personally."

I nodded and resumed my study of whatever was outside the window of my room.

Mai held up her mobile phone. "I think perhaps some music might be in order, don't you think?"

I did not move but said, "Do you think Bukharin listens at his own doors?"

"Well, he taught me never to pass up that opportunity, so I assume you taught him the same."

I shrugged and nodded.

Maiya put her phone on the dresser next to a Bluetooth speaker and selected one of her Spotify playlists. Low, stentorian notes filled the room. Mai adjusted the volume down a bit and sat in the chair facing me.

"Wagner," I said.

Maiya nodded. "*Vorspiel.*"

"Yes, the Ring Cycle. Is there some symbolism to your selection of music?"

"Not really. It's good to cover conversation, but I do rather like Wagner."

"Then, let us enjoy it for a moment."

I closed my eyes as the dueling sopranos began to sing. After perhaps a minute, I opened them and looked at Maiya.

"What news did you wish to deliver in person?" I asked.

"We have in our custody not only the body of the man who killed Olive but his two team members arrested as they removed his body from your house. The Oregon City police chief believes he has turned them over to the FBI."

Another nod. "Have you interrogated them yet?" I asked.

"I thought perhaps you might want to do that."

A head-shake this time. "I have no stomach for that, and I am perhaps still full of anger. Too much anger."

"Well, I was using 'interrogation' as a euphemism. Alexei

usually managed to piss me off before a mission so I could use my anger effectively."

I continued to study her narrowed and discerning eyes, similar to an expression Bukharin often focused on those he wanted to intimidate.

"I've always suspected something more existed between Alexei and you than either of you will admit," Maiya said. "Yes, both of you have denied being lovers, but the bond between the two of you is . . . Well, I have no words for it. Unusual, perhaps."

I shrugged. "You are not Russian or Ukrainian. You have a good understanding of the Soviet culture he and I grew up in, but some nuances escaped you. He and I were teacher and pupil who became friends. Let us return to the subject. Explain what interrogation is a euphemism for," I said, making it sound like an order.

"I know they can provide little useful intelligence, certainly nothing we don't already know. However, they can serve a purpose in teaching someone a lesson."

"Who will be the recipient of this lesson?"

"Who do you think?"

"Kargin?" I shook my head again. "He is beyond the subtleties I think you have in mind."

"No, this will be rather blatantly in his face. He'll get it. If he doesn't, I have something else I can do."

"What is that?"

"First, I'll tell you we've recently cultivated an asset inside Kargin's presidential residence, among the so-called butler's staff."

Kargin's head "butler" was a former GRU assassin who'd become Kargin's close confidante. His official job description was the smooth running of Kargin's household and security detail. Unwritten was the fact the butler was in charge of dealing with whatever enemies Kargin had.

The butler ran a staff of individuals selected from the security services, the Russian Army, the Russian Navy, and from the SVR, FSB, and GRU. Though assigned to the presidential residence, the butler often sent them off to deal with people Kargin had decided were dangerous—to him. Lately, the focus was on defectors. Kargin had decided they had no right to continue living.

"I should not have to tell you to be careful with this asset," I said. "Make certain he is not a double."

"It's a woman, and she came to us. Yes, we treated her as a dangle until we could examine her motivation and her information, but both ring true."

"And that would be?"

"Since Moscow Central assigned her to the presidential residence staff as an under-butler slash bodyguard, the head butler has allowed the other staff, all men, to rape her almost daily. A reward for them; discipline for her."

"Her motivation for treason, then. You obviously have some sort of plan."

"I do, and this asset has already provided key intelligence about what happens inside Kargin's residences. She also has agreed to take an active part in my operation."

"What will happen to her after?"

Maiya cocked her head to one side. "At one time that wouldn't have mattered to you," she said.

"I got old."

"She's to get out of the residence after completing her part of the operation, and we'll exfiltrate her, give her a new identity, provide counseling and any medical treatment she needs." Maiya smiled and added, "You know, all those encumbrances you lectured Alexei about."

I trust my expression never altered. "I was never raped," I said. "A fellow instructor attempted it on my first day as the martial arts instructor at the training directorate. I fought back. No one ever tried again."

Maiya's jaw set, her eyes growing hard and unforgiving. "Sometimes, to survive, you don't fight back, and take it from me, that's difficult. Neither she nor I are you. She thought she'd received a promotion and an opportunity because of her work ethic. Instead, she discovered she was there for the staff's entertainment. And her odds were worse than mine. Three to one and forty-eight hours for me. Eight or more and weeks for her."

"And sometimes, you fight back even in the face of overwhelming odds," I said.

Her tone steely, Maiya replied, "Thank you for your hindsight, which is outstanding for its arrogance."

"Someone displayed such arrogance to me once," I said, "a bitch of a woman. I killed her. Not 'had her killed,' not 'gave the kill order.' I killed her myself. She was the first person I killed."

"The first of many, I suspect," Maiya replied. "Look, if you're not interested in teaching Dmitri Kargin a lesson, say so. I'll turn off the Wagner and leave you to wallow in your grief."

"What would be the point of this?" I asked. "He is beyond any sort of morality lesson. It would be a waste of my time and your effort, not to mention your resources."

"He either gave a direct order to kill you or said nothing when the butler offered you as a target," Maiya said. "And your wife died instead of you, in *your* place."

"Of that, I am well aware."

"And if it had been Alexei he targeted, you wouldn't hesitate to join me in teaching a much-needed lesson, but you hesitate where your wife is concerned?"

"Is this what Americans call a guilt-trip?"

"I'm English, so it's merely pointing out a harsh truth."

I looked away, out the window again. With a sigh, I said, "Very well, tell me what you have planned and what part you think I can play. Make a good case, and I will give an immediate decision."

Maiya outlined the operation in detail and answered the questions I posed. "When?" I asked.

"As soon as possible."

I shook my head yet again. "Your asset needs to be comfortable in this new role, and she has to deflect any suspicion about her behavior. She must be compliant and build the butler's trust."

"The rape will continue," Maiya said.

"As angry and as hurt as she may feel, she needs to bottle that anger and bury it deep enough to hide it, shallow enough she can bring it forth when she needs it. That is the only way this operation will succeed."

"And people think I lower the temperature of a room," Maiya said with a slight smile.

I shrugged again, but Maiya offered no further argument. She said, "I can put off the end game for a while, but your part could still be more or less immediate. We have our own morgue now, with excellent refrigeration facilities."

I continued to stare out the window so long, I suspected Maiya thought she would receive a "no" answer. Then, I stood, followed by Maiya.

I said, "I will need protective clothing, which, along with my clothing worn under it, must be disposed of by burning. I will need a place to clean myself after, and some specialized tools."

"What sort of specialized tools?"

I told her, and I thought maybe Maiya felt uneasy. Her eyes widened in surprise, but she quickly pushed it aside. "All doable."

"Very well."

I went to the closet and removed a small, overnight bag. I

selected a pair of shoes and stockings, a set of underwear, a pants suit, and added all that plus a comb, brush, soap, and shampoo to the bag. All done swiftly, efficiently, in under a minute.

Bag in hand, I said, "I have seen that Bukharin, Alex, and Ivan have now left for a cruise in Bukharin's boat. Let us go."

33

REVENGE

ENTRY 29

United Nations Complex
Geneva, Switzerland

The two prisoners' derisive laughter and comments about "old women" ceased when Maiya handed me a knife and the bone saw. I turned to her, and Maiya's eyes widened ever so slightly again. She saw how I must have appeared to my trainees, to Bukharin: cold, remote, fierce, and fearless.

"I prefer not to have an audience," I said.

"Are you certain?"

"I can handle them." I looked at the two men but spoke to Maiya, "I have kept myself in excellent shape. I would rather do this alone."

Maiya nodded with understanding and replied in English, "What I didn't see, didn't happen."

"Yes. You would have been an excellent KGB officer. Leave me."

Maiya looked at the two men strapped in the sturdy chairs,

their bluster gone, their eyes pleading with her. Maiya spoke directly to the two Russians, repeating what she'd said to me, "*Togo, chego ya ne videl, ne proizoshlo.*" What I did not see did not happen.

Maiya left the interrogation room, closing the door behind her.

I will spare the gory details here to avoid putting off any future readers and also to avoid incriminating myself.

When I had finished, I opened the door and slipped into the hallway, closing the door quickly, so they could not see what I had left inside.

But they could guess.

My hair was dark with blood, which had splattered my face and coverall. The Nitrile gloves on my hands were covered in it.

"I am old," I said. "I forgot that you let the heart stop before beginning the dismembering."

Mason Wallace of UNSECFOR paled so much I thought he might faint, and even Maiya swallowed hard. I hoped Bukharin had planned something bland for dinner tonight.

Maiya brought out her work phone and said, "I'm texting our Medical Forensics Chief. She'll be here shortly."

"Is the shower on this level?" I asked. "I do not want to leave a blood trail."

Blood dripping from my gloves and clothes had left a puddle at my feet.

Mr. Wallace opened his mouth, but nothing emerged. He coughed and said, "Yes, uh . . . Around the corner there. First door on the left. I'll . . . I'll . . . I'll go get your bag from my office." He hustled away in the opposite direction.

"He seemed eager to leave," I said. "You look like you want to follow him."

"How do you feel?" Maiya asked.

"Better. No closure, of course, but I feel better. What now?"

"Now, you clean yourself and redress. Dr. Alford will save the specimens I need and disposes of the rest, and we'll go home, no one the wiser."

"Very well. I will go to the shower. Have your Mr. Wallace leave my bag outside the door. Where do I meet you?"

"Once Dr. Alford arrives, I'll be waiting for you outside the shower room."

I frowned at her. "I said I am all right."

"Adrenaline ebbs," Mai replied.

"For you weak English types, perhaps, but not for a Russian. Did Bukharin not explain this to you?"

❧ ❧

MAIYA ESCORTED me from UNSECFOR all the way back to the door of the guest room of her house and, in the process, I hope she perceived the resentment in my scowl.

"Do you not have job to do?" I asked when Maiya entered the guest room with me.

"Oh, didn't you know? I have a deputy now. A good, trustworthy one. He fairly loves it when I take time off and he gets to be boss."

"As long as he knows who is real boss."

"He does. We get along famously. He's Irish, too. Oh, and the English crack back in the hallway? I'll have you know my ancestors went into battle with at most a sword and a shield, naked except for a neck torque and lime paste, and screaming. Made the Romans shit themselves."

"The Romans never came to Ireland."

"Why do you think that was? Do you want a dinner tray up here?"

"No. I am a bit weary. I will take a nap. Nothing more than that. I will join you downstairs for dinner."

Maiya smiled at me. "Alexei will be glad to see you leaving your room." She turned for the door.

"Maiya?"

"Yes?"

"Thank you."

"Think nothing of it. As I said, had it been Alexei, you would have given me the same opportunity."

"You do understand," I began, "if Bukharin was not on Kargin's list, he will be now. As will you and Ivan."

"Dmitri Kargin is a soulless murderer many times over, but like most Russians, he loves his children and dotes on his grandchildren. I would never harm a child, but, you know, this is a big house with plenty of room. Ivan might like having a brother and sister. And just the right age, too. Three and one. They'd hardly remember their parents. Or their grandfather."

"That is the age of Kargin's . . . Ah, I see."

"And maybe losing his son will temper Kargin a bit."

The expression I gave Maiya made her frown. I hoped it was admiration. Respect. Maybe pride. Maybe all of them at once.

"You had a good teacher," I said.

Maiya's smile was genuine but didn't reach her eyes. "He is. So did he. See you at dinner. Sleep well."

Maiya left me alone.

34

WHY THE KGB?

ENTRY 30

Olive asked me that more than once. She was never quite satisfied with my answers, which she called "platitudes." Once, I replied, "Why does an American join the CIA?"

"Well," she said, "to protect the United States from other countries' spies."

"And there you have your answer," I told her.

Still, she was not satisfied.

Perhaps I can do a better job here.

I joined the KGB because of my father, but that was a partial truth. My role in the Red Circle's plan was to train KGB officers but to also train Red Circle recruits destined for the KGB. I understood duty. Papa had taught me that, even if some of his lessons were extreme—like turning in his own wife because his ego was bruised.

Because of my sense of duty, I accepted the oath I took when I joined the KGB, and I took it to heart. Much as U.S. Government employees swear to "preserve, protect, and defend" their Constitution from "all enemies foreign and domestic," I swore to uphold the socialist state and to protect the worker from all recidivist incursions from foreign intelligence operatives.

Essentially the same thing.

It has been said of the KGB that we were guilty of what we accused others of doing. Of course we were. That is the point of spying. The CIA was guilty of the same. I always shook my head when the CIA or the U.S. Government became outraged upon uncovering one of our operations in their country. Such outrage was hypocrisy seeing as the CIA was doing the same thing in Russia or Beijing or anywhere else in the world.

My duty, then, was to train KGB officers how to spy, how to recruit assets, how to be con artists, and more—the exact same skills CIA case officers use. I, of course, would like to think we were better at using those skills. Sometimes we were; sometimes we were not.

Based on Strakh's mentoring of me, what I taught my officers first and foremost was how to read people and discover their human weaknesses. Then, use those weaknesses and vulnerabilities to recruit them and ultimately force them to do things they would not normally want to do. In Russia, we say, "We are working with people." Meaning we are constantly looking at how to manipulate the humanity of people.

As I have mentioned in an earlier entry, in the old days, for example, the quickest, easiest recruit was a young secretary in an embassy, far away from home in a foreign country, lonely and liable to fall for the charms of a handsome man who paid attention to her and was willing to spend the "quality time" with her. You would be surprised what a secretary reads and has access to.

Based upon experience from observing the male foreign service and military personnel at U.S. Embassies around the world, we determined they were often promiscuous. Most postings did not support bringing a wife and family with them, especially the military guards. So, we sent young women their way—or young men, as might have been needed. Yes, they were our enemies, ruthless to us and we must be to them, but one can put that aside and do what needs to be done for one's country.

Again, the CIA trained its personnel the same way about us.

Even the CIA has admitted there is nothing quite like a KGB officer's tradecraft in acquiring HUMINT—human intelligence. They have also conceded we were often better at understanding which pressure points in a person's psyche were best to push and when. We were also often better at recognizing a person's vices and vulnerabilities while running them as an asset.

Think of it this way: My officers were like a priest you could confess to, a therapist who would guide you, a best friend you could share anything with. However, because my officers were inducing people to do things that they knew could destroy their careers or personal lives, we were their mortal enemy as well. All of this did not happen quickly, like in movies, but, remember, Russians are a very patient people.

Bukharin was one of my trainees who went on to train others, principally his partner (and wife) Maiya. Bukharin has said she was better at spying than he, and I have indeed observed that. Maiya has now incorporated my philosophy—Strakh's philosophy—into training her own operatives. That, in some ways, is an unexpected but profound legacy.

You might say none of this answers why I chose the KGB. In a way it does. I liked the fact that I trained people in what we saw as a life and death struggle against capitalism. I manipulated my trainees the same way I taught them to manipulate assets. And when they recognized that, they passed. There is power in that. Power is an addicting drug, and, again, that makes us no different from anyone else.

So, I will answer the question more succinctly.

Remember, I adored my father. I watched everything he did, listened to every word he spoke, often when he did not know I was listening. Mysterious men came and went at our various residences. There were many conversations behind closed doors, sometimes when I was hiding in the room, unseen. My father would give an order, people would say, "Yes, Comrade!" and execute those orders. My father had power.

I wanted that. I wanted to be my father. I wanted people to respect me and, yes, even fear me.

I knew my father had been one of the founders of the Cheka after the Revolution, and I knew of his long association with the various iterations of Soviet intelligence. He was astute at wielding power to serve his country but also to protect his family—except for my mother, and he used that power against her.

My father had faithfully served the Soviet state since the Revolution, and he had imbued that sense of service in all his children. Each of us served our country in different ways: demonstrating Soviet athletic power, serving in the Red Army, following in my mother's footsteps by starring in movies glorifying the socialist ideal. Those were my brothers' choices. I chose to follow in our father's footsteps.

When I told Papa my intentions, he did not like it. I was, after all, his little girl, and he did his best to dissuade me. It did not take long for him to recognize my commitment to this career, and he accepted my choice.

"You will have to achieve this on your own merit and abilities, Olechka," he said. "I will pull no strings, I will grease no wheels, I will put in no good words. I will not help you."

Exactly what I wanted. I would have it no other way.

For perhaps too many years, I believed it was Strakh who gave me the most understanding of what my job and my purpose were.

In reality, it was observing my father's day-to-day, constant execution of his duty without question, his dedication to his profession, his soulless performance of what the State expected of him, including denouncing his own wife and consigning her to death in a gulag.

That, perhaps, was his ultimate lesson to me—that my position in the KGB was not the place from which to deal with personal enemies. It was my job to eradicate the enemies of the State, internal and external.

Our definition of enemy, however, was different.

Strakh poured knowledge into my head, and I willingly absorbed it. my father's example showed me how to use that welcome knowledge.

In short, I chose the KGB to serve my country.

Ask a CIA case officer, and he or she will give you the same answer—for my country.

35

HARVARD

ENTRY 31

I had no children, but I do understand how a parent feels when a child becomes an adult, how you resist the inevitability of the child fading and the adult becoming predominant. Of course, that does not include the fact the child quite often thinks she is an adult long before she legally is.

Natalia Petrovna has always been wise beyond her years. I believe the sudden death of her mother, the prolonged indifference from her father made her mature sooner than most young girls. She could be the silliest girl, she could be a diva-in-training, but she was far more thoughtful than most children her age.

She was not a difficult child, but she could be annoying, particularly in those pre-teen and early teen years. Her willfulness and Maiya's clashed often, but I seldom disagreed with Maiya's solutions to such issues. Those years passed quickly. Yet, it seemed as if I had barely become accustomed to living in a suburb of Washington, D.C. before we packed my and Natalia's belongings and moved into a duplex apartment in Cambridge, Massachusetts, where Natalia Petrovna would attend Harvard University.

Natalia was both excited at the prospect of leaving home and somewhat daunted by it. Bukharin wasn't pleased at all. He was like most fathers of girls—mine being the exception—he did not want to think of her as an adult but always his "little girl." Maiya was disconcerted, too, but that may have had more to do with the new direction their careers had taken.

I doubted from the beginning the career change would work for Maiya. Some people you know will not successfully transition from an action-oriented job to a desk job. That was Maiya when she accepted the position of Chief of Security for the International Criminal Tribunal in The Hague. Bukharin had been appointed the Secretary-General's special liaison to the tribunal, though in reality, he was there to funnel intelligence to Nelson, head of the Directorate.

I was glad Natalia Petrovna and I were in Massachusetts when the move occurred because the process of convincing Maiya to take her position had been a contentious and occasionally upsetting one. Maiya did not want to give up her operational status. In 1998, she was only forty, Bukharin fifty-five. He had noticed some deterioration in his physical capabilities—reading glasses, aching joints, nothing more than that, but he feared he might falter on a mission and cause harm to come to Maiya.

About the time Natalia Petrovna and I settled in Cambridge, Bukharin and Maiya were moving into a much smaller house overlooking the North Sea outside The Hague.

With Harvard and MIT so close and Tufts not far away, Cambridge was full of nightlife and student life. Natalia took to it immediately—she always made friends with ease—but she kept a good balance between her studies and partying. I was of the philosophy, as was Maiya, that Natalia should experience life, under supervision, of course, my supervision. However, there are negative aspects to being away from home for the first time.

So, yes, she vomited copious amounts of liquor into the apartment's toilet and had the ensuing hangovers, followed by my lectures about underage drinking. The lesson on moderation she learned quickly, more from the vomiting than my pontifications. I kept Maiya apprised of these incidents and their follow-up, and neither she nor I ever told Bukharin. He had mentioned Ukrainian convent schools one too many times.

Thank goodness, Natalia Petrovna had taken a gap year after graduating from high school at seventeen, and she was not a year younger than the other freshmen when she arrived and spread her wings, as it were.

I discovered Harvard is a university with gravitas. Barely a century older than where I studied during my early years at the KGB, Moscow State University, Harvard was one of the highest-level universities in America. The academic standards surprised me —another lie of Soviet propaganda dispelled. On occasion I would sit in on Natalia Petrovna's classes, and both the scholarship of the faculty and the dedication of most of the students impressed me.

Oh, there were those legacy students, as they were called, accepted into the university because, usually, their fathers had attended. I found many of those students lazy and entitled, from families who had more money than they knew what to do with. They displayed arrogance and privilege and few redeeming qualities. I was glad Bukharin and Maiya had raised Natalia Petrovna not to think of herself as better than others because of Maiya's bank balance. Natalia did have a good head on her shoulders, and she navigated the snobbery well.

I found I was not the only bodyguard of a student there. Indeed, a child of a U.S. Vice President attended the same time as Natalia, but the Secret Service detail was more obvious than I was comfortable with, especially with their dependence on guns. Though I had guns at the apartment, I never brought any onto campus. I sometimes carried a folding knife, but I relied on my martial arts skills to protect Natalia Petrovna. Despite being almost sixty when we arrived at Harvard, I had kept myself in "fighting shape," as the Americans say.

That reminds me of my favorite part about being a "civilian" in America. No more damned girdles. Though my physique remained slim, and remains so now, my waist succumbed to the usual Russian woman's curse: It became nonexistent, as wide as my hips and bosom. This plus wearing my hair shorter gave me a somewhat frumpy appearance. However, that was on purpose. Who would suspect a dowdy *babushka* to know how to kill you a dozen different ways with her bare hands?

In all my years as au pair/bodyguard to Natalia Petrovna, I am proud we had no serious threat to her, until her junior year at Harvard. That interlude is painful to me for a number of reasons. It almost broke Natalia Petrovna's young heart, but it is painful for me because I did not see the young man for what he was—an illegal agent of Russian intelligence who had been tasked to kidnap her for revenge against Bukharin. This is an experience no one talks about, though Natalia did confide in me that years later she encountered by coincidence that individual in his new identity provided by the Directorate. She said he answered questions that had plagued her, and she had what everyone seems to want, that ever elusive closure.

Maiya knew of this incident because by then, she was the head of the Directorate, and there was little she did not know.

Again, we kept Bukharin in the dark. As I have said, he is as protective of his granddaughter as he would be of his own child. Anyone who caused her distress was in danger of encountering Bukharin's ire. Who better than I to know how unpleassant that can be? He learned it from me.

As it is for most young people, college, and especially Harvard, was good for Natalia Petrovna. There, she lived the life of an adult and had to deal with the consequences of her own decisions, good or bad. Her already broad mind and curious intellect bloomed there. Unlike some of the other wealthy students, she took her studies seriously. Much like Maiya, who became more her mother than her late mother had the time to be, Natalia Petrovna was a planner. At Harvard, she discovered her career path: law school and a job with the United Nations Human Rights Commission. The summer before her freshman year, she had interned for one of the tribunal judges during the Balkan genocide trials. Her experience that summer, plus Maiya's influence, cemented in her a passion for justice.

I am proud of Natalia Petrovna, as a doting aunt might be. Proud of her choice of careers, of her work for women's rights, of the mother Natalia is. Of the woman she is. Her own, late mother would have been as proud of her as her surrogate mother and her old *Tyotya* Olga.

I learned a great deal at the same time. I learned that the American people are among the finest in the world, as an aggregate. Oh, I saw the bad apples, but every country has those. In my former country, the most rotten of the bad apples is now in charge, but I have already written about this. No need to repeat myself.

Yes, some of America is as decadent as Soviet propaganda said it was, but America also has a somber sense of history, a dedication to democracy, and a deep understanding of its place on the world stage. Russia, even today, will never compare, and, again, that rankles the little man in charge, knowing that the largest country in the world will always be second rate.

I liked the omnipresent aura of intellectuality in Cambridge, that in restaurants and coffee shops, you could overhear intense discussions about political theory, law, or particle physics. It was a vibrant place, in some ways like the Moscow State University of my youth, though far more exuberant and far more free with speech. It was a delightful four years, but 9/11 happened.

And Alex Terrell came back into Natalia's life, and Olive came into mine.

36

DENIAL

ENTRY 32

1999

The Purple Shamrock
Boston, Massachusetts

I sat at the bar and nursed a cup of coffee. I watched to make sure Natalia drank nothing more than an O'Doul's. All in all, this was fairly typical of most American versions of an Irish public house I had visited: a bar, too many tiny tables in too small a space, and pictures of famous Irish Americans on the walls. This was Boston, though, and most of the pictures were of the Kennedys. A loud band played "traditional" Irish music and joked with the customers in faux Irish accents. People downed pints of Guinness and sang along, out of tune. The large, flashing purple shamrock-shaped light on one wall, I assumed, gave the establishment its name.

Couples in groups of four or six occupied the tables, and I watched them all to determine if any of them posed a danger to

Natalia. The couples acted like most did in public. They held hands, looked into each other's eyes, exchanged sloppy kisses, fed each other from their plates of food.

Except they were not man and woman couples. Some were man and man, some woman and woman. A sign inside pronounced that this night was "Gay Pride Night," and I noticed extra security at the door.

I struggled to keep my expression neutral at such decadence. Americans were more tolerant of deviants than Russia. I knew better than to say what I thought. I would simply keep my opinions to myself and hide my feelings of disgust.

Coming here this particular night did not surprise me much. Natalia's group of friends from the drama club had suggested it. Natalia was one of the few people here who did not have someone specific, and from my study of the patrons who were here alone told me they were likely looking for someone.

I was ready to dissuade anyone from harassing Natalia.

Among the singles was a woman at the other end of the bar, a woman who'd been watching me all evening. I had memorized the pictures of the entire faculty at Harvard for security purposes, and I recognized the woman as a professor in the English Department. She had a head of thick, unruly hair, dark brown heading toward gray. I gauged her to be in her forties. On campus, the professor dressed in trousers and oversized blouses and wore flat-heeled shoes.

Tonight, she was a form-fitting dress in dark green, a great deal more makeup, and stiletto heels. Like Maiya, she drank Irish whiskey, neat.

I had noticed this woman had looked my way. Often.

Boizhe moi, I thought, why did I agree to let Natalia Petrovna come here.

I made sure I looked anywhere except at the woman watching

me, while still keeping a wary eye on her. My senses heightened when I saw the woman rise from her stool. She walked the length of the bar and sat two stools away from me.

"I decided you'd sat here all by yourself long enough," the woman said in a husky voice. "I'm Dorcas. Can I buy you . . . What are you drinking? Irish coffee?"

"I am drinking coffee, and no thank you."

Dorcas laughed, low and sultry. "You're in an Irish bar drinking coffee? That's a new one. That accent of yours is quite sexy. Eastern Europe?"

"Excuse me, but I am working."

"Aren't we all, sweetheart? I've noticed you watching that young girl over there," Dorcas said, nodding toward Natalia's table. "Two things. She's way, way too young for you, and unfortunately, she's straight."

A surge of anger made my face flush. "What are you suggesting? Are you suggesting I have perverted interest in that young woman? How dare you?"

Dorcas held up a hand. "Easy, easy. My mistake. It's Gay Pride Night at the bar, you know."

"That young woman is here with her *homosexual* friends," I said. "She is my job. I protect her."

Dorcas' smile faltered. "Wow, that was a lot of disgust in one word," she said.

"What are you talking about?"

"The way you said 'homosexual,' as if it were a dirty word, but I still think you're one damned sexy woman. If you ever want to explore what you're so obviously suppressing, come back some time. Alone."

I leaned toward this Dorcas. "Get away from me, *lesba*, or I will call the police."

Natalia was suddenly at my side. "Everything okay, *Tyotya*?" she asked.

Dorcas answered, all huskiness gone from her voice, replaced with stridence. "Honey, do your gay friends know you brought a homophobe in here?"

"She's not a homophobe," Natalia said. "She's straight and probably didn't appreciate you coming on to her. So back off."

Dorcas laughed and said, "She hasn't figured out yet she's not straight, honey." Dorcas stood and spoke to me, "That self-hate is a bitch, but you'll realize one day what you're missing. Right now, your loss."

Dorcas drained her drink and left the bar.

"Are you all right?" Natalia asked.

"Of course. Why would you even ask that?"

Natalia peered at me, as if seeing me for the first time. "Is she right?" Natalia asked.

"About what?"

"Do you dislike gay people? I mean, like, hate them?"

"I can say I do not even think about such people."

"My friends I'm with are gay."

"That much is obvious."

"What if I were gay?" Natalia asked.

"You are not, so it is no matter what I think."

"How do you know I'm not?"

I drank some coffee, looking at Natalia over the rim of the cup. "Night after Junior Prom," I said.

"Well, okay, yes, that's true, but these are my friends. They're important to me, and their issues are important to me."

"And you are important to me. Your friends are of no concern to me unless they intend you harm."

"But you're uncomfortable here?"

I shrugged. "It is not a place I would choose, but you are here, so I am here."

"Gah, you sound like Popi."

"*Malyishka*, it is more he sounds like me. I was his teacher."

Natalia rolled her eyes but laughed. "I'll be finished with dinner soon, and when the band finishes this set, I'll be ready to go. I've got to hit the library early tomorrow for a paper that's due soon." Natalia turned away but turned back. "Are you going to tell Popi we were in a gay bar?"

Another shrug. "Maiya and I are in agreement that some things he does not need to know. Like night after Junior Prom."

Natalia laughed again and returned to her table. Her friends huddled closer to her, and I wondered what she told them.

37

A PLACE OF OUR OWN

ENTRY 33

2003

Bukharin-Fisher Residence
Mount Vernon, Virginia

Olive liked the kitchen in my apartment. It was spacious, but everything was convenient. The apartment was a pleasant place to live. We could enter from inside the house above or by our separate entrance. We could decorate it however we wanted, and soon Olive felt at home with her books and other things around her.

But it wasn't ours, and she often expressed she felt as if she were a guest in someone else's home. By strict definition, that was what she was, but she was a most welcome guest. Though Maiya and Bukharin respected our privacy, we agreed this place would never feel like our home. I think Olive sensed that I would be content to remain here. My life since I'd left the Soviet Union had been here. I sensed as well that Olive needed to have a conversation with me, a difficult one.

One evening after dinner, Olive brought two cups of decaf coffee from the kitchen to the lounge and handed one cup to me. She settled beside me on the sofa in front of the picture window, which overlooked the large lawn with the Potomac River beyond.

"You're quiet tonight," Olive said.

"I am digesting your delicious dinner."

Olive smiled at me. It had taken her some time to become accustomed to someone who didn't mince words about anything.

"Well, I want to talk to you about something," Olive said.

"Of course."

"I know we've talked about finding a place of our own, but before we do that . . ." Olive paused, maybe her resolve wavering a bit. "There are things about you I don't know, even after all these months together."

I sipped coffee and stared out the window, not speaking.

"See, that's what you do whenever I ask questions. You clam up."

"I have a good reason for that," I said.

"What is that reason?"

"If you knew who I really am, who I was, you would no longer care for me."

"I doubt that, but we won't know unless we try."

I set my coffee cup on the sofa table and folded my hands in my lap. "Olive, I do not wish to lose your respect."

"Again, I doubt that would happen, but go ahead. Try to shock me."

"If I tell you these things, you must understand they are secrets. You can speak of them to no one."

Olive laughed and said, "Were you some kind of enemy spy?"

When I looked at Olive, my expression was so serious she sobered at once.

"I was not a spy," I said. "I taught people how to be spies. For the KGB."

"Are you serious?"

"Of course. I was a colonel in the KGB, and I left the Soviet Union right before it dissolved and came here to be Natalia Petrovna's au pair. However, I was really her bodyguard."

"I'm guessing then, your name isn't Linda Collins?"

"No, it is not. If I tell you my real name, you must be careful not to use it in public."

"Why?"

I sighed, knowing now I should have stayed quiet. "To get myself safely out of the Soviet Union, I had to fake my death. A homeless drunk who froze to death in a Moscow alley lies beneath the headstone that bears my birth and death dates."

"Okay, what is your real name?" I told her, and she repeated, "Olga Yevgenyevna Lubova. I like how that sounds. The Yevgenyevna, that's what's called the patronymic, right?"

"Yes. Yevgeny was my father's name, so my middle name is Yevgenyevna, daughter of Yevgeny."

"Do you have one of those nicknames, like how you and Alexei call Mai Maiya?"

"Yes. For Olga it is usually Olechka."

She smiled at me. "That's kinda sexy."

I know I blushed. I still had trouble speaking of such things.

"Okay, so you taught people how to be spies. What did you teach these newbie spies?" Olive asked.

"Everything they needed to know."

"Like, how to steal things, how to spy on people, trick people into giving up secrets, things like that?"

"Yes, but more. How to survive. How to make certain they

survived." I paused, took a deep breath, and added, "How to protect themselves. How to deal with the enemies of my country."

"Enemies? You mean . . . Americans?"

"Yes, and British, French, West German, others."

"Well, we were taught in school that the Russians were our enemies. Whatever we did, we were defending our country."

"I see that American propaganda worked," I said. "What do you think I was doing? I was defending my country."

"From what? Freedom?"

"We believed our way of life was as good as yours, even better. I worked to restore the revolution that had been subverted by Stalin, to return it to what it was meant to be. The revolution was to free the Russian people from centuries of oppression, to give equal opportunity to all, to put everyone on an equal standing. Rather like the Declaration of Independence, and America was also established by revolution. We were not so different."

"I never thought of it that way, that you were defending your way of life, too. I'm sure you did what you thought was right."

"I did. That is what drove me, even in the darkest of times."

Olive considered, her lips pursed. "Pick one thing, only one, and tell me about it," she said. "You know I will never say a word to anyone."

Twilight was upon us, but I didn't turn on a light.

"I know you would not, but anything you might want to know is classified. I know my country thinks I am dead, but I vowed I would tell no one, not even Bukharin, what I knew. However, one thing you should know about, since you told me about your husband," I said.

"Oh. Were . . . Were you married?"

"No. Never. Though I was asked several times, because they wanted to be close to a position of power. I should tell you of a man named Strakh. He is dead now. Many years."

"Strakh. An unusual name."

"His *nom de guerre*."

"A nom de guerre is usually symbolic of something. Does Strakh mean something?"

"It means fear or terror. He taught me, and I taught others."

"You were lovers."

Not a question.

"Yes. For seven years."

"Wow, that's a relationship. Why did you stop being lovers?"

"He was an encumbrance."

Olive frowned, now looking out the window herself. "By logical extrapolation, then," she said, "I'm an encumbrance, and when you realize that . . ."

"Never. I have learned, you have taught me, that love is not an encumbrance. Without you, I would have no reason to live. Never think that I would walk away from you. I will not. What other questions do you have?"

"I think I have enough answers to last me a while, so I'll ask a different question. Have you thought about what I said about moving to our own place?"

"I have."

Olive bit her lower lip, bracing herself for the bad news, but I rose and retrieved our laptop from a table. I opened it to a web site I had examined earlier.

"These are houses I found for us to look at," I said.

Olive sighed and laid her head on my shoulder.

38

PORTLAND, OREGON
ENTRY 34

For a while after beginning my relationship with Olive, I continued to be Natalia Petrovna's bodyguard. That would be the arrangement until her marriage to Alex Terrell. That was not supposed to happen until Natalia finished law school in 2004 or 2005.

That was Bukharin's condition for him to agree to the marriage. Not that he could have stopped it. Natalia Petrovna was an adult, after all, but she did want her grandfather's blessing. Unfortunately, Bukharin would have withheld that because he was convinced, with no evidence, Alex was like his Uncle Eddie, Edwin Terrell, who would copulate with any woman in his immediate vicinity.

One of those women had been Maiya. Even though Bukharin was not a faithful spouse until well into their marriage, he could be possessive of Maiya, especially where Terrell was concerned. I believe the American colloquialism is "the apple does not fall far from the tree," and Bukharin supposed that of Alex Terrell.

That was not Alex Terrell though. He has been fiercely loyal to

Natalia Petrovna, either from his commitment or my private conversation with him about what would happen to him if he hurt her.

With the prospect of a second war for the United States after 9/11, Natalia wanted to move the date of the wedding up. By two years. Maiya agreed, and she had to convince Bukharin Natalia would not abandon law school. I am certain you can surmise how she accomplished this.

The wedding plans were altered, and they married at a chapel on Alex's base, where both Bukharin and Pyotor Alexeivitch presented her at the altar, Bukharin with a certain reluctance.

Now that my duties as "au pair/bodyguard" were done, I lived for a while in my old apartment in Maiya's and Bukharin's house. They agreed that Olive could move in with me, and she and I had little need to see anyone except each other. We both yearned, however, for our own life in our own house.

I realized then I wanted to start our new life far from my old one. Olive's family was originally from Vancouver, British Columbia, Canada, and she and I decided to live in the Pacific Northwest, an area I knew nothing about, even though my father and we children lived on Kamchatka for a year. That was the closest I came to Portland, Oregon, until I moved there.

At that time, Olive and I had no thought about marriage. It was not allowed in most states anyway, including Oregon, where we decided to settle. We said simply that we would buy our own house and live our lives in peace. We chose Oregon because it was a place accepting of gay people—Olive broke me from saying "the gays." We were very happy there.

The small house we bought had three tiny bedrooms, a living room, and a kitchen. We made one of the bedrooms a "library," as Olive called it, where we would read, drink tea, and be together. The house's backyard was large and fenced in, which prompted

Olive to want a dog. I offered excuse after excuse, but Olive would not be put off.

Olive was only the second person I told about Sasha and Stepi. Even Bukharin didn't know. The only other person was a protege of mine with whom I had to make a point about bloodlines, bad bloodlines. Olive understood and sympathized, but she still wanted a dog.

We adopted a dog from a shelter, and Dolly was a sweet, gentle thing, but, then, we had no children around to torment her. At first, Olive alone was responsible for her because of my reluctance, but I became accustomed to her, and she was like our child.

The man who came to that house to kill me was well-trained. Any dog could be a potential threat and would have warned of a stranger's approach. So, he dispatched the dog first. Dolly would have greeted him with her tail wagging, hoping for a treat, but had her throat slit instead.

The man must have been utterly silent. Olive never stirred from her favorite chair, where she liked to read and look out over the backyard. She had not turned toward any sound but sat still and quiet as she read, her right leg propped on a hassock because she was a month past a knee replacement.

It was quick.

I could read that. Like I would have taught one of my assassins. This killer was too young, though, to have been one of my pupils. If he had been, I would have taught him to be sure of his target before he struck.

If he had checked, I would be the one buried not Olive.

When he realized his mistake and returned to kill me, I killed him.

Then, I left everything I loved behind.

39

GENEVA

ENTRY 35

I came to Geneva to escape the assassin who killed my wife instead of me. Given the notorious Russian homophobia—of which I was once guilty—I suspect the assassin thought all aging lesbians looked alike. He saw a woman with short, gray hair and assumed he had found his target.

As I said, not one I trained. My trainees would not have made such a mistake.

My most successful trainee, Bukharin, had insisted I have a "contingency plan" when I opted to move to Oregon. I told him I could take care of Olive and me.

"Better to have and not need than to need and not have," he reminded me.

He did learn most of his lessons well.

I had prepared "go-bags," containing cash in several currencies, all the paperwork associated with a new identity, credit cards, burner phones (ah, what a wonderful invention for spies and teachers of spies), and several changes of clothing. Everything one would need if it became necessary to leave in a hurry. One for me, one for Olive. It was difficult for her to understand why this might ever be necessary, but she came to accept it might be needed.

The hardest day of my life, harder even than the day my little brother died or the day they took my mother away, was the day I took my go-bag from the closet and had to leave Olive's behind.

I did everything as I'd taught my trainees: laid a false trail, used money and credit cards from my would-be assassin—he was in no condition to ever use them again—drove to a different city, booked multiple flights, and picked one at the last minute. When I arrived in Europe, I took shorter, local flights back and forth across the continent until booking one to my final destination. All good tradecraft. I had sent my coded message to Bukharin, and he awaited me when I arrived alone in Geneva.

I had intended for my stay in Geneva to be temporary. A few weeks, a couple of months. Where I would go after that, I did not know. I only knew it would not be back to the house Olive and I had shared, where Olive had been murdered. As far as I was concerned, my life, such as it was, had ended when hers did. Going back there would have been too painful.

Maiya and her business manager arranged for the sale of the house and the transfer of our belongings to storage in Switzerland. I was sad not to see that little house again, but it was best I did not.

Geneva is a beautiful city, though in the first weeks of my time here, I saw only the four walls of a guest room in Maiya's and Bukharin's home. I left that room only to take meals with Bukharin and Ivan or with the three of them when Maiya came home from work. Natalia and her children would come visit from the second house on the property, which belonged to her and her husband, Alex. Natalia would often bring her boisterous children in an attempt to cheer me up, but what cheer I'd had with Olive was gone.

Maiya and Bukharin, by then, had adopted their son, and I

decided they needed to finish bonding with him without my impeding presence.

"Where will you go?" Maiya had asked when I announced my intentions to leave.

I had no clue, of course, and told her I would "figure something out."

I even thought of returning to Russia, presenting myself to the SVR or the GRU, and accepting their punishment for my defection so long ago. That punishment would likely involve being taken to the basement of the Lubyanka and executed there. A fitting end, perhaps, and an ironic one, as well. Perhaps one I deserved for all the people I had sent to that basement.

I decided against that because my death that way would mean Dmitri Kargin had won.

That is how I came to be in the apartment over the garage attached to Natalia's and Alex's house. I traded the four walls of a guest room for the four walls of a nice apartment, still with no purpose and no plan and a life without Olive.

No. I had a purpose. I was content to die. I wanted to die. Before the pandemic came, the family had a small celebration for my seventy-ninth birthday at a wonderful restaurant, a rare occasion for me to leave my apartment. It was, however, a joyous few hours with a happy Maiya and Bukharin, a happy Natalia Petrovna and Alex, and happy, though noisy, children.

Even amid that, I wanted to die.

I am not religious. That part of Communism I had no quarrel with. I do not believe prayer does anything except waste words. Every night, I think to myself or even say aloud, it will be fine if I do not wake tomorrow morning. My "prayers" were not granted. I did not expect them to be, and that was why I found myself on Bukharin's dock on Lake Geneva, contemplating how long it would take me to drown.

I have even wished for a debilitating disease, one that would take me quickly and without time for treatment. I have contemplated not wearing my mask in public or not washing my hands with my usual discipline. However, I would not want to bring COVID into houses with children. Bukharin is only a few years younger than I am. I would not endanger him.

It seems I am stuck in life. I could start drinking, I suppose, but Alex is recovering from that issue. I would not risk tempting him. Also, I do not want to start down the same path as my father.

I could stop eating, but knowing Natalia Petrovna, she would force-feed me, and I will not be a bad example for her children nor for Ivan Alexeivitch.

I am stuck. Waiting for nature to take her course. I wish she would hurry up and decide that this earth no longer needs me.

FROM A WINDOW OF MY APARTMENT, I watched Bukharin and Alex play with the children. Rachael M and Ivan chased each other about the lawn in an unending game of tag. The two older boys kicked a soccer ball back and forth to each other. Rachael M's hair flew wild about her head as she ran, and that reminded me of me at that age, chasing my brothers with abandon.

The twins, now twelve, had begun to exhibit the sullenness of adolescence. When they did not play soccer with each other, they played video games and shunned their sister, the trigger for many disputes and noise. I remembered Natalia's mood swings and how difficult that was for Bukharin, Maiya, and me to handle, but Bukharin recently said, "It is only fitting that Natalia gets to experience what she put us through."

I could not argue with that. Indeed, I hoped an apology from her would be forthcoming.

Bukharin and Alex stood together and watched the children, close enough to converse, far enough away that no one would ever realize they were related by marriage. I believe that Bukharin believes that if he thinks of Alex merely as Rachel, Alex, and Barrett's father rather than Natalia's husband, he could tolerate Alex as his bodyguard, which was Alex's job now.

Of course, when I saw that the two men would be so close to my apartment, I opened a window so I could hear their conversation. Why, you ask? I suspected they would eventually talk about me, and my old habits are difficult to break.

"Hey, Rache!" Alex called to his daughter. "Five more minutes, then inside for dinner, okay?"

"Okay, Daddy!" she shouted and eluded Vanya's attempt to tag her.

"So," Alex said to Bukharin, "Nat's still worried about Olga."

I am always right about these things.

"What now?" Bukharin asked.

"Same old. She makes excuses not to eat with us. Hardly ever leaves her apartment. I mean, I know it's a pandemic, but she's in our bubble."

"Natalia needs to understand how task-oriented Olga is. Once Natalia put the idea of a memoir into Olga's head, that is the only thing she wants to focus on."

"Well, you know how it is. When the wife's not happy . . ."

"No one is. I am well aware. Far more than you. When you and Rachael M head home, Ivan and I will pay Olga a visit."

"Good. I'm pretty task-oriented, too. I can check 'talk to Popi about Olga' off my honey-do list."

"Such an obedient husband."

Bukharin's sarcasm was easy to discern.

"And you aren't?"

"Alex, the key is to make them think you're doing what they

say while not actually doing it. Anything other than that is being pussy-whipped."

"Considering who my pussy-whipper is, I don't mind at all, and neither do you, old man. Hey, Rache, time to go!"

I heard Rachael's and Ivan's groans of disappointment, but they headed toward the two men.

"Vanya, would you like to say hello to Baba Olga?" Alexei asked his son.

"Yes! Please!"

"Put your mask on, please," Alexei said, pulling his from a pocket and donning it.

The two children skipped down the path ahead of Alex and Alexei, and I listened as long as I could.

"Let me know when you're ready to leave," Alex said to Bukharin. "I'll walk you back to the house."

"I think I can protecting myself for a few hundred feet."

"I don't doubt that. You forget, I work for your wife, and since I'm so pussy-whipped, you know, I do whatever she says, and she says I'm with you any time you're out of your house."

"Here I thought it was because you adored me."

"Ha, ha. You're a funny old coot."

"You're an impertinent, pussy-whipped asshole."

They rounded a corner of the house, and I could hear no more. I closed the window, put on my mask, and waited for the doorbell to ring.

40

TOVARISHCH (COMRADE)

I pretended to be surprised when I opened the door to Bukharin and Ivan Alexeivitch.

"Ah, some company," I said, ruffling Vanya's hair. "And how are you, *mal'chik*?"

"I am good, Baba Olga. We came to see you."

"Yes, I can see. I think perhaps that calls for some tea cakes. What do you think?"

Vanya nodded with vigor.

"Come in, come in."

I took their jackets and hung them in a closet by the door. I removed my mask and left it on a table by the door, and Bukharin stowed his in his trouser pocket. They headed into the living room, and when I looked over my shoulder, I saw Bukharin watching me walk. I knew what he would see: a smooth, strong gait, no limping. My color was good. I looked healthy.

"I had just put the kettle on," I said. "Some tea for my handsome young men?"

"I'd love some," Bukharin said.

"Yes, thank you," Vanya said. "And some tea cakes?"

"What else would you have with tea except tea cakes?" I said, smiling. "I made them this morning. Sit, sit."

Vanya tugged on his father's sleeve. In a stage whisper, he said, "Papa, I have to use the toilet."

"Ask Olga."

"No need. Of course, you may use the toilet. You know where it is," I said from the kitchen.

"And don't forget . . ." Bukharin raised an eyebrow.

"To put down the seat and wash my hands," Vanya said, his tone indicating he'd heard those instructions numerous times.

Bukharin leaned down and kissed the top of the boy's head. "Yes, good man. Hurry back before I eat all the tea cakes."

Vanya's eyes widened at that.

"Do not worry," I said. "I will save some for you if your papa is a *bol'shaya svin'ya*."

Vanya dashed off to the bathroom.

"Shall this big pig help you with the tray?" Bukharin asked.

I turned to him. "Am I a doddering *babushka* that I need a big, strong man to help me?"

"Don't overreact, old friend. I am being polite."

I snorted and said, "Go sit down. You are a guest. I will bring the tray. If I want your help, I will ask for it."

Suppressing a smile, Bukharin snapped to attention and saluted me. "Yes, of course, Comrade Colonel," he said. "I obey."

I snorted again and went back to my preparations.

Bukharin settled on the end of the living room sofa that let him see the Geneva skyline across the lake. Soon, Vanya joined him, resting on his knees, arms on the sofa back. He looked across the lake, too.

"Papa, which one is Mama's office again?" Vanya asked.

"Remember which building it is?" Bukharin asked.

"Yes. That one. With the black windows."

"Good. Her office is on the top floor . . . "

"The fourth . . . No, the fifth window from the left."

"Excellent!"

"Can you text her and tell her I am waving?" Vanya said, as he waved toward the building.

"Of course." Bukharin brought out his phone and tapped a message with his thumbs. "This is what she sent back," he said to Ivan and showed him his phone.

The boy studied the screen and smiled. "Mama sent back a smiley face, a hand waving, a heart, and an emoji blowing a kiss."

"Yes, she did. Now, turn around and sit properly, please."

"Yes, Papa."

"Such an obliging child," I called from the kitchen. "Refreshing, considering the two surly twelve-year-olds on the other side of the wall. You will have a few more years of peace and quiet with Vanya before the adolescent hormones take hold."

"A good thing," Bukharin said, "because I won't be getting any younger."

I came from the kitchen with a wooden tray laden with three silver tea glass holders, their clear inserts filled with strong, almost black tea—except for one. Vanya's was about three-quarters full. I was mindful of the caffeine.

On the tray was a bowl of sugar cubes and a small plate with nine, perfectly round tea cakes. I had been generous with the powdered sugar, making the confection live up to its other name, snowball cookies. A trio of serviettes was the finishing touch.

I placed the tray on the sofa table and sat in an armchair perpendicular to the sofa. I trusted that Bukharin noticed I indeed had no problems carrying the tray.

"Go ahead, *mal'chik*," I said. "Help yourself. I think only three tea cakes because you still have dinner coming."

The boy helped himself to one of the ball-like cookies, as did Bukharin. After sampling his, Bukharin said to me, "Yours have always been infinitely better than mine."

"Yes, your baking is good, but you are better at savory," I told him.

"It's refreshing to see you have lost none of your bluntness."

"I am eighty-one years old. What is the point of changing that now?"

"Baba Olga," said Vanya, "is the book Rachael M and I were reading still here?"

"The one about the black horse?"

"Yes."

"It is in the room I use as my office. In the bookcase."

"Can I . . . May I go read it?"

"Yes, of course. Take your tea and another tea cake with you, if you like."

"And some napkins," his father said.

"*Da, da, Papa. Spaciba,* Baba Olga."

"*Pazhaluista, mal'chik.*"

The boy took another cookie, a napkin, and his tea to the room divided from the living room by a half-wall.

Bukharin popped his third tea cake into his mouth and washed it down with tea.

"Why does he call me Baba Olga? Did you tell him to do that?" I asked.

"I didn't. He's an interesting child. He knows what he wants and needs and has no trouble expressing either. When he first laid eyes on Mai on the day I brought him home, he called her Mama, almost as if he knew he would become our son."

"She did not object?"

"No. I expected her to, but she told me some weeks later it was different from Natalia calling her Mums and she liked it because she had given up on ever being called Mama long ago."

"Was she drinking? That is the only time I have heard her say anything sentimental."

Bukharin smiled at the truth of that. "No, she was quite sober, but it was after some rather satisfying sex. That has always made her talkative."

I shook my head and waved a hand as if dismissing him. "Men do not lose the need to dwell on that subject even in their dotage," I said.

"Far from my dotage, old friend. He started calling you Baba Olga the first time he saw you. No one told him to. Does it bother you? I can tell him not to call you that, if you prefer."

"Baba is what he called his grandmother, yes?"

"Yes."

I stared out the window for a moment and said, "Olive and I would talk about when her son would marry and we would become grandmothers. She picked out what she wanted to be called, but I thought it useless to speculate because the boy was not even dating anyone seriously."

Another smile from Bukharin. "How practical you are. Does Olive's son keep in touch?"

"Yes. He calls every Friday evening when he is not deployed. When he is, he sends an email telling me not to worry."

"I'm glad he's good to you."

"He does not have to be. The only connection there was between us is gone."

"You are all he has left of his mother."

I shrugged. "Well, you know me. I am suspicious of everyone's motivations." I looked at him. "Even yours. Why this impromptu and unexpected visit?"

"Oh, am I to make an appointment now?" he asked, a smile still playing at his lips.

"Of course not. It is your property, after all."

"Don't say that as if I'm some bourgeois landlord come to evict you."

"You are my landlord, and despite your obvious membership in, if not the bourgeoisie, then the elite, you are a good one."

"Thank you. I think."

"So, why are you here?"

"Natalia is still worried about you. According to Alex, you don't leave the apartment and make excuses not to eat with them."

"I never was a social animal. You know this. I rarely dined with you and Maiya in America. I preferred my own space. I love Natalia's children, but they are not as quiet and well-mannered as your son. They can be overwhelming at times."

Bukharin looked toward the room where Vanya was. "Sometimes I think he is too subdued. He plays exuberantly with Rachael, but I do worry he is too serious, that he gets that from me."

"I taught you that. I am sorry."

"The therapist says he's fine. Now, be honest. Why are you not leaving the apartment?"

"Even though I thought Natalia's idea of writing this memoir too fanciful, I find I look forward to devoting my time to it. When I am focused on writing, I do not like interruptions."

"Ah, Vanya and I interrupted your creative endeavors."

"No, I was done for the day. It was simply an excuse not to have dinner with the Hooligans."

"Come have dinner with us. Our house is quiet as a tomb."

"I suspect you will not take no for an answer."

"Did you in your interrogations rooms?"

"Do not try to be comedian in your dotage. You are no good

at it. And Vanya may call me Baba Olga as long as I get to spoil him and return him to you and Maiya full of sweets."

"What? You don't think his bourgeois parents have spoiled him enough?"

I finished my tea, rose, and said, "I could always outdo you, and you know that. Since it seems I have no choice, let me get my coat and gloves."

41

REFLECTIONS

ENTRY 36

In winter, daylight leaves early here in Geneva, though not as bad as the part of Siberia where my father was stationed for a while.

When the daylight fades, my old eyes do not like staring at the computer screen, and I stop this exercise, wondering as I do most days, whether it is worth the effort. Some memories I do not mind. Others are painful, more painful than I expected, and push me to the end of the pier again. Old age makes you sentimental.

Today, I was restless after saving the manuscript and shutting down the computer, and I could not fathom why. Before it was completely dark, I walked up the main path to the main house and invited myself to dinner with Bukharin, Maiya, and Vanya.

Vanya is a boy with a thousand questions. Bukharin's patience in attempting to answer each surprises me. The child will ponder the answer he receives and ask yet another question.

As usual, Maiya was not home yet, though Bukharin has told me her late nights are rare now. Raising a young child provides a reason for not working late, it seems. My experience of small children is that working long hours is an excuse to keep from dealing with them.

While Bukharin's casserole of some sort—it smelled delicious—finished its cooking in the oven, he took the time to observe his son's piano practice. I watched them, still marveling at Bukharin's patience. His criticism was gentle and instructive. His praise was fulsome but not fake, and the boy responded well to such tutelage.

And asked question after question about unrelated things.

That made me wonder if Little Sasha would have been like this, had he lived long enough to talk.

Despite the fact I did my best to beat emotion of Bukharin, it was good to see him happy at last.

With the piano practice over, Vanya took me by the hand and led me to the French doors that opened onto the house's deck. He turned on the deck's lighting and pointed to a birdhouse on a tall pole attached to the deck.

"Baba Olga, I made that house for the birds," Vanya said.

"I know, Vanushka, because you have shown it to me before," I replied.

Vanya turned to his father. "Papa, can I . . . Is it 'can I' or 'may I'?"

"Work it out and tell me," was Bukharin's reply.

Vanya's little forehead furrowed in concentration. "I am able to tell her, but I need your permission, so it is . . . may I?"

"Yes, that is correct. Good work."

"May I give it to her now?"

"Why don't you wait until Mama comes home, so we can all give it to her?" Bukharin said, intriguing me.

Probably a drawing of some sort. Maiya has said he gives her three or four at a time, and she takes them to her office. I would almost like to see how she displays them, these childish drawings in the office of a ruthless spymaster.

"How long before she comes home?" Vanya asked.

"No more than an hour," Bukharin told him.

"May I go FaceTime with Rachael?"

Bukharin looked at his watch. "They won't be eating dinner for a while. Go ahead. Fifteen minutes, understand?"

"Yay! I mean, yes, Papa, I understand." The boy dashed up the stairs to his room.

"Young love is so sweet," I said, teasing Bukharin.

"Do not even think that. One of my blood married to a Terrell is enough."

Together, he and I made some yeast rolls to have with dinner, and about the time we took them from the oven, Maiya arrived home.

More excited chatter from Vanya, to tell his mother all about his virtual school. At dinner, he quieted down, and we adults talked. It reminded me of how Olive and I would chat through dinner, and I was again sad.

After dinner, Maiya and I cleared the table, refrigerated the leftover casserole and rolls, and placed dishes in the dishwasher. She and I talked a little "shop," most likely because Bukharin did not like to, and Bukharin oversaw Vanya's preparation for bed. A domestic scene almost surreal to me.

Bukharin came back downstairs with the child, Vanya in pajamas decorated with images of baseballs and bats, of all things. He carried a medium-sized box and held it out to me when he reached me.

"What is this?" I asked him.

"Natalia was here the other day, talking to Papa, and I heard her say you were sad. I asked Papa if I could make you something so you would not be sad," Vanya explained.

"A present for me?" I asked, surprised by the child's kindness and thoughtfulness.

"Mama said I should wait for the holidays, but I want you to have it now."

I took the box from him and placed it on the kitchen counter. He stood close to me, his eyes bright with excitement. I lifted the lid.

"Oh, my," I said.

Nestled inside the box was a birdhouse in the shape of Olive's and my house in Oregon. Old woman that I am, I could not stop two tears before they left my eyes.

Vanya looked up at his father with alarm. His voice trembling, he said, "Papa, I made her sadder."

Maiya came to the boy and knelt so she did not tower over him. I knew how bad her knees were, almost as bad as my old ones. She took his hands in hers and said, "Ivan, sometimes people cry when they are happy."

I lay my hand on the boy's head, for it would be impossible for me to kneel and rise again with any dignity.

"Your mama is right, Vanya. This is a beautiful gift, and I treasure it. I will make sure it is placed where I can see it from all my windows. When I look at it, it will bring me happy memories. Now, tell me how you made such a beautiful thing."

"Well, Papa cut out the pieces because I am not allowed to use the saw. Natalia gave Papa a picture of your house as a guide, and Papa and I put it together."

"I oversaw the hammering of the nails and the glue, but he did the rest," Alexei said.

"I painted it from the colors in the picture," Vanya said. "Do you really like it?"

"It is something most precious to me, Vanushka. *Spaciba, spaciba.* May I give you a hug?"

Bukharin raised an eyebrow at me. He knew I was not a

woman to demonstrate affection, but a child is a child. Gratitude for a child's gift should never be withheld.

Not long after, Vanya went to bed, and Bukharin, flashlight in hand, walked with me down the hill to my apartment.

"You don't mind the birdhouse, do you?" Bukharin asked. "It was his idea, and he was adamant to make it."

"Of course I do not mind. I meant what I said to him. I will remind me of the happiness I had in that house."

"How's the memoir coming?"

I shook my head. "Sometimes I want to throw the computer into Lake Geneva, but for the most part, it is a positive thing."

"Are you going to let us read it?"

"*Nyet*! Well, only after I am dead."

He laughed softly. "I always thought you'd take your secrets with you. What have you learned about yourself from this literary exercise?"

"Nothing I did not already know."

"Come on, tell an old friend something."

We had reached my door, and the light I had turned on when I left gave plenty of light for me to watch Bukharin's expression.

"All right," I said, "I will tell you one thing. Do you remember Comrade Strakh?"

"Yes, of course. Only you were scarier than he was. Why?"

I looked him in the eye as I spoke. "He was a friend to me, a good friend. A *blizkiy droog*."

I let myself into the house, satisfied by the startled look on Bukharin's face at my use of "intimate friend." I half-expected him to knock on my door and demand an explanation, but he is a smart man. I am sure he understood.

That will teach him not to be nosy, and I could not wait to add this comedic moment to this oh-so-serious memoir.

42

MEMORIES

ENTRY 37

I put Vanya's birdhouse on the fireplace mantel, next to a picture of Olive. The walk had set a chill in my joints, and I turned on the gas fireplace. The restlessness I had felt all day returned, and I knew what was necessary.

Bukharin had closure from his old life as a KGB officer, as a U.N. spy. He had the love of his wife and his child, both of those a second chance for him.

Did people not write memoirs for closure as well? My life had a big hole, where closure still waited.

My mention of Strakh had brought his unopened letter to mind. That wasn't the only memory to emerge. I recalled how I would watch his face as he talked, as he taught me the things I needed and wanted to know. How his eyes would gleam at some key piece of information. How he would stroke my hair or brush my cheek with his fingertips as we lay in bed after intercourse. How we would play our little game of being "only comrades" when we were in public.

I felt an emptiness at those memories. Not quite the abyss I felt after finding Olive dead but close enough. I realized I missed Strakh, that I had missed him from that day I had dismissed him as an encumbrance a half-century before. For several years after that, our encounters were the same as they had always been. I delivered my reports on students to him. He asked questions, and I answered. I asked for advice about a problem recruit, and he provided it.

Then, those occasions became fewer and fewer because, as he told me, smiling his crooked smile, "Olechka, you no longer need me."

When he died in 1975, he and I had not seen each other even officially for three years.

Did I love him after all?

If I did, it was mere infatuation. The love I had for Olive was deeper than anything I'd had with Strakh. If I were with Strakh and had found his murdered body, I would not have found myself on that dock, prepared to step into the water and let myself drown from grief.

However, I cannot help but think that perhaps I "missed out" on something by sending him from my bed.

No, I cannot imagine what that could possibly be. Not sex. I have said before, there was no lack of pleasure with him, but there was also no intimacy, no feeling like I had with Olive, that feeling of this was where I was meant to be.

I went to my bedroom and took a box from a shelf in the closet. I had in it a few mementos of my life in Russia, including that unopened letter given me after Strakh's funeral. I replaced the box and returned to the living room, letter in hand.

In my chair before the fireplace, the heat warmed my bones, and I watched the play of the flames while I thought.

I could achieve closure with Strakh one of two ways. I could

put the unopened letter in the fire now, and let that old relationship turn to ashes, the way it was always destined to be.

Was I afraid of what I might read?

Of course not. I fear nothing.

Not true. I fear . . . I have always feared losing the ones I love.
There are so few left. Burning an unread letter would be like
losing Strakh again. A silly thing to think, since I had never had
him in any way except physically.

Or I could open the letter and read his last words to me.
Would they be words of criticism, of disappointment? Would he
have used that opportunity as he was dying to remonstrate me for
forcing him from my bed?

As Vanya would say, that could make me sadder.

What is wrong with you, I asked myself, you always took risks,
faced any danger. Are you weak in mind now that you are old?

I looked up at the image of Olive's smiling face and could
almost hear her voice say, "Open it."

I did.

43

CONFESSIONS

Kuntsevo, Moscow
October 11, 1975

Dearest Olechka,

How amusing I begin this letter with this cliche: If you are reading this, I am dead, likely already buried in the Kremlin Wall. I know I never seemed the type to want that accolade, but I worked hard for it. Serving two masters—the Party and the Red Circle—was never easy, but you know that.

That day when we parted in your new flat, I had so many things I had planned to say, but I knew you too well. After your declaration, it would have been pointless. Nothing I said would have changed your mind. I knew as well that to keep you as a friend, I had to agree to what you wanted, as much as it pained me to end a relationship I had particularly enjoyed.

Do not mistake me. I enjoyed every part of our relationship, but the physical aspect was more fulfilling and comforting than anything I have ever known. I will tell you what may surprise you. I knew the seven year we were intimate would never be enough for me. I suspect it was far too long for you, but they were the happiest years of my life, far happier than anything I experienced with my wife, who, I daresay, will shed not a tear at my funeral.

My confession continues. Brace yourself for this revelation. I was quietly and discreetly looking into whether my wife would agree to a divorce. You see, my dearest, I had hoped to share that wonderful apartment with you as your husband. The ultimate encumbrance, yes?

I have always wondered if you suspected how much you mattered to me, but I was afraid to ask. I knew I would not like your response. I do understand. How I felt about you would have meant nothing to you. I have never known as dedicated a socialist, as dedicated a patriot as you.

You and I often discussed—oh, how I miss

our conversations after sex—how the West seemed to think it had the monopoly on patriotism, how their spies operated out of love of country, and how they believed we were too evil for such high-minded patriotism. We were always nothing more than one-dimensional villains to them, like that cartoon Boris Badenov. They refused to acknowledge that we loved our country, too, even with its flaws. This is to say, I accepted the whole time we were together that country would always come first for you. Nothing else, not even a besotted man, could compete with that. The Soviet Union and the Red Circle were lucky to have such a patriot as you, and I was proud of that, even if it meant we could not be together.

Because I did not get to say these things to you in person, I will continue my confessions. I have already made two: the happiness you gave me and the fact I considered divorcing my wife.

Here is another. I was not put to death by the KGB or the Party. I died by my own hand. Poison. Clean. Quick. A swallow with taste obscured by a decent shot of good vodka.

When the cancer diagnosis came, the Party informed me I had its permission to seek treatment in the West, under a cover identity. I had made no such request. I would like to think the Party granted me that for my unwavering service. Of course, because it was offered, I could not refuse it, and I did go to London to an oncologist. His prognosis was even more grim than that of my doctor here.

It was beyond hope. All that remained was for me to rest, medicate against the pain, and wait for the end, but you know me. I needed to be in control of my own destiny.

I made peace with the Party, with the Red Circle, with my family, whom I had lived apart from since I knew I could not have you, and I picked the day.

I almost contacted you to ask to see you one last time, but I doubted you would come. Ah, those encumbrances.

Then, I realized I wanted you to remember me as you last saw me, younger, strong, and in control of my bodily functions. Besides, what would it have done to my final days to see what I'd lost and know I would never see you again, that it would be the last time to lay eyes upon you?

Now, we have the final confession. I love you. I never stopped loving you. I hope you are not alone. I could not bear that thought. If you are, I want you to know someone loved you.

My consolation after we stopped seeing each

other was that you were incapable of love. I hope
that is not true. My ardent wish is that you have
someone who cares for you as you, not for the
uniform or the privileges your position in the Party
brings. I can go to whatever happens after death
with no fear because of that hope. Whoever wins the
heart I know you have will be a lucky man, and
if I were alive, I would envy him.

I would like to say I never lied to you, but
in truth, I did. Only once. If I had told you the
truth back then, you would have hated me. I could
live with the fact you considered me an encumbrance,
but I could not bear the thought of your hating me.

Once, you asked me about the death of Alexei
Bukharin's wife, Sofya Krasnovskaya. I told you
it was an accident, nothing more. However, since
Bukharin's unauthorized marriage and the birth of
his son, he was faltering in his commitment to his
part of The Plan. He even spoke to Misha about it.
Misha made him some vague promise about allowing
Sofya and the baby to defect with him. I also
knew if we allowed him to defect with his family,
they would be his focus, not the work of the Red
Circle.

Misha had no knowledge of what I had
decided to do. Until this letter, I am the only one
who knew what I had done.

Sofya Krasnovskaya, as a good and honest citizen and committed socialist, thinking only of the safety of her fellow workers, had reported the issues with the factory boiler many times. She had been reprimanded for her continual filing of safety complaints.

One night, I visited the factory in secret and examined the boiler myself. She was right. It could fail at any time. If that failure happened in the middle of a crowded night shift, it would be a disaster and a humiliation for the Party and the officials who had ignored her warnings.

I also saw it would be easy to hasten the boiler's failure.

She and the rest of her shift came to work that night and worked with socialist diligence a few meters away from the boiler I had sabotaged. I understood the sacrifice of many workers would cover the murder of one.

The Red Circle had always been clear about necessary sacrifices.

Her death was instantaneous. No suffering. Had she survived, however, I was prepared to end her suffering.

I took it upon myself to do what needed to be done to compel Bukharin to fulfill his purpose. I took from him a beloved, young wife, a beautiful woman, a new mother. This gave me no happiness, but I accepted that I did what I'd done for The Plan.

I have read reports on Bukharin's activities with the Directorate. He has fulfilled his duty admirably. That is because he not only had a good teacher but the best teacher.

If you wish to set his mind at ease, do so. Make sure he knows the Party had nothing to do with her death nor the Red Circle. I acted on my own.

For my country.

I have done many things for my country that, to many, would be horrific. Like all of us in the Red Circle, I focused on the "big picture." I killed Krasnovskaya for the good of my country.

I do not ask forgiveness for that but for having lied to you. I like to think there was always truth and trust between us, as much as our positions would allow, and I regret to my dying day that I was the one to break that trust and lie to you. I think, I hope, you understand why I did.

When I take the poison, which sits here at my bedside, within reach, I will hold an image of you in my mind, so I may take that with me into whatever lies beyond life.

Keep yourself safe, my love, and be happy. I love you.

Yours always,
Strakh
(Dmitri Ignatsievitch Borukov)

44

BURDENS

ENTRY 38

I re-read Strakh's letter, slower this time to make sure I had read correctly the first time.

I had. Sadly, regretfully, I had.

I refolded it, slipped it back into its envelope, and held it on my lap with both hands. The glow of the fire comforted me, but I found I breathed hard, fast, as though I had run a long distance.

These words had been written almost half a century ago by a man I'd only recently thought of after decades of not thinking about him. Now, all his words, written and spoken, jostled about in my head. To my surprise, I could bring the sound of his voice to mind, and the letter was as though he sat here before the fire and spoke to me.

Had I missed hearing that voice?

I missed Olive's voice, her laugh. I can still hear her laugh in my dreams, my reveries, but Strakh?

At one time, I longed to hear his voice, the voice I heard on the nights when we lay in bed after intercourse. He would talk about Lenin and Trotsky and the Revolution, the origins of the KGB, its predecessors the NKVD and the Cheka, even the tsar's spies, the Okhrana. Those words stayed with me.

After I ended our physical relationship, I could bring his words to mind when I needed them; when I dealt with a difficult recruit or on the occasions I conducted "special" interrogations. Then, it was as if he were physically with me, speaking to me, still in that oh-so intimate setting. I did not give up that part of him; I did not want to. I also understand now what he meant when he said I no longer needed him. He gave me up without fighting for me so I could be who I was meant to be.

Was that love?

Olive and I talked about normal things: when to go shopping, what color to paint the bathroom, when to take the car in for service, books we had read, television programs we had watched, politics. Never did she and I talk about how to kill people without leaving a trace or how to induce a reluctant subject to spill his or her secrets. I would give anything to have one of those "normal" conversations with Olive again.

Though Strakh, too, is dead, for a long time now, his words are seared into my brain. I needed to access them so often, they will never fade. I must make sure there is space enough in my old head so that Olive's words do not fade either.

Unlike Strakh, Olive had no time to write me a letter. Having now read Strakh's, I wish she had.

An epiphany jolted me, almost as though Geneva had experienced an earthquake. I had used Strakh for whatever I could learn from him to advance my career. I had accepted his attention to sharpen my life's focus—my career, my country. I used him as I had taught others to use an asset. That is all he was to me, and he is not here to grant forgiveness for that.

Olive gave my life purpose and meaning, a life I was able to lead as the person I truly am. I miss my life with Olive in it.

For a short time, Strakh had been the most important person in my life. For a short time, Olive had been my life. When Olive was murdered, I felt as though I, too, were dead, lifeless without her, though I still walked the earth, a ghost, a spirit, a zombie. I have felt that way every moment, every second since I found Olive's body.

That was why I had stood on Bukharin's dock and contemplated sinking into oblivion. My life had left this world when an assassin crept into our house and slit Olive's throat.

Writing about this has brought everything I tried to suppress back. Strakh. All the men and women I taught to be spies, to be killers. The things I have done for my country, which no longer exists. At the time, I was proud of every action I took. It seemed right at the time. Now, I am not sure.

Is it too late for remorse, too late for redemption?

Yes, for all the people who suffered and died at a word from me, from my signature on an official form with a raised seal. Too late for Olive, who died in my stead and by the orders of a man I had trained. I believe that is what people call irony.

I had my revenge on Olive's killers. Maiya had assured revenge on the man who had planned my death. The man who had ordered it still lives. Is it, I wonder, worth living longer to see that mediocre KGB officer who fancies himself a tsar pay for his marking me an enemy of Russia?

If Strakh were alive, a word from me and Dmitri Kargin's head would become the centerpiece on my table.

My laugh is short and guttural. If he lived, Strakh—also Dmitri—would be one hundred three years old.

He had loved me.

Olive had loved me.

Had I been home when the assassin arrived, had I died instead, would Olive have avenged me?

Strakh would have.

An unfair comparison. Olive would not hurt a mouse. Literally. She used humane traps and released the mice at the far end of the yard, no matter that they would soon turn up again to repeat the process. Olive named them.

Strakh would have dispatched them with poison, with his pistol, with a knife. And I would have learned technique from it.

The two people who loved me were so different from each other. One I loved. One I used.

I have some anger that Strakh confessed both his love and his despicable act to me, placed both burdens on my shoulders. His love is a burden because I never could have returned it. Then, I did not know why. Now, I do.

The burden of what Strakh did to Bukharin's first wife . . . That is perhaps too much to bear. If Olive were alive, we would still be in Oregon, and I would not have to see those exotic blue eyes that can still show me Bukharin's grief. If I were never to see him again, I could carry that burden. Here, when I see him almost every day, the weight of that burden will crush me. If I had known Strakh's secret on the day I stood on the dock, that weight would have sunk me quickly.

Bukharin overcame his loss and found happiness again, something I will never experience. However, that one event in his life will trouble him to his last breath. He has lived all this time with the lie Strakh told me, the lie I perpetrated.

Did not my oldest friend deserve the truth? Should he not be the one to decide whether this is a secret he needs to know?

What good would it do now? It would become his burden, and I will not let it bear him down.

As I controlled his destiny so many years ago, I will decide for him.

I looked at the letter, let a fingertip brush my name, written in

Strakh's smooth handwriting. I would know it anywhere. I had seen it countless times on official documents. The letter is all I have left of Strakh, who was once the most important part of my life and career.

I looked at the picture of Olive, next to Vanya's magnificent birdhouse. I have Olive's things, the books she loved, her paintings, her embroideries, and her crocheted pieces. I have something of her.

All I have of Strakh are my memories of him. That will have to be enough.

I tossed Strakh's letter into the fire and watched it burn to nothing, a small swirl of dark smoke rose, disappearing into the chimney. I closed my eyes and imagined that smoke streaking across the night sky, reaching for the stars as it passed over the Kremlin Wall until it dissipated in the rarefied air.

Some secrets should die with me.

45

ENCUMBRANCES
FINAL ENTRY

Throughout this memoir, I have written of how I avoided encumbrances, anything I thought would hold me back from my goals. If I was not clear before, I will be now.

I wanted to be the highest-ranking woman in the KGB, and I was, though not in the position I wanted. I wanted to be head of the KGB, an ambition the Red Circle likely suspected but had no proof of. As head of state security, I could have reshaped the KGB to achieve the Red Circle's plan sooner. I explain because I would not want you to think me power-hungry.

Power, in its own way, is an encumbrance because once you have it, you are too busy keeping it to do anything useful.

I left the KGB nearly thirty years ago as the Soviet Union died, as Marxism, Leninism, socialism, all the things that had defined me, died. That is a sadness I will never lose. My country, in the right hands, could have truly been a worker's paradise. It could have fulfilled Marx's and Engles' vision of a proletarian state, again if the right people had been in charge, if the state had not been co-opted by a power-hungry, paranoid, self-important Georgian petty thief and thug.

In the four decades from Stalin's death to the Soviet Union's, my country never escaped its Stalinist yoke. Perhaps the Red Circle's carefully conceived plan was but a dream after all. We have a nightmare now.

I was writing of encumbrances.

I rid myself of my encumbrances. As many as I could, but not all. My father removed the encumbrance that was my mother, and she would have been my encumbrance. As the look-alike daughter of an accomplished and award-winning actress, the Party would have had me as her successor, would have attempted to push this square peg into that round hole.

On the word of my father, she became a traitor, and he spared me from that future.

I rid myself of the encumbrance of my father, even though he inspired my career. That encumbrance would have been the expectation that I would be like him, like a man who had sent his innocent wife to a certain death in a gulag. Yes, as I have said, I sent people there, and worse, but they either deserved it or it furthered the Red Circle's plan.

My brothers . . . More encumbrances, of course. I shrugged them from my shoulders. Any or all of them would have borne me down. To be free, I cast them off without a thought.

Friendships, potential lovers, a long life with Olive, encumbrances all. Olive is the only one I regret losing. That is a pain that will never cease. She was an encumbrance I welcomed and wanted and then lost so horribly. Unbidden and far too often, the image of how she looked, sitting dead in her chair, her life's blood soaking the book she was reading—*The Tattooist of Auschwitz*—comes to me. That anger, along with the pain, I will gladly relinquish at death.

And Strakh. Dmitri Ignatsievitch. No, Strakh. I never knew his real name until after he was dead.

All those years in the KGB and I could have looked that up and read his file, but as my dear friend Bukharin has said, "Mystery heightens the sex."

I have said enough of Strakh. Even dead all these years, he "gifted" me with one last encumbrance, the knowledge of what really happened to Bukharin's first wife. I have tried to hate Strakh for that, but I could not because, damn me, I understood why he did it.

You may ask, what if Bukharin reads this?

He will not. I have already arranged that it will not be published, if it is ever published, until after I am dead and he is dead. Of course, I hope that is long enough from now that Natalia Petrovna will have forgotten she bullied me into doing this in the first place.

Or I could toss the laptop into Lake Geneva instead of myself.

All in all, not ending my life when I thought I wanted to was a good thing. I look around me and see all the things and the people I would miss. I accept now that because of them, I have many, many reasons to live.

That is an encumbrance I bear with joy.

End of Book 2

For My Country
November 2020 - June 2024
Staunton, Virginia

ACKNOWLEDGMENTS

Thank you to the usual cast of characters: my Beta Readers extraordinaire, Allison K. Garcia and C. A. O'Neill; my editor, Mary-Ellen Jones; my writing groups; my writer friends who bolster me, and the readers who messaged me wanting to know more about Olga V. Lubova.

Also, thank you to Vasili Mitrokhin for defecting in 1992 and bringing the KGB archive with him. I relied on Mitrokhin's and Christopher Andew's book, *The Sword and the Shield: The Mitrokhin Archive and the Secret History of the KGB* for this book.

And much gratitude to Allison K. Garcia for making sure the "gay" was correct. It's a good thing to be inclusive, but you've got to get it right. She held my feet to the fire. Thankfully.

ABOUT THE AUTHOR

The author of 30+ published historical espionage works and one mystery, P. A. Duncan is also a former commercial pilot, government aviation safety official, and stodgy bureaucrat, albeit one with a highly overactive imagination.

A graduate of Madison College (now James Madison University) with degrees in history and political science, she lives and writes in the beautiful Shenandoah Valley of Virginia. History and politics often find their way into her writing.

Her short fiction has been featured in numerous literary journals and anthologies and has won or placed in several contests. Her novels consistently reach the top 25 on Amazon bestseller lists, with one rising to #2 twice in one year. She has also edited the works of several award-winning and bestselling authors in a variety of genres.

When not writing, she cheers on the New York Yankees (yes, even after the 2023 season), watches Formula 1 and NASCAR, and spoils her grandchildren.

ALSO BY P. A. DUNCAN

Find all of the author's work at

Short Story Collections

Blood Vengeance, 2012

Spy Flash, 2012

The Better Spy, 2015

Spy Flash II, 2016

Spy Flash III: The Moscow Rules, 2021

Novelettes

A Face in the Crowd, 2017, mini-sequel to *A War of Deception*

Old Love Does Not Rust, 2022

Prologue to Terror, 2022

Prologue to Revenge, 2022

Prologue to Treachery, 2023

Prologue to Rendition, 2023

Novellas

The Yellow Scarf, 2015

My Noble Enemy, 2015

A Change for the Better, 2020

Dateline: Belgrade, 2020

Quintet, 2022

Standalone Novels

A War of Deception, debut novel, 2017

Love/Death, 2021

A Spy's Legacy, 2024

For My Country, 2024

The Devil Passed By, coming 2024

SERIES

A Perfect Hatred

End Times, 2018

Bad Company, 2018

Descending Spiral, 2019

Collateral Damage, 2020

Self-Inflicted Wounds

Welcome to Belgrade, 2020

Dangerous Truths, 2020

And Justice for All, 2020

Meeting the Enemy

Terror, 2022

Revenge, 2022

Treachery, 2023

Rendition, 2023

Box Sets

Quintet, 2022

PROLOGUES, 2024

Secrets, 2024

Writing as Phyllis A. Duncan

Supreme Madness of the Carnival Season, debut mystery novel, 2023

AUTHOR'S SOCIAL MEDIA

Follow me here:

Amazon Author Page: amazon.com/author/phyllisduncan
BookBub: https://www.bookbub.com/profile/p-a-duncan
Facebook Author Page: www.facebook.com/unspywriter
Facebook Reader Group: www.facebook.com/group/RealSpies
Goodreads: http://bit.ly/GRPADuncan
Instagram: www.instagram.com/paduncan1
Substack: https://paduncan.substack.com/
Website/Blog: www.unexpectedpaths.com
X (formerly Twitter): www.twitter.com/unspywriter

NEWSLETTER SIGN-UP

SECRET BRIEFINGS

Bimonthly Issues

Stay up to date on what I'm reading, featured books by other authors, my book events, my preorders and sales, and—this is the best part—*free* excerpts.

Sign up at: https://unexpectedpaths.com/contact-the-author-2

"REAL SPIES, REAL LIVES PODCAST"

"Where we talk about writing, spies, and writing about spies."

Find the "Real Spies, Real Lives Podcast" on your favorite podcast
provider: https://linktr.ee/paduncan
Listen to the latest episodes at www.realspiesreallives.com
Join the podcast's Facebook Page:
www.facebook.com/RealSpiesRealLives

DON'T FORGET THE REVIEW!

I'm sure you've heard all the cliches, and I'm a writer so allow me to indulge in a few.

Reviews are a writer's life's blood. We live for them. We weep for joy over the good ones. Bad reviews are inevitable, and we express (inwardly) righteous indignation at them. Without reviews, how would we improve as writers?

Bottom line? All those cliches are reality for us. I will continue to write and publish what I write whether people love my writing or hate it, but putting a few kind words on Amazon or Goodreads or BookBub is all you have to do to make me smile.

P. A. Duncan

DISCUSSION QUESTIONS
FOR MY COUNTRY

1. Do you accept the premise that most KGB agents carried out their duties for love of country much as CIA case officers did?
2. Beta readers have remarked that Olga Lubova's affair with Strakh diminishes the credibility of her coming out later in life, that she is bi and not a lesbian. Do you agree?
3. While she was KGB, was Olga 100% true to her pledge of no encumbrances?
4. Was Olga right to burn Strakh's letter?
5. What do you think became of Olga's memoir after her eventual death?

July 23, 1961

Directorate Headquarters

Everyone settled around the conference room table until one chair only was empty, the one at the head of the table, reserved for Sir Nigel Hume, director, boss, head honcho, spymaster of the United Nations Intelligence Directorate. Quiet chatter filled the room. Several times, men looked at Grace then spoke in whispers to each other and laughed.

Grace could imagine what they were saying. She'd grown up on Naval bases, after all. Granted, no one would have made salacious comments where the base commander, her stepfather, would have heard, but she knew the men around this table weren't discussing her mission-planning skills or analytical acumen.

She sat next to Pierre, her boss, who scowled at the men looking her way. One man, however, didn't engage in the speculative discussions—the senior headquarters operative, Nelson. More than one clerical in the Directorate had pointed him out. In truth, he was easy to notice. Six feet tall, fit, with leading man looks, Nelson would turn heads regardless of the observer's gender.

He'd definitely stirred Grace's interest, but she'd decided she wouldn't get involved with anyone at work. Not only could it be used against her—and only her, never the guy—but, as her stepfather often quaintly put it, "Gracie, it's never good to shit in your own backyard."

Nelson's scrutiny was neutral, despite his reputation, which the clericals had also related. No roving eyes or sexy smile for Grace. The man next to him had studied Grace, licked his lips suggestively, and made some comment to Nelson. Whatever Nelson said back to him made the man shrink away.

For credibility, she knew she'd have to have an ally among the operatives, and maybe it could be Nelson. She hoped so. He was like the captain of a baseball team, second only to the manager, but he also had his fellow operatives' respect. Yes, he'd definitely be a good ally.

The conference room door opened, and Sir Nigel Hume entered. His suit, custom-made, was at least twenty years out of date; three-piece, charcoal in color with a lighter charcoal pinstripe. A crisp, white shirt, black tie, a gray pocket handkerchief. He had a pipe clenched between his teeth and a stack of file folders under one arm. His neatly trimmed mustache and his slicked back hair had to have been dyed, they were so black; his eyebrows, too. He took the chair at the head of the table, a signal to the others to sit. He'd been knighted for his SOE service from World War II, though no one except his "girl Friday" referred to him as "Sir Nigel." It was always "Hume" or "Mr. Hume" or, informally, "His Nibs."

He placed the files on the table before his chair and sat, saying, "Good morning, gentlemen."

Several murmurs of "Good morning, sir," answered him.

Beside Grace, Pierre cleared his throat, and Nigel looked at him.

"Ah," Hume said. "I see you've brought along our keen, new girl analyst."

All right, she'd endured a long five minutes of adolescent behavior without reaction, but this was too much, the last straw that broke the fucking camel's back.

"Actually, sir," Grace began, "I started menstruating at the age of thirteen, and I've considered myself a woman since then. I'd appreciate it if you would, too."

The reaction around the table was a series of gaping mouths, blushes, and recoils. Pierre said nothing nor did Hume. Nelson smiled at Grace and gave a slight nod.

She had an ally.

Secrets Book 3
Taking Her Bows
Coming in August 2024